Murder Book

Murder Book

By

Frank F. Weber

Joyce,
Thank you for your interest. It all starts here in rural MN...
I hope you enjoy!
Frank

NORTH STAR PRESS OF ST. CLOUD, INC.
St. Cloud, Minnesota

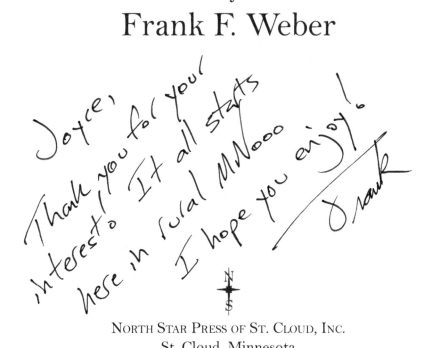

ISBN: 978-1-68201-068-6

This project was made possible by a grant provided by the Five Wings Art Council, with funds from the McKnight Foundation.

First edition: May 2017

Printed in the United States of America.

Published by
North Star Press of St. Cloud, Inc.
19485 Estes Road
Clearwater, MN 55320
www.northstarpress.com

Dedication

Brenda, nothing I accomplish will ever compare to the tenderness, grace, kindness, and beauty you bring to me.

Thank you, Tiffany Lundgren, for your feedback, insight, and efforts to change a grammatically incorrect world.

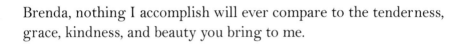

Chapter One

Jon Frederick
5:12 p.m.
Friday, March 28, 2014
Bureau of Criminal Apprehension, St. Paul, Minnesota

The missing person's report, from a decade earlier, read that Mandy Baker was last seen leaving the Little Falls High School on Friday, February 6, 2004, in Little Falls, Minnesota. It was assumed she returned home after school, as there was a postmarked letter lying open on her bed. The picture stapled carelessly to the report showed Mandy with straight light blonde hair, light-blue eyes, and a rounded face with distinctive dimples. She was a slender five feet, eight inches tall. The then-sixteen-year-old had moved with her mother and her mother's boyfriend from Fresno, California, to Minnesota at the beginning of the 2003-2004 school year. They lived near the railroad tracks on the west side of Little Falls, in a low-income neighborhood. A light-colored compact car pulled up to the home the day she went missing, at approximately 8:00 p.m. It was reported that a neighbor witnessed someone of Mandy's shape and size leave the home and get into the car. It was dark, and the neighbor had no view of the car's driver. Mandy Baker had not been seen or heard from since. Mandy enjoyed charcoal drawing, painting, and other creative activities. She did not own a vehicle. She did not own a cell phone. Mandy was last seen wearing a white tank top and blue jeans.

Mandy Baker was the biggest mistake of my life. Ten years ago, I was the seventeen-year-old boy who wrote the "Dear John" letter investigators found on Mandy's bed. This made me the prime suspect in her disappearance. It's always the ex-boyfriend, right? But there was no evidence, beyond the letter, connecting me to her disappearance. The problem was, there was no evidence connecting anyone else to her disappearance, either. Little Falls is a rural Minnesota town of around twelve thousand people, about a ninety-minute drive north of Minneapolis. The disappearance of a young person in a small town never stops haunting its residents. People lived there because they thought it was safe. Unlike the anonymity of large cities, small-town crimes are committed by people residents typically know and interact with. When the case went cold, people simply assumed I had gotten away with it, so I didn't stick around. I became determined to become an investigator myself. In college, I managed to secure an internship with the Bureau of Criminal Apprehension (BCA). After agreeing to help out on every undesirable shift that needed an extra set of hands, I was eventually offered employment. Today, I had been promoted to investigator status. My business card would read JON FREDERICK, BCA INVESTIGATOR. This promotion was significant, as it had finally given me access to the cold case room.

My shift had ended, and I stood in the unfinished basement of our office, where the cold case files were stored. The room was a large, cement space, filled with rows of floor-to-ceiling metal shelves housing boxes of evidence. The term "cold case room" applied well. The winter of 2014 had been one of the three coldest in the history of Minnesota, and we were slowly coming out of it. It was a balmy thirty-five degrees, and we had received six and a half inches of snow in the last two days. Throughout the winter, we had more than fifty days where the temperature dipped below zero, and numerous days where the windchill was a painful thirty to forty below. To put it in perspective, this is about seventy degrees colder than one's freezer. At this temperature, even a heavy winter jacket feels like a plastic windbreaker. The cold case room was unheated, and felt about fifty degrees. I held Mandy Baker's missing person's report in my hand, carefully going through the "murder book." The murder book is a twenty-first century term for the box holding all the evidence of a case. While Mandy's "murder" was never confirmed, there was no evidence she ever contacted anyone after that night. The BCA handles all of the homicide and abduction cases in Minnesota, similar to the manner in which the Federal Bureau of Investigation (FBI) handles investigations which cross state lines.

I cannot honestly say that being accused of murdering Mandy when I was in high school made me the obsessive person I am. I think the door to that room opened years earlier, and Mandy's disappearance settled in to occupy the space. At the very least, it exacerbated my obsessiveness, leaving the contents of the room difficult to contain. My thoughts tormented me at times, but overall, I did pretty well at keeping them in check. In my work for the BCA, I'd been in a hundred homes owned by obsessive people, which were filled with trash. That would never be my scenario. My hyper-awareness of my obsessiveness prevented me from going down that road. People who don't keep their obsessiveness in check start collecting items they feel are essential, and soon they're weaving through piles in their homes. I keep things simple to compensate for my craziness, so my home is clean and uncluttered.

I'm a little lanky at six feet, one inch, but clean-cut, lean, and in good shape. No crew cut, though—that's a little too militant for me. I work out three days a week and, for the most part, eat healthy. At times, I feel like working out more frequently, but I don't allow myself to, as I gravitate toward overdoing everything. But I do work my body hard on those three days. I've been told since I was young that my bright-blue eyes are inviting and friendly, which is a little embarrassing, because it basically means that it's the rest of my personality that keeps people at a distance. In my twenty-eight years, I've kept my body clean of tattoos and jewelry. I don't particularly care if others choose to paint or hang ornaments on their bodies like a Christmas tree, but it's not for me. If I started, it would never end. Perhaps having everybody assume I was a killer since I was seventeen extinguished my need for attention.

I reached into the cold case box and picked up the list of items discovered in Mandy's room. As an investigator, I began to think of her clothing differently than I had when I dated her. Her Forever 21 brand clothing wasn't surprising, but Victoria's Secret underwear was expensive for an unemployed teenager with alcoholic parents. I remember sitting on her bed when her parents weren't home talking about our lives. It was memorable, because I was never allowed in the bedroom of the small-town girls I dated. It's funny when you consider what parents worry about and what teens actually do. We never had sex in her bed! When I told Mandy I picked rocks in the hot sun during the summer, for five dollars an hour, she laughed and pulled a pair of lace underwear out of the drawer and threw them on the bed. Being a naïve country boy, I was too embarrassed to even look at them for long. She told me she had bras that would have cost me more than five hours of hard labor to buy, and all she had to do was flirt with Ray's friends—Ray was her mom's boyfriend—and they'd buy them for her. I wanted to tell her that they weren't buying lingerie for her, it was for them, but I didn't want to make her feel bad. Maybe I should have.

I set aside the list of Mandy's clothing. Reaching into this box was like stepping into a time machine. I found a picture of Mandy at a 2003 New Year's Eve party. I smiled for a moment. Mandy confidently posed, hands on her hips, revealing long legs below her short, black skirt, showcasing the rose tattoo on her ankle. There was something dangerously mesmerizing about Mandy's ice-blue eyes. As a teenager, I had never noticed the dark roots showing beneath her blonde hair. Her pale orange tank top melded to the curves of her breasts. She reminded me of an arrow just shot free from the bow—enjoying the flight, without considering that the odds of a pleasant landing were slim. Ten years ago, Mandy exuded sexuality in the midst of rural Catholic girls, who were painfully repressed. Like every other post-pubescent boy, I was drawn to her. I blew out a long exhale and asked, "What the hell happened to you, Mandy?"

I was at that New Year's Eve party with Mandy. The party was in the small, Catholic farming community of Pierz, Minnesota, just east of Little Falls (also in Morrison County), my hometown. It was a place where people still went out of their way to help each other with a physical task. The idea of seeking emotional help was still pretty foreign, however, as it was assumed that hard work would basically solve everything. It was an area where people worked with dangerous farm equipment, but if someone got hurt, it was just an accident, not a lawsuit. People were expected to reap the rewards, and suffer the consequences, of their choices. Men often wore baseball hats, although I didn't, unless I was playing baseball. The "good old boys," with their curved visors and the "wannabes," with their flat visors, both wore hats for no logical reason. Comfort was always the fashion in Pierz. People wore jeans, t-shirts or hooded sweatshirts, and sensible shoes without heels. Contrary to movies about Minnesota, people didn't typically wear vests unless they were hunting. There simply weren't times where one's torso was cold and one's arms were hot. Pierz folk did say "Yep" a lot, so I made it a point to always say "Yes." The old Germans in town also started a lot of words with the letter "D." For example, every Sunday, the church lector would end the reading with, "Dis is da word of da Lord." This man wasn't ignorant; he was bilingual. He spoke primarily German as a child, and there is no "th" sound in the German language. Much of life is not as it appears. Hell, "Germany" doesn't even exist, in Germany. The country we call Germany, Germans refer to as Deutschland. I apologize for that obsessive tangent. It's how I'm wired. You'll need to bear with me.

As midnight approached that New Year's Eve, Mandy slid onto my lap in worn, warm jeans, and whispered, "Let's get out of here." I was just seventeen years old at the time, and the heat coming off her body was beyond anything I had ever experienced.

In the dark of midnight, I drove us through a light snowfall to a secluded dirt road, until I found a remote place to park. The surrounding woods were thick with pine trees, branches tiredly swaying with snow. Mandy dreaded the darkness of the rural Minnesota nights, so she clung tight. Once parked, Mandy quickly shed her jacket, and with hormones cascading through me, I clumsily followed suit. Neither the cool air nor the cloying floral smell of her perfume was going to dissuade me. Her not-so-subtle hints had promised that tonight was going to be my "first time." My urgent desire made her touch feel like a warm blanket on a bone-chilling night. Still, I fought my eagerness, to make certain she was okay with each step, while she graciously led me along. Mandy suggested we move into the backseat, to avoid the steering column, and I said something like, "Of course," pretending I'd been in this predicament before. We simultaneously peeled out the front doors and into the back. She insisted I lock the doors, so I complied. With a smile, Mandy then felt safe enough to proceed. I wasn't convinced a locked door would dissuade a psychopathic killer standing outside my car in the dark, secluded wilderness, miles away from where anyone could hear a scream, but if it eased her mind, so be it.

Mandy helped me pull off my shirt, and I returned the favor. She started undoing my belt, and when I took over, she shed her jeans and underwear with one quick swoop. It was at this point our behavior stopped feeling natural and quickly became awkward. With my length of six-one, and Mandy at five-eight, our long limbs weren't ideally suited for getting horizontal in a sedan. Mandy battled the stickiness of the vinyl seats against her bare skin as she squeaked into position beneath me. I was propped with my head pressed against one door, and my pants tangled around my feet. Still, the warmth of her bare skin on mine, now lubricated with tiny whispers of sweat, made immediate body contact crucial, so we wrestled into the missionary position. Mandy assured me I wouldn't need a condom, because she was using a foam form of birth control. I remember thinking, *They land planes on foam when they can't get the landing gear to drop. Probably not the same stuff, but this would explain its lubricating qualities.* Unfortunately, my burning passion was followed by a torrential deluge that felt amazing for a moment, and then quickly put the fire out. Well, so much for that. I apologized and slowly sat up.

I leaned against the door, pants still down, and after a ragged breath considered that the experience wasn't exactly like I imagined it would be. I sort of expected her to be mad at me, and wouldn't have been surprised if she would have slapped me. Mandy wasn't one to hide her frustration.

Instead, Mandy gave me an understanding smile. Still naked, she snuggled against me, kissed me on the cheek, and seductively comforted me, whispering, "That's how it's supposed to be the first time."

With her forgiveness, I decided there was no point in pretending I knew what I was doing anymore. It wasn't a relaxing embrace. Imagine someone you don't know, hugging you—naked. I found myself counting in my head as I considered the appropriate length of time a person should wait after sex before suggesting it was time to go home. Mandy seemed to be enjoying the warm security of lying against me, and I felt I owed her this comfort. So I silently counted on. *Two hundred thirteen, two hundred fourteen, two hundred fifteen . . .*

Mandy's smile turned devilish as she finally looked up and said, "Let me show you something."

Before I could respond, she dropped her head into my lap and started doing something sinfully pleasurable. I pondered whether that foam was safe to consume orally. When it became apparent there wasn't going to be an immediate, tragic effect, I wondered, *Is this a sin? Probably not a mortal sin. Maybe a venial sin. The type of sin you might get slapped for, but they'd probably still let you into heaven, anyway.* No doubt worth it.

Once Mandy achieved the desired result, she lay back and guided me back on top of her. This time I was able to relax and enjoy sex with her. She positioned me by guiding my buttocks with her hands, until she finally breathed, "There."

For a moment, I felt like the luckiest guy on earth.

I tossed the picture back into the cold case box. Looking back through the eyes of a twenty-eight-year-old, her behavior was disturbing. She was only sixteen. My decision to be involved with Mandy placed me at center stage in an unfolding tragedy. My life probably would have played out better if my first experience would have been with someone just as naïve as I was, if indeed that person existed.

The reality of Mandy's life became obvious when I pulled up to her home to drop her off. Her mother was screaming in a jealous rage inside, followed by the sound of glass breaking. I envisioned glasses shattering and cascading down a wall. Mandy had no reaction to it, suggesting this was a relatively common occurrence. She caught me flinching and asked if she would ever see me again. I wanted to get the hell out of there and never come back, and I admonished myself for thinking this.

I was starting to seriously question if she had used birth control, so I blurted, "Do you still have the box for the spermicide?"

Mandy warily responded, "No. I made sure it was tucked away in the garbage before we left." Defensively, she asked, "Do you think I lied about that?"

I didn't want to say "Yes," so I responded with, "I just wanted to know how effective it is."

Mandy was keenly aware that this wasn't a loving conversation. It was the kind of conversation we should have had before having sex. Dejected, she said, "You don't need to worry. It works. I did read about it. I think it said seventy-nine percent of the time, which means a pretty low chance of getting pregnant."

My interpretation of "seventy-nine percent effective" was different. The odds of getting pregnant, using it once, weren't very good, but the reality was if you had sex three times, the odds were against you. And we'd had sex twice. I hastily explained that I had no free time until Saturday. I hated myself for the sadness in her eyes as the words left my mouth.

Crestfallen, Mandy nodded. She was about to exit my car when I reached out, grabbed her wrist and asked, "So, would you be interested in eating at Charlie's Pizza next Saturday?"

Her eyes immediately glistened with renewed life. She smiled and kissed me, gently placing her hand on my cheek as she breathed, "You're everything Serena said you'd be."

My drive home that night took me to a depth of despair I hadn't known existed. As an adolescent, I couldn't comprehend that even terrible situations are finite, and life eventually goes on. It had stopped snowing, and had become dark and bitterly cold. My contact with Mandy left my clothing and skin with an unpleasant, residual smell of a bathroom deodorizer. My mom might give me the "You're headed to hell" lecture if she got a whiff of it. More likely, I'd spend some time in purgatory with all those guys who ate meat on Fridays before the rules changed. Regardless, this was the least of my worries. I had released sixteen million sperm into a girl I now realized I didn't want to date, and I wasn't prepared to take care of one of them. I prayed to God she wasn't pregnant, and swore I'd never put myself in that predicament again. My older sister, Theresa, referred to this as "The Prayer of the Teen Catholic."

The parting comment Mandy made about my best friend, Serena, had shaken me. Serena Bell was more than just a classmate. She was the one person who honestly knew me in high school. We had spent hours walking and talking about every issue we could think of. But every time I'd express interest in formally dating, she would always put me off. Serena wasn't at the New Year's party, so when Mandy pursued me, I decided it was time for me to consider someone who wasn't afraid to acknowledge publically that we were together. I didn't want to be alone when high school ended. Isn't it funny how we have a way of making what we fear most come true? That night, I thought if Serena found out I had sex with Mandy, the feud we'd have would be the worst thing imaginable. When I became the prime suspect in Mandy's disappearance, I realized the absolute silence between us was much worse.

The problem with the Mandy Baker case was that, while everyone in my hometown remembered her, Mandy's disappearance had faded from the memory of the agency responsible for investigating it. The BCA always had new cases to work on, and Mandy didn't have any family in the state pushing to keep the case alive. But I would never forget her.

My quiet reflection in the cold case room was interrupted when my supervisor, Maurice Strock, entered the room. Maurice was a white-haired man in his early sixties, closing in on retirement. He always wore a gray suit with a white dress shirt and a solid-colored tie as his "work uniform." Today, the only spot of color on him was his royal blue tie. Maurice was a small man with aardvark-like features—a pointed nose and small, marble-like eyes. Maurice did a double-take when he scoped his nose down the long row of shelves and spotted me. In a nasally voice, he asked, "Shouldn't you be out celebrating your promotion?'

"Yes. I just have to check on something before I go." Not wanting to call attention to my supervisor that I was once a suspect in a girl's disappearance, I tried to find something useful in the evidence box before closing it. Numbers were the easiest for me to remember, as I configure stories out of them. I can't really say my ability to memorize numbers is a blessing, since the numbers continue to run through my head on lonely nights, wearing grooves in my brain as I miserably pray to be rescued by sleep. I quickly found three social security numbers and memorized them. "Biological Father: Cade Freeman 639-92-6484. Biological Mother: Carrie Baker 546-79-8832. Mother's live-in significant other: Ray Benson 652-71-2937." I'll try to explain how my system works with Ray's number:

6 is the shape of a pregnant woman; 5 is giving birth; 2 indicates the baby is gone (so 652 in my brain is the birth process); 71 is a sharp and straight man; 2 is a woman, so 29 is a woman holding the baby instead of carrying it in her uterus (as 9 is the upside down of 6); 3 means that, as a result of her pregnancy, she now has larger breasts, and she's still with her sharp, 7, husband. This story occurred in my brain in two seconds, and I would remember it as 652-71-2937. It was an odd system and, admittedly, not necessarily politically correct from a gender-sensitivity standpoint.

I closed the box, placed it back on the shelf, and went to Maurice. Shaking his hand, I told him, "Thanks for giving me the opportunity to work as an investigator. I won't let you down."

Maurice smiled at my exuberance.

I headed back to my office on the first floor, determined to celebrate my promotion, at least for part of the evening. I've been told it's important to mark positive events in your life. The negative events seem to mark themselves.

My immediate problem was that I didn't have anyone to celebrate with. I hadn't been on a date for four months, and I deliberately avoided friendships with coworkers. My obsessiveness was an asset on the job, but hyper-aware it had to be irritating to others, I didn't socialize with peers outside of work. Ninety percent of promotions at work were based on social interactions with coworkers, and I wasn't going to let my annoying personality cost me a promotion to investigator. I was polite, professional, and respectful to everyone, and avoided the office gossip. Sucking up to the person in power made one look pathetic when the power structure shifted, and supervisors worked harder to please assiduous workers who didn't blindly follow. At least that was the theory I operated under.

I decided to call Clay Roberts, an old friend from high school. Clay and I played high school football and basketball together. When all else failed, we would look each other up, typically after months of no contact.

Clay had been raised rough and rugged by his father and liked to pretend to be a tough guy, which I always felt was a veneer covering a salvageable soul. He had been abandoned by his mother in his early teens, when she left the family for a man she'd met online. Clay was the one friend who had stood by me without reservation when Mandy disappeared. He now had his own construction crew, which worked in the suburbs around Minneapolis. We had little in common. Clay loved four-wheel-drive trucks and hunting, and bedded a lot of different women. I didn't. If we hadn't grown up together, it's unlikely our paths would have crossed. I liked the fact that, in small towns, you're forced to befriend whoever's around, rather than having the option of seeking out like-minded people. I think it prepares us better for the variety of personalities we encounter at work.

Clay answered the phone with a clipped, "Yep," and after our usual banter, congratulated me on my promotion. "That was fast work."

"If you call one thousand, four hundred, eleven days of work fast."

"You and those damn numbers," he groused. "Have you ever noticed you talk more about numbers when you're single? The only number that matters right now is the number of women lining up to celebrate with you."

I considered this and said, "I don't know that the number of women a man dates is an effective way to measure happiness. It could be argued that the correlation is negative—as one increases, the other decreases."

In his gravelly voice, Clay chided me. "The number's significant when it's zero. So, no dates since your fallout with Jada?"

"I've been busy at work." Jada Anderson was an attractive and assertive African American woman I had dated for four years.

Clay continued. "I get why you wanted to be with her. She had that Mandy Baker body type. Same height, same—"

It wasn't rude to interrupt Clay. I considered it to be a moral obligation, as he tended to become progressively more inappropriate if you let him ramble on, particularly about intelligent women. "I know you weren't wild about Jada, but she was good for me. Deep down, she has a good heart."

Clay laughed. "So deep down that it's not visible."

"I don't think either of us should judge her moral character."

Clay casually responded, "I beat up a guy for picking on a retard once, so I think I'm good with God."

The best chance Clay and I have of getting into heaven is through an unlocked window.

"You need to find someone and settle down," Clay continued. "You're going to end up wandering around alone at night like your crazy brother does."

Ready for a subject change, I said, "I'm looking into Mandy Baker's disappearance. I've been thinking about calling Serena Bell. I know it sounds desperate, calling her ten years later and asking, 'Remember me from high school?' But I want to find out how she met Mandy. Serena was the one who first invited Mandy to our parties."

Clay was uncharacteristically speechless for a moment. "That's worse than desperate. That's pitiful."

"I know. But I need to start somewhere."

I was quickly lost in the memory of her for a moment. Serena Bell was a true beauty—pretty and petite, with long, dark hair. She was often mistaken for Hispanic, but was actually of Polish descent. She had large, tear drop–shaped green eyes that scintillated when she smiled—and her smile was contagious.

Clay went into a sermon about how Serena was "a wolf in sheep's clothing." This lecture was triggered every time I brought Serena's name up. Not every "kind" woman is a wolf in sheep's clothing. After all, what do sheep wear? I, in turn, responded with a conversation he didn't want to hear. I reminded Clay he needed to get over his mom's departure. It was a dozen years ago. Now frustrated with each other, we decided not to go out for a drink. It sounds harsh, but it was how we communicated. The next time we spoke, this conversation would be ancient history, which was both good and bad. It was nice to always be able to start over, but it also meant nothing ever got resolved. It's what men do.

I decided to call my parents to tell them about my first day of work as an investigator. My dad always answered the phone, and then would immediately hand it to my mother, without saying anything in transition. I once mentioned to Dad that this felt like a control issue, but he pointed out that not all calls to our home had been pleasant since Mandy disappeared. Once my mother, Camille, was on the phone, she gave me the usual who's-ill-among-old-people report. I learned a long time ago that it didn't pay to tell her I didn't even know those people, because this would only lead to a twenty-minute explanation of how I should know them, still followed by the report. I did manage to find out that Serena's family had moved to the St. Paul area.

I had a legitimate reason to talk to Serena. She had information on Mandy Baker, and I finally had the ability to investigate Mandy's disappearance. But in all honesty, Clay was right. Part of me had a desire to chase the ghost of "what could have been" with Serena, and that was pathetic. I didn't try to access her phone number through work, as I didn't want anyone suggesting I used my new employment status to look up an old girlfriend. I decided to take on the challenge of calling Serena's parents to ask for her phone number. Serena's mother refused, and I understood—I was once accused of being a murderer in their community. I did manage to get her to agree reluctantly to give Serena my phone number. Nothing ventured, nothing gained.

6:15 p.m.
Birmingham Apartments, Minneapolis

Back at my apartment, I untucked my white shirttails and, with restless energy, bounced on my toes like a boxer in my black work slacks and stocking feet. I threw some punches in the air as if I was sparring Manny Pacquiao on the beige carpet in my living room. Like a boxer, I'd had an extended period of abstinence. I abandoned my contrived fight and played "All Along the Watchtower," by Jimi Hendrix, on an old record player I kept in my living room. My dad was always in a good mood when he played music on the record player, so I kept it when they were ready to discard it. It's possible I still hung onto that memory because it wasn't always pleasant at home.

My apartment on the fifteenth floor gave me a great view of Minneapolis at night. Going out to eat alone felt a little depressing, so I decided to make myself an extravagant meal as a reward for my accomplishment. As I searched recipes off of the Food Network, my mind returned to thoughts of Serena. I wondered what she was like today. I wanted her to be content, as opposed to suffering through the restlessness I struggled with, because she was truly the nicest person I had ever met. I printed the recipe for pan-seared salmon with a citrus glaze and chilled mango salsa.

After I picked up my groceries, I found myself in Robbinsdale, driving by Travail, Jada Anderson's favorite restaurant. Why? I'm not sure. I didn't even want to talk to her. I think I wanted to see someone I cared for happy. Not necessarily with me. Just happy. No matter how I spun it, I couldn't ignore that I was now more alone than ever. After a moment of anguish, I reached a conclusion. I would give myself one year from today to solve Mandy Baker's disappearance, then I would start my own family. The remedy was obvious. The first step would be to stop putting off dates for work. The second would be to start dating women who actually wanted children.

Midnight
Birmingham Apartments, Minneapolis

I spent the night on the couch with my laptop, gathering what I could on Carrie Baker, Ray Benson, and Cade Freeman. Cade Freeman, Mandy Baker's biological father, committed suicide with a handgun in 2001 in Fresno, California. Mandy claimed she was afraid of the rural darkness because she was a "city girl," but Fresno wasn't exactly New York or LA. She lived with her biological parents at the entry point for Yosemite National Park. If Mandy had early sexual victimization, as I now suspected, I'd bet it started in the darkness of the park. It would help explain both her fears and her father's suicide. But Cade's suicide happened three years before Mandy moved to Little Falls, so Cade had nothing to do with Mandy's disappearance. Strike one.

Carrie Baker, Mandy's mother, had been involved in court-ordered chemical dependency treatment in 2002 and 2004, after she was charged with writing bad checks. She died in 2006, from a series of strokes, renal and liver failure. Her autopsy showed the presence of methamphetamine and opiates. Carrie's abuse of alcohol and drugs apparently became a death wish after Mandy disappeared. Carrie was in detox when Mandy went missing, so she was not involved in Mandy's disappearance, either. Strike two.

Ray Benson, Carrie's live-in boyfriend at the time of Mandy's disappearance, was now serving time in Florida after being charged with lewd or lascivious battery (statutory rape) in 2013. The victim was the fourteen-year-old daughter of Ray's lover at the time. Odds were, Ray Benson had also sexually victimized Mandy. He looked like a promising suspect. Ray never had a reported income, but had performed tree-trimming work for cash. Tree trimming was big money in rural Minnesota, but many of the crews burned up the cash on alcohol and meth as fast as it came in. They drove nice cars but lived in crappy houses, because you can't get a home loan without an identified income. But Ray Benson was incarcerated on the night of February 6, 2004, the night Mandy disappeared, for driving while intoxicated. Carrie went to detox and Ray went to jail when they were pulled over earlier that afternoon; Mandy was still at school at the time. Strike three.

In most cases, you could use Facebook for information and direction. That wasn't a possibility with the three names I had, as two were dead and one was in prison. I thought about the information I had hastily scanned from the cold case box. My name had been written down and circled. My paranoid schizophrenic brother's name, Victor, was also on the list. There were two names written down and crossed out: Clay Roberts and Randall Davis. I was familiar with Randall's name, as I had researched sex offenders living in Morrison County over the past decade. Randall was accused of raping a fifteen-year-old girl the year before Mandy disappeared but pled it down to a statutory offense. Randall apparently had an alibi, Anna Hutchins, for the night of Mandy's disappearance. I wanted to talk to her.

Chapter
Two

Jon Frederick
1:30 p.m.
Saturday, March 29
Highway 10, headed north toward Little Falls

Saturday at noon, I received a call for my first official case as an investigator. An eleven-year-old girl had gone missing in rural Minnesota. Unsure how long I'd be away from home, I quickly hauled all of the perishable items from my refrigerator out to the garbage, packed, and headed north. With two days in a row of temperatures hovering around forty degrees, the snow was departing fast. Late March and early April in Minnesota can be unforgiving, with cold, gloomy, overcast days. April is the purgatory ending the hell of winter, before the green of May brings everything to life once again. The trees were barren, and the color was drained from all the foliage by the bitter and exhausting winter. Patches of snow littered the burlap-brown prairie.

As I drove through Little Falls, I adjusted the rearview mirror to double-check that my insulated, watertight boots were in the backseat. They were. I had packed in a hurry, and hoped I hadn't forgotten anything I would need. Warm or not, I would be spending time outside.

I turned right onto Highway 25 from Main Street and headed east out of the city. Sean Reynolds, a BCA colleague, called and told me I'd be working with an investigator from Morrison County named Tony Shileto. I would be the liaison between the BCA and local investigators. I got the liaison assignment because I was the rookie. Sean gave me a brief description and historical rundown of Tony's past, as he wanted me to be adequately prepared. Tony had a history of hostile relationships with others. The story was that he beat a citizen, after the individual was found not guilty of a sex crime. Tony had a friend in administration who helped him keep his job; however, local investigators had been reluctant to partner up with Tony, out of fear that the prosecution of their cases could be muddled up by his history. The Morrison County investigators used terms like "Shileto Justice" when an officer overreacted to a situation.

Three miles east of Little Falls, toward Pierz, I approached a gravel road that had been recently named 210th Street. The city managers had elected to give the small roads street names, to make it easier for families to direct ambulance drivers when accidents occurred on the farms. Two police officers had blocked off the road, so I showed them my identification and was waved through. Gravel crunched beneath the weight of my tires for a half mile before I reached three squad cars parked by the side of the dirt road. Based on Sean's description, the man not in uniform standing among four sheriff's deputies was Investigator Tony Shileto. Tony was in his late forties. He had thick, black hair streaked with gray, which he wore combed back. His face bore strong Italian features, despite Sean's suggestion that he was Irish. Tony fiercely shouted directions to the deputies through the bitter wind.

I quickly stepped out of the car into the cold spring air, and swallowed hard as I studied Tony. His tan trench coat was open and waved with the wind as he scurried about in scuffed brown hiking boots.

Attempting to portray an illusion of confidence, I approached him and held out my hand. "Jon Frederick."

Tony eyed me with irritation, which I assumed to be frustration over having been assigned a rookie for a partner. He smirked as he registered my new black tennis shoes. In my haste to get to work, I had forgotten to change into my boots. "Brittany Brennan was last seen walking out of a driveway half a mile back," he said in greeting. "She was headed to her folks' farm another half mile down the road. She never made it home. We found this on the road, here." Tony held up a dark-brown leather jacket. "Any idea where it's from?"

I shrugged. "No."

Tony said, "It's an Express leather men's jacket. My guess is it's about a decade old."

That was a lot of information to have on a jacket that was just discovered. I wasn't sure what to say, other than, "Okay."

"Did you ever own one?"

"I don't think so." I couldn't help wondering where he was going with that question.

Tony scowled at me and said, "Think hard."

"No, I didn't. I couldn't afford a leather jacket when I was younger, and I don't own one now. Is my attire relevant to this case?"

After glaring at me for a beat, Tony nodded. "Tell me what you were thinking on your way here."

"Okay . . . If she was abducted on this dirt road," I speculated, "she's probably with someone from around here. This isn't a road tourists would be traveling. That doesn't necessarily make her safe, but it may mean she's still close by. I also thought I want to find her alive, and prove I can do this job. People don't realize how hard it is to find a child, until it becomes your job to find one."

"Ain't that the truth?" Tony rolled his shoulders. "The only guaranteed way to find her is to bring everyone in the world to Morrison County, and ask the person standing on her to raise his hand."

The problem with giving me hypothetical proposals was that they started a series of numbers tumbling through my head. I felt compelled to respond. "Actually, if everyone in the world was in

Morrison County, it's possible that nobody would be standing on her."

Annoyed by my response, Tony growled, "What?"

"There are eleven hundred, twenty-five square miles in Morrison County. There are twenty-seven million square feet in a square mile, and about thirty billion square feet total in Morrison County. Assuming each person took up three square feet while standing, you could fit ten billion people into Morrison County. There are only a little over seven billion people on earth, so it's possible no one would be standing on Brittany." I wasn't sure how Tony was taking my oration, so I added, "But we could ask them to look around."

He furrowed his eyebrows and said, "No shit. Everyone in the world could fit in this county, with room to spare?"

"Yes."

"What, are you some sort of savant?"

"No, I just have a thing with remembering numbers."

He gave a couple of quick head-shakes, as if he was trying to clear the conversation out of his mind and, switching gears, pointed toward the ditch. "Brittany's parents organized a search when she didn't come home. They feared she was hit by a vehicle and was lying in the ditch somewhere. So, we have a mess. If we have a crime scene, it's contaminated. This jacket could have come off the man who abducted Brittany, or it could've come off one of the searchers." Tony turned in a slow circle and said, "Walk a little down the road with me, as Brittany did, and tell me what you think."

As we strolled, Tony told me, "Brittany Brennan is an eleven-year-old white girl with dark-brown hair. She was wearing a pink jacket and pink sweatpants. The Downings gave Brittany a pair of pink-and-white tennis shoes that no longer fit their niece, and Brittany was excited to show them to her mom. Her parents are Al and Mary Brennan, and she has a brother, Jason."

The gravel road was lined by ditches with long strands of dead, brown grass haphazardly twisted at various angles by the winter storms. Beyond the ditches stretched long fields so dark and muddy they looked like could have been composed of finely ground coal. The cold air bit at my ears. The local farmers were waiting for the water from the melted snow to completely run off the fields so they could start planting. About a hundred yards from the road sat a row of poplar trees jutting from the muddy ground like dried sticks. I looked down the gravel road and thought out loud, "That's a long walk to the next farm for an eleven-year-old girl."

"They said she did it all the time." Tony looked at me curiously. "Any visions or premonitions?"

I finally realized what he was getting at, so I explained, "I'm not psychic. I just have an obsession with numbers. It's not anything special. Anyone could find out what I know with an iPhone."

"The square footage of Morrison County?"

"I grew up on a farm near here."

Tony smirked. "For a moment I thought you were going to make it easy for us. That's too bad." He looked out at the muddy fields and said, "I've lived here for two decades now, and no one can explain to me why everyone plants corn. So, farm boy, tell me. Why does everyone plant corn?"

Tony apparently had done his research on me, too. I looked out at the field and with a half-smile, said, "They just do. But it hasn't been planted yet. It's too wet."

He stared at me for a few seconds, and with histrionics, waved his arms as he said, "Now I get it—they just do! Next time I put a criminal in front of the judge, I'll tell the judge, 'He did it.' When the judge asks how I know, I'll tell him, 'I just do.' That should work."

I grew up with a father who would furiously ruminate on issues, so I had little tolerance for this kind of ranting. Determined to end his tantrum quickly, I explained, "Okay, there are more profitable crops that could be planted in this soil. But a farmer in this area plants corn because his dad did and made money, and his dad's dad planted corn, and he made money, too. Planting corn is profitable, but not the best option."

Tony seemed to find perverse pleasure in agitating me, but he quickly acquiesced. "Okay, I get it. So, 'They just do,' is simply the best answer."

"Yes."

As we walked down the road, Tony commented, "Another day standing out on a dirt road. Welcome to rural Minnesota. They say the road to hell is paved with good intentions. Well, at least it's paved." Tony directed me, "You walk the ditch north for a bit, and I'll head south. Yell if you find anything."

Becoming progressively impatient, I half-jogged as I searched. The three-hour mark had passed since Brittany's disappearance. Three hours after an abduction, the odds of finding the victim alive drop below fifty percent.

Chapter
Three

PANTHERA
1:38 P.M.
SATURDAY, MARCH 29
GRAVEL ROAD

BE SOBER, BE VIGILANT; because your adversary the devil walks about like a roaring lion, seeking whom he may devour." Peter 5:8

Panthera is my name for myself, a name I will never hear outside my head. *Panthera Atrox* was the scientific name of the North American lion. It's not to be confused with Pantera, although I did like the title of their first CD, *Vulgar Display of Power.*

Sharp, frozen clumps of dirt and ice cut into my knees as I kneel in the frozen ditch. Her breathing is shallow, but it's still there. There's a rosy redness to her cheeks and nose from the cold. I speak to my silent prey. "The cops are searching just a mile down the road, so it's time for us to part. If you would have just listened, it wouldn't have ended like this."

I lay a blanket out in the ditch and roll her body into it.

I can see in their eyes when it's to the point they think they can defy me. They have all entered my life uninvited, and I was initially polite to every one. It's ignorant for them to expect there won't be consequences for intruding in the life of a predator. Eventually, I speak softly into their ears and my words penetrate their thoughts as unforgettable. It ends with them, to quote Israel Keys, "Begging to be my Stockholm sweetheart." Keys thought he learned from studying Ted Bundy, but he obviously didn't learn enough. Keys cut his wrists and hanged himself in his cell in 2012, when he was caught. Bundy escaped twice before he was finally fried. Still, Bundy spent his last night of life crying and praying. *Sigh* . . .

I run my thumb over her forehead and give her one last kiss.

"I don't want to kill you, Brittany, but I'm out of options. I could say it's the crap I went through as a teen, but it's about survival. Nietsche. Social Darwinism. It's about the need to either stand for something or simply disappear into nothingness. It's not about recognition. If you think that, you don't know me. No one really knows me. But I have done something for you, Brittany. Because I picked you, people will talk about you forever."

I cradle her body and begin to carry it down the hill.

I hate it when the adrenaline wears off. I used to spend days worrying, but now I'm smart enough to clean up the mess instead of relying on blind luck and intimidation. I just need to finish it. My life goes on.

I slide her body into its final resting place, then return to open the floodgates.

I did get one piece of useful information from watching ID, the Investigation Discovery channel. Israel Keys buried a murder kit so he would be prepared when he had the need to kill. I'm too smart to get this close to getting caught again.

I carry the five-gallon bucket containing duct tape, a handgun, needles loaded with an animal tranquilizer, industrial plastic zip ties, and an awl to the black, muddy field. I use my phone to get the GPS coordinates of the bucket and then commit the numbers to memory. I shut my phone off, toss it in the bucket, wipe it all down, seal the cover, and then bury the bucket.

The murder kit is in place, and now I need to depart.

Chapter
Four

Jon Frederick
1:56 p.m.
Saturday, March 29
210th Street (gravel road)

We needed to talk to the girl's mother. I followed Tony's beat-up, brown Chevy Celebrity down the gravel road. It was the first unmarked car I'd ever seen with rust eating through it. I wasn't sure how much benefit there was to having an unmarked car in Morrison County—everyone knew everybody. All the local criminals likely knew what Inspector Shileto drove.

After parking the cars in the Brennans' dirt driveway, we started the long walk to the farmhouse. Tony glanced at my hand and commented, "You're not married."

"No." Deciding to take the focus off me, I asked, "Are you?"

"I was. I married this fantasy of having a fulfilling job and some wonderful time alone with my beautiful wife. Instead, I spent long nights interrogating slimeballs, and she just got tired of being alone. When people tell you 'we both grew apart' or 'it was mutual,' you know they're just giving you a line of crap. It's never mutual. Someone always wants out and the other person can't stop it." Tony took a cleansing breath and blew it out in a white vapor. "No one likes spending a lot of time alone. I don't hate her for leaving."

"But you hate her for other reasons?"

Tony glanced over at me, as if trying to figure me out. "You might have some potential," he chuckled. "Go through a divorce with a kid involved, Jon. You have reasons to hate that person. I have a boy who worshiped me once, who now can't stand me for reasons I'm not aware of." Tony squeezed his shirt pocket and muttered, "And I quit smoking." He was silent for a moment, likely grieving the loss of his nicotine, then got to the case at hand. "Greg and Denise Downing picked Brittany up to go to church with them at eight o'clock this morning, as they do every Sunday. After returning from church, Brittany stayed to play with their ten-year-old daughter, Kayla, until about ten thirty, and headed home. After Brittany left, Greg Downing bundled his daughter up, and they went outside. He watched Kayla jump on the trampoline for fifteen minutes before he decided it was too chilly, and they headed back in. The Downings are a nice, Christian family. There is no evidence of any kind of a struggle in or around either the Downing home or the Brennan home. We've searched the barn and the sheds. To sum it up, we don't have a hell of a lot."

I added, "Except the jacket you found on the road?"

"We do have that. I do know the jacket was only recently left here. If it had been here overnight, it would have been soaking wet."

WE REACHED THE FADED brown door of Al and Mary Brennan's home.

Mary Brennan was a big-boned, sturdy woman. She had thinning, reddish-blonde hair, pale, weathered skin, and small eyes set back behind plump cheeks. She was only five years older than I was, but looked a decade beyond her years. She sat at the worn oak kitchen table with several school pictures of a petite, dark-haired girl spread out before her. A stained dish towel was bunched in chapped hands. The linoleum floor had likely started out white, but had yellowed over the years. This helped it blend with the walls, which had started out yellow, and faded closer to a shade of off-white. Gingham-checked curtains gathered to the side of double windows gave view to an expansive mowed lawn, edged by pole sheds. On a happier day, I'd expect to see an apple pie on the table.

Tony put a finger on one of the pictures and told her, "Thank you for finding the pictures of Brittany."

Mary nodded, fighting back tears. "On Sunday mornings, we all just kind of do our own thing. I was going through our mail. Al went and checked out the south field, and came back a muddy mess. There's just too much water in the fields to plant."

"Where is Al now?"

"He changed his clothes, and is tryin' to get some chores done so he can assist with the search."

Tony thought for a moment before continuing, "Mary, do you have any proof that Al and Jason were in the yard after ten thirty?"

"Yeah, I heard Al returnin' in the truck, a little after ten. The muffler's got a big hole in it. It's pretty bad when you can't watch TV in the house because the truck's runnin' outside."

Tony frowned. "That doesn't really tell us much, because that's before Brittany left the Downing's home."

"But it shut off and never started up again. You can't ignore the thunderin' sound of that thing startin' up. The van isn't runnin', so the truck's the only workin' vehicle we have."

I asked, "Were you messaging with anyone on the Internet this morning?" Communicating online could open up a home to a variety of predators.

The question took Mary by surprise. She glanced at Tony and then back at me before responding. "What's that got to do with Brittany? I didn't talk about Brittany."

Tony asked her, "Who were you talking to?"

Mary busied herself wiping the table and avoided eye contact when she answered. "I was just checking my emails."

She was obviously lying. Tony callously said, "I don't care about your online boyfriends. We can't afford to be wasting time right now. You need to be honest with us, Mary, for your daughter's sake." I held my breath as I considered telling Tony to show some compassion.

Mary's cheeks reddened, and she responded, "He's just a friend, from another state. It has nothin' to do with this. I don't want to be blamed for distractin' you guys, when Brittany might still be saved." Mary's flushed face became a portrait of guilt. She took a shuddering breath, and tears began to trickle down her round cheeks.

I softly asked, "Where was Jason at ten thirty?"

Mary sternly answered, "Jason was in the shed tinkerin' with the van. It's not runnin' because Jason's a teenage boy, and he's hard on things." She softened her tone. "But he's a good kid, and he was out there tryin' to fix it. He came in about eleven thirty. When I told him Brittany wasn't home, he was frantic. I think he was afraid she got hit by a car. So I called Al and told him to come in."

Tony asked, "What time did you call Al?"

"A little after eleven thirty, and he came right away. We called the neighbors. They put off their Sunday dinners and everybody went out searchin'. Al led them and they walked the ditches the whole way, both sides, lookin' for her." Mary's voice became gritty. "Please, just go find her." Drowning in genuine grief, she put her head down.

Tony cocked an eyebrow. "You called the police before you searched? You knew something bad had happened?"

Mary was losing patience. "Brittany's never this late."

Tony thought out loud. "Is there an officer with Al right now?"

"Al's doin' chores with Jason. They'll be in as soon as they're done. We still need to feed our animals."

Tony's frustration was mounting; he slapped the table, and I jerked back in surprise.

Mary looked at him like he was crazy and implored, "Please, just go find her!"

I was in a dilemma. I wanted to tell Tony to simmer down, but as a rookie, I didn't feel it was my role. At the same time, I didn't want to be part of a duo of investigators who would be emotionally abusive to a woman who just lost a child. I stood up and put my hand on Mary's shoulder in an effort to console her. In my gentlest tone, I told her, "If anything occurs to you that you think might be helpful, call. I know this is hard. We want to help any way we can." I set a card on the table with my number on it. "Where can we find Al and Jason?"

She studied my card for a second and sarcastically replied, "I said they're doin' chores, Jon Frederick."

I found her contempt toward me gratifying, as it was evidence of resilience.

Tony sat motionless. It was his way of telling me he'd decide when the interview was over. He studied Mary in silence as she wiped away tears with the back of her hand. Without another word, Tony turned and left the home.

When I stepped outside, I expected him to yell at me for ending the interview.

Instead, he simply fell into step beside me and said, "By the way, an officer checked out the van. It wouldn't start, so that part's true. It pisses me off that the deputies let them start the chores, unsupervised. Are you a computer expert?"

"No."

"So you're just a numbers-in-your-head guy. No superpowers."

"Basically. Sean Reynolds will be here. He'll have no problem finding what she's been doing on the computer."

Tony unconsciously reached to his shirt pocket for his cigarettes, but after realizing it was empty, stated, "Let's take Al and the boy downtown for the interview, so we can record it." He scratched his head. "Do you think she called the police pretty quickly?"

"I understand her panic. Brittany should have been home. It's interesting that Jason initiated the search."

Tony looked out over the road. "You never know where the break is going to come from, so you keep asking questions until you've asked the right one. Pay particular attention to the first contradiction in someone's story." Tony was now by his car. He asked, "How many cars have gone by this place since we've been here?"

Now I felt stupid. Tony had been observing much more than the interview during our time with Mary Brennan. He was testing me, and I had failed. Embarrassed, I reluctantly answered, "I don't know."

Tony smiled. "That's a good answer," he said. "Don't ever pretend to know something you don't." Tony left me hanging for thirty seconds before he declared, "Not one car has passed by since we've been here. I told the police to let the traffic through, but no one has driven down this road."

I added, "And if no one drives down this road, it has to be the people here."

"Yeah." Tony got on his cell phone and asked, "Where the hell are Al and Jason? They should have been accompanied by a police officer . . . Well, find them, and bring them back to the house." As Tony listened, he motioned for me to get into his car. "Okay, all right. But let's at least have an officer stay with them until they've been interviewed. I don't want to give anyone an opportunity to destroy evidence." When Tony hung up, he said, "We have cops stopping at all the farms in this area, to see if anyone's noticed anything suspicious. An old farmer, Eldon Meyer, who has a farm half a mile north of here, said the bales of straw in his ditch had been moved. We're probably the closest investigators to the scene, so we should stop there before the interviews with Al and Jason. The problem with going to people and asking them about suspicious activity is that they notice things that may have been changed weeks ago."

Tony and I headed half a mile straight north, down the dirt road past the Brennans', and stopped on the top of a small hill. We approached two BCA investigators standing in the middle of the gravel road by their unmarked, silver Crown Victoria. Tony swore in disgust, and then added, "Just what I need. Two more state employees to tell me how to do my job."

I grimaced at the implication that I, as a state employee, was somehow already telling Tony how to do his job.

Officer Paula Fineday was in her early forties and slightly overweight. She had thick, shoulder-length dark-brown hair, heavy eyebrows, and Native facial features. She wore a navy-blue North Face jacket. I'd worked with Paula before. She was generally oblivious to fashion trends. I respected her effortless and unembellished style, as it contradicted her complex and labyrinthine processing of language. She was an articulate and observant woman, who gleaned information from casual conversations that other investigators often failed to catch.

Sean Reynolds was an African American man in his late thirties who maintained excellent physical condition. Sean wore his hair closely cropped and was meticulously groomed; his black pants always held a sharp crease. His attention to detail made him an excellent crime-scene investigator. Sean wore a black stocking hat and a designer black leather jacket. Sean and Paula worked very effectively as partners for the BCA.

Tony and I joined them and the four of us walked along the water-filled ditch, looking down at the bales of straw. Someone had broken a path through the bales on Eldon Meyer's land, allowing the water to flow through and fill the ditch. A farmer would notice this the first time he drove by.

After the initial greetings, Sean asked me, "You grew up around here—can you tell us why they have these bales in the ditch?"

"When it gets above freezing, the snow melts and there's a lot of water running from the fields into the ditches. The bales of straw help regulate the flow of water," I explained. "They slow down the runoff, and this keeps the water from flooding the culvert at the bottom of the hill. If this happened, it could freeze water over the road." I jogged down the hill while the other investigators followed, curious.

We had now reached one end of the culvert that ran underneath the road. Sean bent down and peered into the deep water that had covered the culvert below. At the bottom of the hill, the ditch water was almost as high as the road. The temperature had dropped just below freezing, so a skin of ice had formed over the water. Sean punched his gloved fist through the ice and said, "It looks like someone deliberately moved the straw to flood the culvert."

The thinness of the ice indicated this water had only recently frozen—perhaps in the last hour. I quickly walked across the road to look into the water on the other side of it. This side wasn't frozen. As I bent down, I caught a glimpse of a pink-and-white tennis shoe floating in the murky water. "She's here!" Without thinking twice, I jumped feet-first into the icy water. The three-foot-deep water quickly muddied around me, which made it necessary for me to submerge completely underwater and feel my way to the culvert opening. With my entire body now immersed, hands quickly going numb, I felt what I believed to be a child's leg. The cold was so absolute, I could feel sharp pains radiating through my ears and into my lungs, like claws of ice piercing through me. As I felt around blindly, I noticed Brittany's body felt somehow mummified. I carefully pulled her out of the culvert and lifted her stiff, lifeless body above the surface. She had been tightly wrapped in a red blanket. Dark hair spilled from the top of the blanket, and when we uncovered her face, there was no doubt we were holding Brittany Brennan—a pretty face devoid of expression, with lips tinged blue against her colorless skin.

Sean helped me gently set the small girl on the road, and I crawled out of the ditch. My teeth chattered as I told Sean, "We might be able to save her." I had difficulty speaking, as shudders began to rip through my body. There is a phenomenon called the "mammalian dive reflex," which emergency medical teams from cold climates are aware of. A body can survive in cold water for a long time, if the conditions are right. Mammals immersed in frigid water have an instinct which shuts off the bloodflow to the extremities, in order to preserve their hearts and brains. This can occur before they drown, and can help them survive cold water immersion. I prayed this was the case for the prone little form in front of us.

Tony had retrieved a dry blanket and spread it out on the gravel. Sean knelt by Brittany, carefully peeling away the wet blanket as he prepared to transfer her to the dry one.

I stood by, shivers convulsing through my body.

Sean cautioned me, "You'd better get in the car. We don't need two bodies out here."

"I need to know how she died first," I said, clenching my teeth to still the chattering.

Sean carefully looked her over. "Let's not decide she's dead yet. I'm familiar with the dive reflex."

Brittany was wearing a pink winter jacket and pink leggings. There was a large blood stain high on the left leg of her pants.

Sean turned her stiff body slightly as he told me, "It looks like she was shot in the leg. There's an aperture wound clear through. But I don't think she bled to death. And there are no ligature marks on her neck." Sean opened up her jacket and pressed two fingers to her neck. "There's no heartbeat. I need to start CPR on her. Now get in the car—I know what I'm doing." Sean directed Tony, "Help me with CPR. Paula's getting directions from the hospital to guide us."

I finally got into the Crown Victoria and cranked the heat up. Shivers seized my body in spastic jerks through my limbs.

I could hear Sean tell Tony, "She has to unthaw slowly." I reflexively opened my mouth to correct his use of the English language, but now was not the time to educate him on the difference between "thawing" and "unthawing."

Paula drove me to my car, which was at the Brennan farm, so I could change into dry clothes. My hands shook as I fumbled out of my frigid, saturated layers.

When I returned to the scene, Sean continued to rhythmically administer chest compressions. Tony looked exhausted from his efforts to breathe life into Brittany's lungs. I stepped out of the car and nudged him gently aside as I took over for him.

Tony coughed and then spit on the ground as he stepped away. He muttered, "Just give me a minute to catch my breath." Tony took out his phone and directed a police officer to bring Al, Mary, and Jason Brennan to the station to have their hands tested for gun residue.

I don't think people fully appreciate how law enforcement officers put their own health in jeopardy to save others. Brittany had aspirated her stomach contents through her mouth, which is typically the case with CPR, but Tony had cleaned most of it out. I breathed air into her lungs, and Sean followed with five chest compressions, over and over. This is the standard CPR for a child of Brittany's age. "Come on, Brittany," I panted, "come back to us." I'd rather facilitate the breathing (even though it's gross) than the chest compressions, as you had to be careful not to break the ribs of children. There was no doubt in my mind that Sean's compressions were exactly one inch, as they were supposed to be. I wasn't sure if it was wishful thinking, but I thought I felt an independent breath. I was tremendously relieved when the ambulance crew arrived and took over.

After a brief conversation with Tony, Sean, and Paula, I headed to the hotel. Sean thought Brittany's heart had started beating on its own, as well. We gave Brittany a chance, and I prayed for her recovery.

I checked into a room at the AmericInn and stood under a hot shower until my chills subsided. Maurice Strock called and told me he was setting up a news conference. I told him I knew a reporter for WCCO, and he said he didn't care who I spoke to, as long as I followed his guidelines. I decided to do an old friend a favor. I called WCCO and requested to speak to Jada Anderson.

Tony stopped by to pick me up. We went to the sheriff's office to make our statements, then to complete our paperwork at our BCA makeshift headquarters, which was still in the process of being set up in the basement of the Morrison County courthouse.

Jada Anderson arrived at the courthouse with a camera crew, and quickly worked to set up the interview. Jada's mocha brown eyes, slightly curved nose, and bright smile were camera-friendly. Her thick, black hair was combed back, and her dark skin was flawless. Her gray suit jacket, gray slacks, and red sweater fit her perfectly. We hadn't seen each other since our break-up, so after some awkward greetings, we addressed the press conference. Jada confessed she was a little nervous, but excited for the opportunity. She excelled in the limelight, and I had no concerns over how this would go.

Jada interviewed me on the steps of the government center. She gave me a quick, friendly wink before we started, and then was all business. As instructed, I said nothing of Brittany's aperture wound or of her being wrapped in a blanket. I stated that we were optimistic for a full recovery for Brittany, and that the doctors had indicated she was showing promise. The truth was the doctors told us that, at this point, she had about a fifty-percent likelihood of surviving. Maurice wanted people to believe she would survive, because he wanted the perpetrator to sweat over the possibility that Brittany could identify him. He thought it might get someone who had information to come forward. I didn't like doing this to the family, but it wasn't my call. I stated that the quick discovery was made possible by the BCA working closely with local law enforcement. This allowed everyone to receive credit. As anticipated, Jada was at her best, both genuinely concerned for Brittany and appreciative of the work of law enforcement.

When my interview was done, Jada continued to speak to the camera while I snuck out. I was exhausted, cold, and had a headache. Maurice ordered me to take Sunday off. I returned to my hotel room. Numbers began swarming around in my brain like angry hornets, and it took me a minute before I realized the timeframe of Brittany's disappearance and discovery was tormenting me. I wasn't aware of any cold-water immersions where someone had survived after being submerged for hours on end. The paramedics confirmed that we got her heart beating. It was faint, but it was there. This meant her body had been submerged for fewer than thirty minutes. If this was the case, Brittany didn't go into that culvert until after the police arrived at the Brennan farm. Someone had wrapped an eleven-year-old girl in a blanket, entombed her in a culvert, and then flooded the culvert, less than a mile from where I was standing. It was disturbing, and my soul ached for Brittany.

Sunday, March 30

I agreed to meet my parents at St. Joseph's Church in Pierz. I loved driving into the town. In 1888, early Pierz settlers erected an enormous brick Catholic church on a hill in the middle of town. The community then grew around it. The result was a beautiful view of the church, rising above the houses from every direction. It was a common practice in Germany to make the church the highest structure in the community.

Driving into Pierz always made me think of Serena Bell—sharing an ice cream cone with her at Sue's Drive-In or just walking Main Street in the small town, which consisted of a handful of houses and businesses. I considered that the best-case scenario today would have Serena married to a nice Christian man, and mother to a couple of healthy kids. She would be the kind of loving parent who always put her children first. She had probably put on a few pounds and had let herself go a bit; she would talk about her children incessantly. The worst-case scenario would be that she was still a thin, available, ravishing beauty, because it could mean some other factor might have kept her single, like gambling, alcoholism, or sex addiction. By the way, this is what obsessive folks do. If we fear rejection, we convince ourselves that we never really wanted to see them anyway (rather than accepting that most single women are healthy and stable). Serena could be all kinds of wonderful, but for my own purposes, I reduced her to two potential scenarios: married and frumpy, or beautiful but deeply disturbed.

St. Joseph's had large, arched stained-glass windows of saints all along the sides, and when the sun was out, as it was today, the windows glowed in a glorious display of colors. As I turned to make the sign of peace in church, I spotted her two rows back. Worst-case scenario. Serena's long, brown hair flowed with a natural curl past her shoulders. Her green eyes were radiant, framed by her olive skintone. At a diminutive five-foot-three, she was still petite, but was now a stunning twenty-eight-year-old woman who instantly took my breath away. Her black wool coat was open, revealing a peasant-style blouse, decorated around the edges with colorful embroidered flowers. Serena had a classy, if a bit folksy, style.

Serena was waiting on the steps as I exited the church. With a combination of heart-hammering excitement and disbelief, I blurted, "What are you doing here?"

She bit her lip, and I was transported back to high school, fondly remembering how that little mannerism used to make my stomach flip. "This from the man who used to tell me religion should be a way of life, not something you attend."

The Shakespeare sonnet, "If I could write the beauty in your eyes, and with fresh numbers, number all of your graces, in days to come they'd say this poet lies," came to mind. Like Shakespeare, I found this woman unbelievably ravishing. But instead of saying anything along those lines, I clumsily said, "I didn't realize you still lived around here."

Serena smiled. "I don't. My parents were renting out their old place, but now that they've lost the renter, they've decided to sell it. I drive back to Pierz from St. Paul, when I have time, to make it look nice for them. So, I'm staying at our old house tonight." She cocked her head to the side and added, "You look good, Jon."

"You look amazing." I was a little embarrassed over how easily the words left my lips.

She hesitated for a second, then extended her arms for a hug.

I savored her warmth and felt my spirit recharge. It felt wonderful to hold Serena. Her presence and clean scent felt as fresh as the air after a much-needed summer rain. Without conscious awareness, we held hands for a moment after the hug ended, before we both glanced down and awkwardly let go.

I swallowed nervously. "I've been thinking about you," I admitted. "I've often wondered how your life turned out. I imagined you were married and had a couple kids by now."

"Well, I haven't been married and I have no children. I have business management and psychology degrees from St. Ben's, and

I'm managing a clinic for Fairview now. The MNsure insurance stuff is a huge headache at the moment. This system doesn't work, and, instead of making IBM fix the crappy system they created, the state has simply hired more people to answer the phone and apologize to people who can't get help." She stopped herself. "But I enjoy most of my work, and the people I work with are great. I was living in Eden Prairie, but I let my lease end and moved in with my parents in St. Paul until I find a house. I'm ready to buy."

"I knew you would do well." If she was ready to invest, she didn't have gambling issues.

I invited Serena to dinner at my parents', then spent the day with her at her parents' old farmhouse.

10:30 p.m
Pierz

Later that night, we were sitting on the floor in front of her parents' old brown couch playing Scrabble. We had quickly lapsed into comfortable conversation, and it felt as if no time had passed since we last saw each other. She had been working on the same glass of wine all evening, so she wasn't an alcoholic. I loved the way Serena's eyes lit up when she shared stories about her family. She had always made me feel like I was an important person, even though I'd honestly never been one. I reveled in her affection and did my best to reciprocate it. Suddenly, our conversation reached an awkward silence.

She fussed with the hem of her blouse, then met my eyes and quietly asked, "What are you thinking about?"

"I'm thinking of asking if I can kiss you." Although we never defined our relationship ten years ago, we had shared more than a few kisses, and I felt we had once mastered the art of kissing. I wanted to be close to her again.

Holding my gaze, Serena slowly leaned forward, then hesitated just before our lips met. I took that as a "yes," and closed the distance.

What began as a tentative kiss quickly intensified. As I leaned into her, Serena responded by reclining to her back on the floor. Our breathing deepened as our kissing became more passionate. After several minutes, I tenderly brushed her hair to the side of her face and gazed into her eyes. "God, I've missed you."

She closed her eyes for a moment, softly kissed me, and then gently pushed some space between us. "I'm sorry, Jon. This is just too fast. I have so many questions."

We worked our way back to a respectable arrangement, side-by-side, on the couch. She probably wasn't a sex addict. I admonished myself, thinking, *Why did I have to interrupt this wonderful kiss by talking?* Like most guys, I didn't want to talk about a relationship. I just wanted to have one. But I took a deep breath and prompted, "Ask away."

With sadness in her eyes, she responded, "Why did you stop talking to me?"

I considered how to present this. "Have you ever slept with someone you shouldn't have?"

Serena busied herself trying to smooth new wrinkles from her blouse, and without looking up, said, "I'm a Christian, but honestly, I haven't been a great Christian. But I keep trying, and I hope there's some redemption in that. Maybe I'm even the cliché of the hypocritical Catholic girl. So, have I slept with someone I shouldn't have?" She looked up and shrugged. "Honestly, yes—and yes." She slowly shook her head back and forth, as if settling an uncertainty, and then added, "And yes."

I thought, *Okay. Point made.* I wasn't sure if this meant everybody she had slept with, or just the people she shouldn't have slept with. Regardless, I needed to surge forward.

Serena sat posture-perfect and turned to face me as I sat next to her, leaning forward. I was simply going to be honest with her and let it play out. "Okay. Mandy and I had sex on the first night we were together."

Serena nodded. "I assumed that."

"She said she was on birth control, but I don't know that she was. I was worried she might get pregnant, so I stayed with her. I needed to be responsible for the choice I made." If Serena would have slept with another guy at that time, I would have been devastated. But I was too immature and self-centered to have considered this back then. "When it was clear that Mandy wasn't pregnant, I ended it . . . and she disappeared. After everybody started accusing me of murder, I didn't want to burden you with my garbage. You're just nice enough that you would have stood by me, and you didn't deserve that."

Serena studied me for a moment, and with genuine compassion, she sighed, "Psalm Thirty-One."

"Okay." I wasn't going to pretend I knew what she was talking about.

"It reads, 'My life is spent with grief. I am repulsive to my acquaintances. I am forgotten like a dead man. I am a broken vessel, for I hear the slander of many.' It was all so unfair." When I didn't respond, she added, "You should read Psalm Thirty-Two."

Okay, maybe she was still single because she was a religious freak. It's interesting that we never refer to atheists as "freaks." After all, isn't it incredibly egocentric to only believe in what you can comprehend? I smiled sadly and said, "I have nothing against reading the Bible, but it's not going to solve this for me. I didn't kill Mandy Baker."

"I know," she sighed. "I've missed our long walks and conversations by the fire, huddled in a blanket."

I agreed. "I should have confided in you. It seems so obvious, now, but at seventeen, everyone else's life seems so far from your own."

Serena softly conceded this. "Yeah." She placed her hand on my knee. "I didn't know you were going to leave, for good, the night after graduation."

I looked over the scars on my arm I had earned from working construction as I replied, "I didn't have you to talk to anymore, so there was no reason for me to stay. After the graduation ceremony, my family came home to the word 'Killer' painted on the side of our house. Dad said, 'That's enough. I'm getting you out of here before one of these judgmental zealots shoots you.' The next day, I moved in with an uncle who lived two hours away, and worked in construction until I started college."

With a sad acquiescence to opportunities lost, her shoulders sank in resignation. "Have you ever heard of Facebook?"

"Do you have any idea how tired my family is of mindless gossip about my involvement with Mandy Baker? I wouldn't go on social media for their sake."

I saw a painful sorrow in Serena's eyes as she sadly said, "In the Hmong language, they'd say 'Kuzee.' It means a lost opportunity with someone you admired. It's spelled *k-h-a-u-r x-i-a-m.* Not how I would have spelled it."

I couldn't stand seeing her so melancholy. I took her in my arms, held her close, and said, "I'm sorry." For a moment, I wanted us to be who we used to be. I wanted to lie next to her and not think about anything other than how good it felt. Serena was neither married nor damaged. She was just a normal, beautiful, healthy, single woman. After a long embrace, I finally ended our silence, once again, by offering, "I think tonight, the best thing I can do for you is to make sure you're safely secure here and head back to my hotel to get some sleep."

Chapter
Five

JON FREDERICK
MONDAY, MARCH 31
AMERICINN, LITTLE FALLS

AT 7:00 A.M., TONY KNOCKED and entered my hotel room. He was comfortably dressed in faded jeans and hiking boots, ready to take on another day's work. Tony announced, "Brittany began breathing independently last night. The lab results came back, and whoever abducted her injected her with some sort of animal tranquilizer to sedate her. It wasn't a lethal dose, maybe just enough to put her out until her abductor decided what to do with her body."

"Anyone who has worked on a farm could have taken syringes of the tranquilizer from a veterinarian," I said. "The vets typically need help from the farmhands with holding the animals still during examinations, and they keep extra syringes in the kit."

Tony agreed. "Yeah, I know. I've already contacted a veterinarian who serves the farmers in this area. He admitted that several doses were stolen months ago, but he was unable to confirm exactly when they went missing. He provides services to a lot of these small farms in Morrison County, so it basically confirms what we already believe, that it was someone local. The doctor thought Brittany may have only been submerged for twenty minutes. That means we," Tony pointed a thumb to his chest, "us Morrison County guys, messed up, because we can't account for Al or Jason Brennan during this time. It likely happened when you and I were standing on the dirt road, talking about fekking corn."

I wondered out loud, "Why didn't the neighbors find her when they searched?"

"She was about a quarter mile beyond where the search ended. They only searched between the Downing and Brennan farms. Brittany was north of the Brennan farm." Frustrated, Tony ran a hand through his hair. "We don't deal with a lot of homicides in Morrison County. We're still trying to avoid heat from the last one."

On Thanksgiving of 2012, Byron Smith had shot and killed two unarmed teenagers who broke into his home in Little Falls. He was currently on trial for murder, since he fired "kill shots" into the teens, after he had already wounded them and they were incapacitated. Attention had been brought to the Morrison County Sheriff's Department over a report that Smith sent a memo to the department, one month before the shooting, requesting they check into break-ins on his property. None of this was related to our case, and employees of the sheriff's department were not allowed to discuss it. With this in mind, I asked, "Where were Al and Jason twenty minutes before we found Brittany?"

"Al insisted they had to get some chores done, so they could help when the investigators arrived, and our local cops just let them go. Do farmers typically do chores alone?"

"Yes. Somebody gets silage and somebody throws hay down. And you fix and do some of the many things that need to be done. You're never completely caught up. I doubt they started milking at that time. You can't change the cows' schedule."

"Everything was done but the milking," Tony confirmed. "Neither Al nor Jason can account for the other's whereabouts, since they both had their own chores, but they did get all of the work done."

I explained, "You get done with chores quicker if each person works independently. There is no time wasted in conversation. Maybe this is why farmers are notoriously quiet."

"What exactly is silage?" Tony asked.

"Chopped up and fermented hay. It's stored in silos to reduce its exposure to oxygen, to allow for fermentation and to maintain its nutrients. It's poured out as needed, each time you feed the cattle."

Tony scratched his head. "None of the Brennans tested positive for gun residue. We know it wasn't Mary. She was with us." Tony found some gum in his shirt pocket and, as he unwrapped it, said, "There were no decent prints on the jacket left on the road. Who leaves a leather jacket on the road when it's freezing out?"

"Someone who wanted to leave the area quickly."

"I interviewed Al Brennan last night," Tony continued. "He's an odd duck. The man eats northerns out of Green Lake."

Green Lake, a small lake completely surrounded by farmland, just a couple miles south of the Brennan farm on 195th Avenue, wasn't even labeled on a map. It had no rivers or creeks running into it, so the water was stagnant and infused with pesticides. If a person drilled a hole in the ice on Green Lake in the winter, green fluid would fizz out onto the ice. All the northerns out of this lake were skinny, "snakes," and they were all particularly slimy. I tried to give Al the benefit of the doubt by responding, "Maybe he just catches them for the sport of it."

Tony shrugged. "He claims they taste the same as any other fish. Al started college, but dropped out because he felt it was 'all bullshit,' which, of course, it mostly is. Then he got sixteen-year-old Mary pregnant, and she dropped out of school. They ended up taking over his parents' farm. Al whined that we should have issued an Amber Alert. He didn't quite understand that Amber Alerts only search for the victim, and we had the victim. Al also was upset that the reporter on the news pointed out that you were a farm boy. He told me, 'We don't need more farmers, we need investigators!'" Tony paced a few steps before he asked, "Are you in a relationship?"

"I'm not sure," I responded carefully. Serena and I planned to talk again soon.

Tony smiled. "I'm not sure if I'm dating, either, but I do know a woman who'd be angry if she heard me say that. So, how do you know the reporter?"

"What makes you think I know her?"

"You gave an unknown reporter an exclusive. And she kind of gave you some cutesy eyes during the interview. She backed off when you were uncomfortable. That's something a lover might do, but it's an opposite instinct for a reporter. So, you have a history with Jada?"

I had to admit, Tony was good. I told him, "We used to date."

Tony grinned like the cat that swallowed the canary. "You're trying to date someone else, then?"

I nodded. "I am."

Tony said, "I thought so. You said you didn't know if you were in a relationship. That translates to you wanting a relationship with a woman, but you're not sure if she's interested. If you didn't want it, you would have just said you weren't in a relationship."

Going along, I simply said, "Okay."

Tony looked a question at me. "You don't see an issue with inviting an old lover to a small town where the investigators and the media are probably all going to be staying in the same hotel?"

I was embarrassed. "I guess I hadn't considered that."

Tony pointed at me. "Well, my vote goes to the beautiful black reporter." He waited for a response but tired of the game when I didn't offer one. He finally got down to business. "There was no DNA on Brittany Brennan because of her submersion, but it's clear she'd been vaginally and anally penetrated. The problem is, we don't know when, and she's not talking." Tony considered this for a beat, then continued. "Maurice wants Sean and Paula interviewing Al and Jason Brennan. Evidently, the family complained that I'm a little too harsh," he said with a sneer. "I'm going to stop at all the farms along 210th Street, and the sheriff's department is getting me a list of all of the registered sex offenders in the area. We'll see what comes out of that."

I was frustrated that being partnered with Tony cut me out of interviews with the prime suspects, so I offered to do some investigating alone. "I've given this some thought, and maybe it'd be best if I went to Brittany's school to speak to her teachers," I offered. "It would be interesting to know if Brittany exhibited any inappropriate boundaries around peers. Unless you want me to go with you."

Tony's short night was wearing on him. He stifled a yawn and waved me on. "No, go. When I'm done, I'll check out Jason Brennan. You try to retrace Al's steps from yesterday morning. As a farm boy, you'd know exactly how long it should have taken for him to do everything he did. I want to see if either Jason or Al had time to dispose of Brittany."

At Little Falls Middle School, I discovered Brittany had been written up in third grade for French kissing a boy in her class. There were no other reports of inappropriate behavior. Brittany didn't share where she learned the behavior. The teacher felt it was something she may have seen on television. Sometimes, when a child is sexually abused, she exhibits poor boundaries in other environments. It's referred to as "sexually reactive" behavior. The hardest part of any investigation is sorting out the relevant information from the distractions.

It bothered me that Brittany didn't have any close friends, other than the younger neighbor girl. No friends from school came over to play at her home; nobody knew her. Every child should have a friend outside of her home. A stranger who is clever and appealing might seem pretty interesting when a child isn't getting attention from anyone other than her mom—regardless of what she's been told about strangers.

School records indicated that Jason was a C-student at Little Falls High School, where he did well in shop classes, but avoided the college preparation coursework. He had received after-school detention once, two years earlier, following a shoving match with a peer. The other student had apparently started it. Jason had no other disciplinary reports. He was described as quiet and sullen.

Mary Brennan had dropped out of school her junior year after she became pregnant with Jason, and never earned her GED.

I also learned that Al's legal name was actually "Alban," an old German name, common in medieval times but rarely seen today. Alban Brennan had been a B-student, and had been suspended twice for possession of chewing tobacco. None of the Brennans were ever involved in after-school activities.

As I finished going through the school records, I saw Al and Jason Brennan trudging into the office, so I sought them out to see what they were doing. They had stopped to see Brittany at the hospital and Al was making sure Jason wouldn't be in trouble for checking into school late. Al had gaunt facial features, dark, thick, wavy hair, and set back, dark eyes. He seemed to have a little extra space between his teeth. In his thirties, he reminded me of a young Willem Dafoe. He was in good shape and stood about five feet, ten inches tall. Al was not particularly good or bad looking, just different. Jason had dark hair as well, which he wore long in the front and shaved in the back. His facial features were sharper than his father's, and he looked like a typical gawky teenager. He kept his head down and avoided eye contact by hiding behind his hair.

When Al saw me, he said, "I guess I owe you thanks." The comment seemed forced and not particularly genuine.

My thought was that Al was just one more local farmer of stoic German ancestry who lacked emotional congruence when he spoke. I could understand his frustration. His daughter had almost been killed, and only God knew if she would ever recover.

Al squinted and asked, "Do you think Brittany was hurt because someone was mad at me?"

"Is someone mad at you?"

Al looked away as he spoke. "It has me thinking. You make a lot of deals on a farm, buying and selling equipment and crops. Not everyone ends up happy. I sold Eldon Meyer some hay two years ago, and loaded it in a shed for him. It was green, and his shed burned up."

The term "green hay" is used to refer to hay that's still wet when it's baled. The storage sheds can get to over one hundred degrees in the summer, and bales that are wet on the inside generate a lot of heat, sometimes catching fire. Every farmer knows you shouldn't bale green hay.

Al continued. "Eldon and I haven't spoke since. And now Brittany turns up on Eldon's land, hidden in a culvert? It has me thinking."

I told him, "We'll check into it."

Frustrated, Al said, "Checking isn't enough. Do something about it!"

I'd be frustrated too, if I'd just learned that my daughter was left for dead, and my wife had subsequently been badgered by an investigator.

Al added, "There are lakes around here where you could leave a body, and no one would ever find it. Why leave her body in a culvert under a county road? It had to be convenient for him."

"I promise we'll look into it." I said, then asked, "How is Brittany this morning?"

Al looked down the hall as Jason headed off to class, responding, "Still the same—just lying there. If I find the man who did this . . . he's dead."

I asked Al to let us handle this and then took my leave, assuring him that I wouldn't rest until I found out who abducted Brittany.

I called Tony and shared the information I received from the school and Al Brennan. Tony indicated that Eldon Meyer had an alibi for the time Brittany disappeared. After church, Eldon ate Sunday dinner at his sister's and was on his way home when he noticed the bales in the ditch had been disturbed. "I need you to meet me at the investigation center," Tony said. "I found an elderly couple who met Brittany walking home. This'll take our focus in a new direction. Don't waste any more time on the Brennans." He sighed heavily. "It's gonna be a long night."

Tony walked into the investigative center with a couple who looked to be in their early seventies, wearing matching red-and-black-plaid wool coats. Tony introduced them, saying, "This is Richard and Martha Boser. They were checking on their son's farm yesterday. Their son and his new wife were off on their honeymoon. The Boser farm is on the same road as the Brennan and Downing farms, south of both. Richard and Martha had gone for a long walk and were on their way back when they met Brittany walking toward her parents' farm." Tony turned to them. "What time did you say it was?"

Richard scratched his bald head and looked over to Martha.

Martha was a thin, silver-haired woman with a timid voice. She quietly said, "It must have been a little after ten thirty."

Richard nodded in agreement.

Tony asked them, "Do you want to tell my partner, Jon Frederick, what you told me?"

Martha would have preferred to remain silent but knew her husband was expecting her to start the conversation. "About ten minutes after that little girl went walking by, we saw a blue Ford pickup speeding down the road in the same direction as Brittany. The girl had walked over the hill, so we couldn't see her anymore. I remember Rich saying, 'I hope that maniac doesn't hit that poor girl.' I never say things like that out of fear they might come true." She gave me a knowing look.

Richard continued. "The Ford pickup was a 1993 or 1994 model. Dark blue. It said 'Ford' on the tailgate in silver letters, except the 'R' was missing."

"That's a pretty good memory," I commented.

"I'm a Ford man. I take care of my trucks. That 'R' would have been replaced on my truck."

"Did you get a good look at the driver?"

Richard shook his head. "No. I was looking at the truck."

His wife said, "I was pulling Rich to the side of the road so he wouldn't get hit. That man was going way too fast."

Tony asked Martha, "Did you see the driver?"

Martha gave a faint look of being lost. "I don't recall, but I must have. I believe it was a young man, but I can't really remember what he looked like. I'm sorry. I'm getting old."

I thanked her. "Both of you have greatly helped us by coming forward. And by the way, I drove by your son's farm yesterday and it looks very nice. I'm a former farm boy myself, and you can tell when people do good work just by looking at the grange."

Rich smiled with pride and said, "You know, we used to have a farmers' union called the Grangers. You don't hear that word used for the farmyard anymore." Richard rubbed his head. "If there's anything more we can do to help, let us know."

Tony told me he was going to the sheriff's department to cross-reference trucks that fit Richard Boser's description with registered sex offenders in the area. Since I wasn't part of their agency, and they were skittish about information getting out on the Smith trial, I was asked to wait for him. Tony thought this would take about an hour, so I made a quick decision to drive Brittany's journey from the Downings' to the culvert.

I stopped at my hotel room and filled a large glass with ice and Dr. Pepper. I still had a bit of a headache from yesterday's ordeal, but I was hoping caffeine would carry me through the day. The glass fit snugly into the cup holder in my car. On the way, I drove by the south field, where Al Brennan's day started, and decided to take a look at the field. Sometimes, finding nothing is productive, as it allows you to rule out possibilities.

My eyes burned as I drove to the field. I felt a bit overheated and nauseated from yesterday's chilling immersion, but I wanted to work. The sky was overcast, and it had started to drizzle. We were above freezing, so we wouldn't have snow—just freezing rain. I pulled off the tar and onto the dirt approach to the field.

Before getting out, I leaned back and closed my eyes for a moment, then looked over the wet fields and muttered to myself, "Okay, no discarded guns lying around."

My phone buzzed.

Serena said, "*Gemutlichkeit.*"

"Ga-meet-la-kite?" I sounded out the unfamiliar word.

"*Gemutlichkeit* is a German word that means you make me feel as comfortable as if I were at a warm, caring home. My hobby is finding words for emotions in other cultures that we don't have the English equivalents for. It's the word that came to mind after enjoying yesterday with you. Do you have just a minute?"

"Sure."

"Are you alone?"

"Yes, I'm just checking out a field south of the Brennan farm."

Her voice became softer and muffled. "Shoot, I've got another call," she said. "If I can handle it quickly, I'll call you back."

Chapter
Six

Panthera
Monday, March 31
Highway 25, east of Little Falls,
Near the field south of the Brennan Farm

You never should have invited yourself back into my life. As soon as I saw you pull into the field I knew I'd have to dig up that damn bucket, and it's only been a day since I buried it. I'm not Keys or Bundy or any other sick, perverted ass who gets off on taking someone's life. I'm just exercising my right to express my sexuality in the manner I choose, and to exert the dominance I've reaped in my territory.

I click the nine-millimeter handgun off of safety.

I'm not racist, but that black reporter sticks out like a sore thumb. Like the Counting Crows said, "'Round here we all look the same . . . no one notices the contrast of white on white." Still, she's pretty—a seemingly unattainable beauty. We'll see . . .

The rain makes it easy to pull my vehicle unobtrusively over on the opposite side of the road from Jon Frederick. Since his vehicle is down by the field, he can't see mine.

Jon, you should have gone to prison ten years ago. I saw your letter on Mandy's bed, buttons from your jacket on her bedroom floor, and her body by your home. They had you dead to rights, and somehow you wormed out of it.

Chapter Seven

Jon Frederick
Monday, March 31
South field

After a minute, Serena called again. In a soft, troubled voice, she told me, "I normally wouldn't call you at work, but I need to tell you something about Mandy's disappearance."

The rain was picking up, and a steady beat of raindrops drummed on the roof of my car. The dirt field in front of me was getting darker, fed with the downpour. I grabbed the glass of soda, now wet with condensation, and took a sip. I held the perspiring glass to my left cheek to cool my headache, and waited for her to continue. I sensed something behind me, so I turned to look.

Serena went on, "I was the one—"

Suddenly, a concussion rocked the car, and the driver's side window exploded into my face. I reflexively dove across the seats, then quickly scurried over and opened the passenger side door. My hand burned. Staying low, I slid out onto the cold, wet ground as three additional shots hammered into the driver's side door. Lying on the ground, I pulled my gun from my shoulder holster and began firing into the air. I wanted the attacker to know I wasn't going down easily. The left side of my face was hot and I could feel my gun kick in my hands as I fired it, but I couldn't hear my own shots. A loud ringing stung through my ears. I positioned myself behind my passenger door, sitting on the wet, gritty earth. I suspected the shooter was on the road above me, but I couldn't afford to be wrong. I wanted to stand up and fire in that direction, but this could cost me my life. The shooter knew exactly where I was and was waiting for me to re-emerge. Officers died being overly aggressive. My life depended on recognizing I was at a disadvantage. The intelligent choice was to make him come to me. I remained behind the door and fired two more shots in the air. The shots sounded far away, but at least I heard them this time. The painful ringing in my ear continued to pulsate through my skull.

Blood and rain ran down my shirt and, after putting my hand to my face, I could see watery blood dripping off my left hand. A bullet had apparently gone through the bottom of my left hand, and some raw tissue hung grotesquely loose. I didn't feel anything yet. I wondered how bad my head injury was. When I reached up, I could feel shards of glass prickling out of the left side of my face. I took a deep breath and focused on survival. I needed to get to my cell phone.

I reached into the car and found my phone on the floor. My call to Serena had ended. Holding my phone in the dry car, I dialed 911. "Officer shot! South field by Brennan farm. Let Tony Shileto know immediately." I was afraid the phone would be damaged if I held it in the rain, and it was my lifeline. I set the phone back inside on the seat, careful not to end the call so it could be traced. I quickly looked back and forth down each side of the car, ready to fire. I could feel the contrast of freezing-cold rain with the warmth of blood sluicing down my face. My left hand started to burn with the sensation that a hot poker had just been skewered through it.

Where was the shooter? Who was the shooter? The hearing loss was unnerving. I felt like I was in a dimension separate from the rest of the world. I could hear, somewhat, with my right ear, but the ringing was so loud in my left ear, it was useless. Hearing out of only one ear makes it impossible to determine the direction of a sound. I was getting tired and reminded myself, *Don't be stupid. Wait for him to come to you.* The south field is along Highway 25, a fairly busy road, and this would force the shooter to run. I should clarify that a "busy road" in rural Minnesota means that a car drives by about every five minutes. After several more minutes, the sound of sirens penetrated through the ringing in my ear, which brought me some comfort.

The next thing I remembered was being loaded into an ambulance.

Chapter Eight

Serena Bell
9:30 p.m.
Monday, March 31
Highway 25 between Little Falls and Pierz

I was worried sick, and I didn't know exactly where to find Jon. I called 911, and then drove to St. Gabriel's Hospital in Little Falls. When I arrived, I was greeted by sheriff's deputies who stood me up against a wall and with humiliating force, searched me for weapons. A rugged, crew-cut deputy brought me to the sheriff's department and interrogated me. He accused me of setting Jon up. He wanted to know why I hung up and called him back, suggesting I had notified someone of Jon's location between calls. Then, as suddenly as I was whisked to the office, the deputy was called out, and I was told I could leave. They obviously had something more pressing. Jon was an investigator, so law enforcement was anxious to respond "with the necessary force to neutralize the threat," as they say.

Wanting to avoid being swept up in the manhunt, I hurried out the door and called Camille Frederick. She shared that they were secretly allowed to bring Jon to their home. This was good news, so why was I crying? I raced out to my car and headed to the Fredericks' farm. I tried to keep my mind occupied by reminding myself to breathe, and by praying Jon was okay.

I PARKED IN THEIR DRIVEWAY and ran toward the house. My haste turned to panic when a red dot of light flickered across my blouse. Someone had sighted a gun on me! I dove to the ground by a busted bale of hay that had been left in the yard. I quickly crawled behind the hay and crouched, ready to spring into a run, when I heard Bill Frederick yell, "I'm sorry!"

Five minutes later, I was sitting at the kitchen table with Bill and Camille Frederick. Bill had escorted me into the house, repeatedly apologizing. My silk shirt and blue slacks were now damp and covered with itchy flecks of hay. I imagined my hair had suffered a similar fate.

Bill Frederick was a strong fifty-three-year-old man, with thinning hair and a slender frame. His skin was tanned and leathered from years of outdoor work. Bill's style hadn't changed in ten years, consisting of a worn flannel shirt, Wrangler jeans, and a pair of worn but sturdy brown leather boots. I remembered Jon saying his dad would spend the big money on a pair of boots once, and would simply have them resoled whenever it was needed. Bill was talking about how he and Jon had put phone books inside of Jon's front car doors, after watching a *Mythbusters* episode about the practice, to protect him from gunfire, which might have saved Jon's life.

Bill explained, "The cops say they're closing in on the guy who shot Jon. But I'm still not taking any chances here. I'm sorry, Serena, but rest assured, I wouldn't have killed you."

As nice as that was to hear, I found it particularly interesting that he didn't say he wouldn't have *shot* me. I was just glad to hear that Jon was going to be okay and was sound asleep upstairs. Camille continually apologized and fussed about, offering me food and a variety of beverages as I told her about having been aggressively searched, interrogated, and then almost shot before landing at her kitchen table. Bill suggested I take a drink of something hard to settle my nerves, but I agreed to Camille's offer of decaffeinated tea instead. I asked to take a peek in at Jon, and sensing my concern, Bill finally agreed. He escorted me to the upstairs bedroom and then stood in the doorway, observing as I went to Jon's bedside.

Seeing Jon's battered face brought tears to my eyes, and I bent down and kissed the top of his head. His day had been worse than mine. I found some comfort in watching him sleep.

When I turned away, Bill surprised me by saying, "Jon still has some clothes here. Why don't you grab a t-shirt and a pair of sweatpants out of his dresser and go shower. That hay will make you itch like crazy."

I felt too rattled to leave. I wiped away my tears and went to his dresser. "Thank you. If you don't mind, I will."

Jon suddenly awoke from his deep sleep and looked directly at me, blinking sleep out of his eyes. "Serena, what are you doing here?"

I felt like a criminal caught red-handed, standing by his dresser holding a t-shirt and a pair of his sweatpants. I smiled and said, "You were talking to me when you were shot, remember? I had to see that you're okay."

He patted the bed and wearily said, "Come sleep with me."

I blushed and wasn't sure what to say. He obviously didn't see his dad, and probably wasn't even aware that he was in his parents' home. Fortunately, I didn't have to respond as he fell back into a deep sleep within five seconds.

Bill was smiling when I tip-toed out of the room. He said, "We have an extra bedroom if you want to spend the night."

Grateful for the offer, I said, "That's okay. I'm staying at my parents' old place. But I'd like to stay for a couple hours, if it's all right."

After showering, I sat at the kitchen table with Camille drinking another mug of tea while Bill stalked in and out of the house like a special ops soldier. Camille's slender frame was wrapped in a thick pink robe. Her auburn, shoulder-length hair was probably dyed, but looked good on her. Camille had entered her fifties in good health, as a result of eating a lot of home-grown vegetables. She had smooth and kind facial features. Camille was a combination of empathic mother and hardcore Christian, which is perhaps the best type of Christian.

Camille spoke conspiratorially. "I told that militant hillbilly husband of mine it was you out there, but his response was, 'I don't care if it's Moses. Everyone's getting searched.' Bill is always trying to do things for Jon to make up for . . . well, I'm sure you know." Camille looked back to make sure Bill was outside, before asking, "Can I tell you something *sub rosa*?"

"I'm not familiar with that term. Is it Latin?"

Camille nodded. "The rose was a symbol of secrecy in ancient times, so a statement *sub rosa*, or 'under the rose,' was a phrase meaning you could not repeat what you were told."

I took a slow sip of tea, leaned in, and listened attentively.

Camille said, "It wasn't easy when Victor was young. He was ill and didn't understand what he was doing. Sometimes when we were both working, after Theresa left home, Jon was left in charge of Victor. When I look back, it seems ludicrous that we left a nine-year-old boy to take care of a schizophrenic twelve-year-old boy. But Jon was always so responsible. One day, when we were gone, Victor found Bill's old military items and urinated all over them. Victor didn't know what he was doing. Let's just say it was a bad night in our home; Jon took the brunt of Bill's punishment. He had bruises on his butt, legs, and arms. I told Bill that if he ever hit Jon again, he was not only losing the farm, but losing his family, too. He knew I was as serious as sin, and it wasn't negotiable. Bill never struck Jon again."

It made me sad and made perfect sense at the same time. Victor was paranoid, and an easy target for bullies at school. Jon would always defend him, but because Jon was three years younger, and the bullies were older, they'd usually get the better of him. He would end up with destroyed school projects, get his face washed with snow, or would take some hard punches. I admired Jon's loyalty to his brother but, like everyone else, was too afraid to get involved. It finally ended in junior high, when Jon got the better of the worst bully and beat him bloody. When I told Jon I understood his harsh reaction, he told me it was a sin of "false pride," and that decent

Christians had handled more severe situations better. Now I realized Jon couldn't tell his parents Victor was being ostracized in school. He was already in trouble for not taking care of him at home. My heart hurt for him, and I just wanted to go snuggle with him in bed. It also made me think more seriously about the possibility that Bill or Victor had contributed to Mandy's disappearance.

"Where is Victor tonight?" I wondered out loud.

Camille said, "Theresa picked him up. He's going to stay with her until Jon's okay." Sick of farm work, Theresa had left home the day she finished high school and hadn't looked back.

I stopped to check on Jon one last time before leaving. The right side of his face looked good, but there were small cuts, stitches, and specks of dried blood on the left side, making him look like a kinder version of the villain Two-Face from *Batman.* I carefully sat on the edge of the bed beside this strong, slim, and damaged young man. I kissed his forehead and whispered, "This time I'm fighting for you." An unexpected lump formed in my throat.

Camille peered in on us and whispered, "Are you okay?"

I felt silly as a tear escaped and trailed down my cheek. "It's scary."

Camille joined me on the edge of the bed and took my hand in both of hers. "I know. I went through the same thing when Bill was in the Navy. Wondering if it was worth it to be with someone who caused me so much concern. But then I remembered that if he was willing to risk his life to make the world better, I could handle the task of caring about him. He deserved that."

I sniffled, then smiled. "That's a good point."

Camille squeezed my arm and said, "I always thought the two of you were good for each other."

By 11:30 p.m., I was in my pajamas and robe, back at my parents' old house. I hated this house, and I was glad to help my parents unload it. It never got warm, and I'd had nightmares every night I'd slept here since Mandy Baker disappeared. The sound of the doorbell quickly chilled me to the bone. The scary thing about farmhouses is there often is no one living close enough to even hear a scream. I tried to think logically. No one, other than the Fredericks and my parents, knew I was here. I dialed 911 on my cell phone, ready to hit the send button as I turned on the outside light.

Clay Roberts stood under the light in a tight, white Under Armour shirt and designer jeans. He was hazel-eyed, with tousled brown hair naturally streaked with highlights women paid big money to achieve. He looked like a muscular version of Brad Pitt, in his long-haired days. I imagined the sweat being wicked away by his immaculate white shirt. He had to be cold, so he was obviously trying to make an impression. Not wanting to invite him in, I threw on my wool coat and stepped outside to speak to him. Clay had gotten wind of Jon's shooting, and had gone to the Fredericks' to check on him. This wasn't surprising, as news travels fast in small towns and is amplified by the Internet. After some forced small talk, Clay finally asked, "I just thought I'd stop by to say hi. Are you going to invite me in?"

Clay was charming, but if he was kind, it was by a chance circumstance, rather than a moral choice. Clay was the "bad boy" who attracted girls like moths to a porch light. This was a symbiotic relationship, as it seemed to work well with his attention span for them. When daybreak came and artificial light was no longer needed, he was gone.

I answered, "No, I'm going to sleep," as I prepared to go back inside.

Before going, he shook a finger at me and warned, "Don't ever tell Jon about us. You know how he is. He'll never let go of it. And after you come and go, he'll still be my friend."

Regretfully, I'd been one of those misguided moths. I shot back, "I'm not going to lie to Jon."

Clay smugly said, "You mean *anymore*." When I opened my mouth to reply, he cut me off. "Look, I didn't come here to argue with you. Out of everyone I know, Jon annoys me the least. So let me keep that."

Tuesday, April 1

I had a horrible nightmare again last night. I was lying still, and a white man in his early twenties with thick, long, dirty, dark hair, combed straight back, stood looking down on me. He had small eyes, big teeth, and a skeleton-like face. Like a puppet, he had heavy marionette lines around his mouth. I was helpless and he was leaning over me, studying my face. And then I was in a claustrophobic's hell. It was completely black, and I was in a wooden casket, unable to move. I panicked when my warm exhale blew right back into my eyes. The wooden cover had closed and was less than an inch above my face. Barely able to move my hands, I gestured the sign of the cross with my fingers, and then, mercifully, jolted awake.

Psychological studies suggest the thoughts we have throughout the day are sorted, then sometimes revisited, during our dreams. We don't dream about the Revolutionary War—we dream about our lives. I may have seen this guy at our clinic. Between my claustrophobia and Jon investigating Mandy's disappearance into nothingness, the nightmare shouldn't have surprised me.

This was just further evidence that repression, as Carl Jung suggested, wasn't a long-term solution. The past needed to be addressed. Failing to do so could result in my mindlessly positioning myself to face my worst fears. Thoughts of a future with Jon brought me a combination of dreamy, school-girl elation, and anxious pangs of dread. Jon was sweet—in a neurotic and intense sort of way. Complicated, but sweet. I wasn't sure how he was going to take it when I told him I had information about Mandy Baker's disappearance that I'd never shared. I needed to bring resolution to this. That much I knew.

Chapter
Nine

Jon Frederick
Tuesday, April 1
Pierz

I woke with a searing headache. I vaguely recalled Serena sitting on the edge of my bed during the night. I picked up my cell phone and noticed a text from her, which read, "Next time we're alone together—*manja*."

I had to find out what "*manja*" meant. I called a coworker at the BCA in Minneapolis who took pride in interpreting foreign words exactly how they are used in a specific culture. I told him it wasn't work-related, but I'd appreciate the help when he had time. He had already heard I'd been shot and asked if I was okay. I appreciated the camaraderie or, as Serena might say, espirit de corps, among the people I worked with. In a manner of minutes, I received a text from my colleague, saying, "'*Manja*' is a Malaysian word that refers to playfully provocative love." It brought a painful smile to my face. I could use some *manja*.

Tony called to tell me I could put my mind at ease. They had apprehended a convicted sex offender named Jeff Lemor who lived by Hillman. The dirt road by the Brennan farm was a shortcut from Little Falls to Hillman. Further, Jeff's probation officer verified that the "R" was missing on the tailgate of Jeff's truck, making Jeff the man the Bosers had seen driving toward Brittany Brennan. Jeff also had a prior probation violation for being a felon in possession of a gun. Tony told me Jeff took off running into the woods when the squad cars arrived, but the police hunted him down with search dogs. One of the officers was convinced Jeff was holding a gun to his side, but didn't actually see it. When he was finally captured, Lemor was weaponless. So, the officers had a day of searching ahead of them. Jeff insisted he was at home by himself at the time I was shot. Tony told me Jeff's truck engine was still hot when they arrived. Jeff claimed he had been working on it. He had no one to corroborate his alibi.

I had a lot of questions, starting with, "Any idea why he tried to kill me?"

Tony exhaled loudly into the phone. "He must have thought you were onto something. Do you have any recollection of seeing him? He's about six-three, twenty-six years old, with longish black hair and a few days' growth of beard. Skinny, but wiry strong."

"No, I didn't see the shooter," I answered, which was met with a frustrated sigh from Tony. I thought out loud, "Killing isn't this guy's primary goal. If it was, Brittany and I wouldn't still be alive—he kills to cover up. I want to get back to working this."

"Sit tight. For now, the best thing you can do for this investigation is heal. I don't anticipate you'll be back to work in the next few days."

BY THE TIME MY CONVERSATION with Tony was over, I felt weak and drifted back to sleep.

Dad came in to check on me and asked if I needed anything. I told him I was going back to Minneapolis tomorrow, so we had a discussion about making my apartment safe. Dad obliged me, because he believed I was happier off the farm. He told me to give him the day, and my apartment would be ready by tomorrow evening. He and friends planned to install solid oak doors on my bathroom and bedroom. They would reinforce the frames around the doors with metal plates and put a solid bolt lock on the doors. This would mean that, if I was locked in my bedroom, an intruder would have to go through the wall to enter. Having a secure door from the hall to both my bathroom and bedroom allowed me to keep the door between the two rooms open at night, without having to mess with locks.

When I finally made my way downstairs, Mom was holding paint samples against our kitchen blinds and asking for Serena's opinion on the colors. Praying and painting rooms were Mom's go-to moves when she was stressed. I was trying to ignore the radiating pain from my hand. Instead of taking my pain pill, I had settled on naproxen, as I wanted to stay alert.

Mom held out a bright orange color chip and asked, "Jon, what do you think?"

I grimaced and said, "I think this kitchen has been repainted so many times, it's starting to affect the square footage of this house."

Mom smiled and muttered, "You're a lot of help. Are you feeling okay?"

"I just need to sit for a little bit." I meandered into the living room and sat on the couch.

Serena smiled as she stepped around the corner. Like an embarrassed, love-struck teenager, I found myself stumbling over my words as I greeted her. Serena was an enticing work of art. She wore a teal t-shirt that featured thickets of briar shaped into a heart. Her full lips were highlighted by a sheer plum lip stain and looked luscious. I wanted to feel her soft embrace again, but all of those thoughts left my brain and came out as, "Nice shirt."

"It's just something I picked up on sale," Serena said with a playful curtsy. "How are you?"

I softly told her, "Okay. Thanks for being here. If you need to head back to work, I understand."

"No, I'm okay. I like the idea of spending the day with you." Serena glanced back out of the living room to make sure Mom wasn't in earshot. Serena shared, "I thought I saw Mandy Baker at the Mall of America a couple of years ago. I yelled her name and the woman looked at me but then disappeared."

"Did you really think it was Mandy?"

"No. I don't know why I thought I'd be able to recognize her now, even if she is alive. I think the woman left because I was staring at her. I probably scared the hell out of her." Serena nervously twirled her hair around her index finger as she revealed, "I was thinking about Mandy, because I was thinking about you." She studied my battered face in silence for a moment before continuing. "Your mom mentioned you used to date that reporter, Jada. Why did you break up?"

"I want to a have a child. Jada doesn't." I thought I saw a slight smile playing at the corners of Serena's mouth.

Serena took my good hand. "That can be a tall order. I'd like children, too, but what if I found out I couldn't have one?"

"You don't have to make them; they're everywhere."

Serena chided me. "Yeah, I could just steal one."

"Working investigations has put me in contact with a lot of unwanted kids. They don't have to be babies."

Serena moved closer to me. "Okay, that was definitely the right answer. I still feel like you're the only one who ever honestly understood me. If we're headed where I think we are, maybe we should start with a real date," she smiled.

The floorboards announced that Mom was casually meandering closer, pretending to adjust a picture as she listened in.

Not certain if Serena noticed her, I decided to change the topic. "I think it's time for a funny story."

Serena was already smiling. "That would be perfect."

"Okay, when I pulled into the law enforcement center last week, I saw a guy crawling into his trunk. He told me none of the handles in his car worked anymore, so the trunk was the only way in and out of the car. Then he added, 'It's really embarrassing getting groceries, but my girlfriend is pretty understanding of it.'"

Serena laughed out loud. "I wouldn't go anywhere with a guy who expected that of me."

I teased her, saying, "Come on, just get in the trunk."

Trying unsuccessfully to compose herself, Serena said, "I don't remember the last time I've giggled like this!"

"I suggested to the guy, 'Maybe it's time to get a new car.' He told me, 'Are you kidding? This is a Mustang!'"

"Well, if I would have known it was a Mustang . . ." With a contented sigh, Serena put her hand on my leg. "I should be cheering you up."

Mom peeked in at us. Uninterested in my story, she turned and went upstairs.

Serena stood up for a moment, then pulled her hair into a ponytail. "Can we talk about Mandy Baker?"

I always enjoyed watching Serena put her hair back. It reminded me of how naturally beautiful she was. I still trusted her, so I shared my thoughts about Mandy Baker's disappearance.

Serena was intrigued. "Who do you suspect?"

"Mandy used to flirt with a group of guys who played Texas Hold'em at her house on Monday nights, but there was nothing about those guys in the cold case file. They all had nicknames—Chino, Sliver, Whitey, Onion, and 'Say Hey' Ray. Over the past years, I think I've hunted them all down."

I ticked them off one-by-one on my fingers. "Chino was actually Native, but got the nickname from the crew's racial ignorance. He was in Mandan, North Dakota, when Mandy disappeared. Sliver was a meth addict. It took a bit of work, but I eventually found some guys who partied and crashed with Sliver on the night Mandy disappeared, so I was able to rule him out. I'm not one hundred percent certain I got the right Whitey, though. There's an abundance of guys nicknamed 'Whitey' in rural Minnesota. The most likely candidate was a toe-head named Joey Gilbert, who was killed driving drunk five years ago. I never found anyone who was with Joey the night Mandy disappeared. He lived by himself in a trailer, and was probably just home alone. He was a very relaxed, pot-smoking dude. I haven't cleared him, but he doesn't seem right for it. It took me years to find Onion. He wasn't around as much."

Serena commented dryly, "Imagine writing a wedding invitation to, 'Onion and guest.'"

"Onion was a paraplegic who was in bad health and didn't drive. He couldn't have picked Mandy up. All of these guys are criminals, and none of them will talk to the police. So, I'm stuck. I may need to eventually talk to Say Hey Ray Benson. Even though Ray's been cleared as a suspect, because he was in jail that night, he might have insight into other unsavory characters who hung around their house back then."

When Serena was perplexed, she got two little creases between her eyebrows. I had forgotten how cute that made her look. She asked, "Why would Say Hey Ray help you?"

"He's in prison in Florida," I explained, "and it may look good for him in front of the parole board."

"Jon, I want to help." Her face softened and there was sadness in her eyes as she said, "Remember, I went through this, too."

Chapter
Ten

Jon Frederick
Wednesday, April 2
Pierz

Serena was back in St. Paul at work today, so I called Tony and told him I was heading back to Minneapolis. He offered to stop over at my parents' and update me before I left.

Tony was a filthy mess when he stepped out of his rusty brown Chevy. He looked like someone had slathered honey on him, then rolled him around in the yard. Mom peered out the window and pursed her lips at Tony, not sure what to make of him, as he trudged toward her house. I asked Mom if we could have a few minutes. With a last pained look at Tony, she left us alone.

Tony marched unapologetically into the kitchen, covered in sticky dirt. He was excited, and a little loud, so Mom probably heard him anyway. "We found the gun in the branches of a pine tree. It was absolutely miserable, digging through pine trees, getting that sticky sap all over us. Now I know what the inside of a popcorn ball feels like." Exhausted, Tony slumped. "Mind if I have a seat? It's been a long day of standing." Using my foot, I deliberately pushed one of the chairs without a cushion toward him, knowing Mom would have a large mammal if he put his dirty behind on any of her upholstery.

Tony picked a few pine needles free of his sleeve, making a neat pile of them on the table. "It's a nine-millimeter, double-action stainless revolver, similar to the one that fired bullets into your car."

My statistic-ridden brain immediately registered that the nine millimeter was also the most popular handgun sold in the United States.

Tony continued. "Lemor's denying any involvement with Brittany, and he's denying shooting at you. But he doesn't have an alibi for either. All we have to do now is match the bullets in your car to his gun, and he's done. We already have him spotted driving down the road toward Brittany."

"He's in jail?"

"Yeah. We can hold for him for seventy-two hours. By then we'll have the ballistics report. Plus, possession of a gun is a probation violation, so he'll be sitting behind bars until his trial. This is going to be an APE case." APE was the term investigators used for an "acute publicity emergency." It meant it was essential that prosecution begin as quickly as possible to satisfy an angry public.

Tony went on, "Maurice liked the way Jada Anderson handled the interview, so he gave her the exclusive on Lemor's arrest. Saving Brittany, and now the quick arrest, has been great publicity for law enforcement. Maurice is strutting around like he's the man, and he plans on squeezing as much glory as possible out of this case. A happy day for the gangster of love."

Tony was making reference to a Steve Miller hit from the seventies, "The Joker": "Some people call me the space cowboy, some call me the gangster of love. Some people call me Maurice, because I speak to the pompitous of love." By the way, "pompitous" wasn't actually a word. But apparently no one told Steve Miller that.

Tony continued to pull pine needles from his clothes. "Brittany's improving, wavering in and out of consciousness. We're keeping a guard with her twenty-four hours a day until Lemor is officially charged with attempted murder."

My gaze fixed on the growing pile of tree detritus, but I no longer saw it. "I feel bad for the Brennans. Their little girl was raped and left for dead. It ignites a fire in me. I can only imagine how it's affecting Al."

Tony shook his head sullenly. "If I'd have been the one who ran Jeff down, he'd be in a world of hurt. I don't take kindly to guys who open fire on investigators."

I rubbed my eyes and, with the honesty that often stems from exhaustion, asked, "Why did you beat up Troy Halzberg?"

Tony ignored me initially, as he silently processed a thought. Finally, he asked, "What?"

"Why did you beat up Troy?"

"Are you kidding me?" Tony threw his hands in the air and then dropped them on the table. "What is with you? Nobody's had the balls to ask me about that." Tony glared at me. "You got a pop? I'm going to need something to sip on if you want to hear that story."

I went to the fridge and grabbed a caffeine-free Diet Mountain Dew. "The only soda my parents have is caffeine- and sugar-free. They don't keep anything around that'll make it more difficult for Victor to sleep at night."

Tony accepted the soda and muttered, "No nicotine, no sugar, no caffeine, no fun." He cracked open the can, took a long drink, pondered the question, then slyly grinned. "I guess there really isn't that much to the story. Troy raped my fourteen-year-old niece, after she drank too much at a party."

I waited for him to continue. When he didn't, I added, "So you assaulted him."

Tony scratched his sap-spattered head. "Not immediately. Troy's daddy bought him an attorney who convinced the jury my niece made the story up, because she didn't want to get in trouble for drinking." Tony was progressively becoming more agitated. "My niece didn't report the rape until two days later, and she had already showered."

I could imagine Tony pursuing justice on his own.

Tony leaned forward, his lips forming a thin line. Baring his teeth, he continued. "I initially left him alone. But then one night, after Troy was out using with his buddies, he walked into McDonald's when my niece was working the counter alone. He taunted her with some of the things she said while he was raping her. She stepped into the back and called me." Tony gave a small shake of his head. "So I found Troy. I told him I was her uncle, and I'd be visiting him anytime he came near her. Oh, yeah, and I hit him." Tony shrugged. "It just seemed like the right thing to do. Then he made a smart-ass comment, so I hit him again." Tony held his hands out. "Just like that he was on the ground. So I bent down and told him that, next time, it might not be so easy for him to crawl away. The next week, I was called into my boss's office. I told him what happened. He told me to go back to work and never speak of it again. There were no charges, but it never goes away. I'm just one more dumbass cop who abused his power. That's the story."

"I can understand your frustration. I think a lot of guys would have responded the same way."

Tony considered what I'd said. "But you wouldn't have."

"Honestly it's difficult to say what I'd do, until I'm in that situation. I . . ." my voice trailed off as I decided it would be better if I didn't finish this sentence.

Tony wouldn't accept my retreat. "Speak up. What were you going to say?"

"Whenever I hear about a cop beating someone up, I always wonder how much of it has to do with the situation, and how much has to do with what's going on in the cop's life."

There was an extended, awkward silence before Tony admitted, "Honestly, my marriage wasn't going well at the time. My wife was having an affair. I was working my ass off, and nobody appreciated it, even at work . . ."

When Tony was done sharing, I said, "Thanks for telling me. You've already earned my respect, but it's nice to know the truth."

Ignoring the compliment, Tony changed the subject. "So what's your story?"

"What do you mean?"

Tony was tired, but he still managed to smirk at my ignorance. "Ten years may seem like a long time when you're twenty-eight, but when you're forty-nine, it's like yesterday. I wasn't the main investigator, but I worked the Mandy Baker case in 2004, and you were our prime suspect. If you didn't kill her, who did?" Tony challenged me. "Her friends in Little Falls said Mandy was hell-bent on getting to Pierz that night."

Surprised by this revelation, I nervously repositioned myself in my chair.

Tony continued. "Maurice told me you went through the murder book. You know the killer, and maybe somebody out there knows you know." Tony studied my reaction. When I didn't respond, he continued. "The Mandy Baker investigation was abysmal. It was the biggest damn clusterfuck of an investigation I've ever participated in."

"Why's that?" He had my undivided attention now.

"Nobody could decide whose case it was. My boss thought it belonged to the BCA, so after a couple days of asking around, we gave it the BCA. The BCA thought it belonged to the FBI because even though Mandy had been in Minnesota for six months, she wasn't a Minnesota resident. The FBI thought we should have kept it. But Mandy wasn't a local and had no family around, other than her drug-addict mom, so nobody cared. I think everybody thought Mandy was just shackin' up with a guy, and would eventually pop up."

I found little comfort in knowing that, while the Little Falls community was ready to lynch me, nobody was looking for any other suspects.

Tony went on, "People in Pierz had nothing to say to us. I've always felt the Pierz crew knew more than they let on. It's a pretty tight-knit community, and they tend to protect their own. Your brother was pretty evasive."

"Victor is schizophrenic and a little developmentally disabled, but he's not violent."

Tony studied me for a moment. "He's family. I get it. You're more like me than you'd like to admit."

"Victor never hurt anybody. He was always afraid, and Mandy would have torn him apart if he tried anything."

Tony argued, "Victor, you, and your dad are all strong farm boys. Mentally ill people can be uncontrollably strong, because they fear for their lives in situations where it isn't warranted."

He was right, but I pointed out, "Victor wasn't psychotic at the time, and he was never violent."

Tony sighed and pushed his chair back, making to stand up. "Okay," he conceded. "But you're going to need to open your eyes to possibilities close to home, if you honestly want to resolve Mandy's disappearance. Get some rest. I'll keep you informed. "

"Before you leave, I need to ask the relevance of the jacket found on the dirt road by the Brennans. Why did you ask if I owned it?"

Tony scooted his pine needles into a more compact pile. "When we searched Mandy's bedroom, we found two buttons on the floor by the bed that had been torn off of a man's jacket. I was able to prove it was from a specific type of Express men's leather jacket, but we never found it. And then, by some twist of fate, one of the searchers the Brennans sent out to look for their missing daughter, ten years later, finds an Express men's leather jacket in the ditch, missing two buttons. And I think God's given me another chance at the Mandy Baker case. I looked all over for that damn jacket a decade ago, and now a perfect match is dropped on my lap. I think Mandy was wearing that jacket the night she disappeared. Her friends at school said she wore a leather jacket that belonged to a guy she was dating from Pierz, and, hello, that's you. So, I called the space cowboy and asked for you, specifically, to work this investigation with me. Are you an investigator because of your guilt or your innocence?"

Shame washed over me, but I kept my composure and asked, "Do you think Mandy's disappearance is related to the assault on Brittany?"

Tony said, "Not anymore. It certainly would be easier if all the bad crimes were committed by one guy, but I think we're dealing with a couple different perpetrators." Tony slapped his thighs and stood up as a cloud of dust puffed from his pant legs. "Okay, no work for you tomorrow. We'll see how you're doing in a couple days."

Needing more information, I said, "I have one more question."

"You're pushing it."

"What do you have from the Mandy Baker investigation that never made it into the case file?"

Tony swept the needles into his hand and dropped them into the nearby garbage can. "Not a lot, because we didn't have the case for long. I wanted to talk to Victor again, but your dad lawyered him up. I guess the biggest thing is we initially had a pretty good description of the car. Small, white four-door with red pinstripes. Likely a Chevy Cavalier. When the BCA re-interviewed the witness, she wasn't as sure, so, ultimately, a vague description of the car went into the file. I didn't find anyone related to the case who drove one, so it wasn't particularly helpful."

I calmly said, "Thanks," but it bothered me immensely. I knew someone who drove a white Cavalier with red pinstripes ten years ago.

As I drove to Minneapolis, I spent an hour considering a variety of scenarios involving my Cavalier-driving friend and Mandy Baker. While I wanted to confront this individual in person, I needed to fight my obsessive desire for an immediate answer. I forced myself to wait patiently for the proper opportunity.

Chapter Eleven

Panthera

I'm shut down for a while, but I vow to remain disciplined. I need to sit back and enjoy my success for the time being. I needed Brittany silent and Jon Frederick off the case, and I have achieved both.

Jada Anderson has to be the best-protected person in the state of Minnesota. As one of the few black professional women in central Minnesota, everybody pays attention to her. You can't be near her without being observed. She's also staying at the AmericInn with all of the investigators. Going after her would be my undoing, and getting her would only resolve my curiosity. I need to be smart. So, she's safe for now, but if she interferes with my life, game on.

I have better options to consider. One I've had before, another is highly rewarding, and both would ease my resentment. Balance the world again. I could have ravaged Serena, but I opted to just watch her sleep beneath me. She had become available to me unexpectedly. This time, I'll have her on my own terms. Acting yields a powerful reward, but there is also powerful satisfaction in restraint. I have the power to say, "I spared her life tonight." Exercising options makes an attack all the more exciting.

Chapter
Twelve

Jon Frederick
7:15 p.m.
Wednesday, April 2
Minneapolis

On my way back to my apartment, I decided to stop at the BCA office for one more look at Mandy's murder book. While I could greatly benefit from some *manja*, the white Cavalier troubled me. My hand throbbed, and I no longer envisioned this evening going well.

The cement cold-case storage room was quiet, aside from the humming of the fluorescent lights. As I carefully worked through the evidence box, I searched for details I might have missed in my first overview. I held up a Ziploc bag containing two brown buttons. According to the report, there were no partial fingerprints found on them, and that bothered me. Mandy's bed was unmade, but it was always unmade. There had been no sign of a struggle in her room. Whose jacket was it, and how did it suddenly turn up ten years later? I may never find that answer, so I needed to sort through the remaining contents of the box.

A number of registered sex offenders living in the area were also investigated, but alibis were verified for all. One offender, Randall Davis, had a victim with similar physical characteristics to Mandy. Randall pled guilty to criminal sexual conduct in the third degree in 2003, for having sex with a fifteen-year-old girl. While he pled guilty to a statutory offense, the victim reported fearing for her life as he forcibly raped her. A plea was taken in this case because the victim was labeled "promiscuous," and the prosecutor didn't want to take it to trial. The DNA testing on Davis's victim suggested the girl had sex with more than one man in the previous twenty-four hours, which could simply mean she had a boyfriend. Davis's alibi on the night Mandy disappeared was his live-in girlfriend—a woman he had a previously assaulted. Randall would be worth revisiting.

I smiled at the thought of Tony interrogating my brother. Victor was a paranoid schizophrenic, so you could ask him the time of day and he'd be suspicious. In addition, thoughts flew through his head like divider stripes by a car cruising down the freeway.

Continuing to go through the box, I found the note stating that Mandy was picked up in a white car at about eight o'clock in the evening. Visualizing that car gave me a sick feeling. What was I doing here? I had wanted to be with Serena for as long as I could remember, and here I was in the cold-case room instead. The unknowns about Mandy's disappearance had already consumed a decade of my life. I used to worry this case would never be solved; now I worried about who it was going to implicate. I started this trouble by getting involved with Mandy, and when you start trouble, you have no control over how others respond. I had a bad feeling about this.

I called Serena and told her I had some work to attend to, so I couldn't be with her tonight. That call was difficult. She wanted to take care of me, and I wanted to be with her, but I wasn't feeling well, and I had to carefully consider my next step.

8:30 P.M
Thursday, April 3
Birmingham Apartments, Minneapolis

Today was not particularly productive. I went to the gym and worked out the best I could, avoiding the use of my left arm. I was never a fan of passive healing. I bought some groceries and took a nap but was no closer to knowing how to address my concerns.

The best distraction from my pain tonight was Serena, sitting next to me in an off-the-shoulders, lacy white blouse and black jeans. Her beautiful dark hair flowed to her smooth shoulders and her green eyes shimmered. A hint of lipstick gave her lips a satin sheen. Was she a semblance of pulchritude, or did that beauty radiate within, as well? My headache wasn't completely gone, but it seemed irrelevant, and the pain in my hand had dissipated to the point where it was only a minor distraction.

Serena softly observed, "Something's bothering you."

"Tony gave me a little more information on the car that picked Mandy up on the night she disappeared. It was a white Chevy Cavalier with red pinstripes. How many cars, would you guess, met that description in Morrison County ten years ago?" I had given her a baited question, based on my suspicion. There were actually more than you'd think—thirty-seven, to be exact.

She swallowed hard and glanced down for a moment. "I wanted to talk to you about that. I was the one who picked Mandy up that night."

My stomach burned acid. "Tell me what happened."

"Mandy called me, because she knew I was close to you. She wanted to be in Pierz when your team got back from your game. I was home alone at the time, so I drove her to my house and we talked."

I patiently waited for her to continue.

Serena looked agonized. "She told me how sexually naïve you were. It was miserable. I was trying to be nice to her, but she was so spiteful to me. Mandy was wearing the leather jacket you gave her."

Frustrated, I said, "I never gave her a jacket. I've never even owned a leather jacket."

She nervously nodded in agreement. "Okay." Serena paused, then said, "Looking back, I think she said a lot of things because she knew they bothered me, and she wanted me to hurt just like she was hurting. She said it was urgent that she talked to you, so I thought maybe she was pregnant. I didn't know when I picked her up that you'd just broken up with her. Mandy found a bottle of Windsor in my parents' liquor cabinet, and we had a couple drinks. I asked her if she should be drinking and she laughed. I wasn't a drinker, and she mixed them strong. After a couple, I told her I needed to stop. My head was spinning, so I laid down on the couch. I wanted to rest a little before I gave her a ride home, but I fell asleep. When I woke, she was gone. I never saw her again. I assumed she walked over to your house. You would have been home by then."

I tried to speak calmly and softly as I said, "Why didn't you tell the police this?"

"No one ever came to talk to me," she said.

"You didn't call to check on her the next day?"

"I had no desire to talk to her again. She made so many nasty comments about me and my faith—always followed with 'I'm just kidding.' But she wasn't, really. Out of anger, I told her she was wasting her time with you. If you said you didn't want to date her anymore, it was over. You've always been stubborn—sometimes in a good way." Serena took my good hand. "Looking back, I wish I wouldn't have reacted as I did. My life was easier than hers in so many ways. But you don't think about that when your heart's broken."

I studied her in silence.

Serena squeezed my hand a little harder. "Don't be angry. My first instinct was to protect you."

With my thumb, I wiped a tear off of her cheek. "You thought I had done something to Mandy," I said sadly. "So, why are you here? Why risk being alone with me?"

"Because I think I was wrong, and I turned my back on the best friend I've ever had. I told my parents about my encounter with Mandy two days later, and they said it was too late to go to the police—they'd just think I did it. 'Let them come to you,' they said. They never came. I didn't know what to do. I was seventeen and freaked out. My parents kept warning me to stay away from you."

I sighed and shook my head. "So where did Mandy go?"

"I wish I knew. We searched every inch of our land and couldn't find her. I know the police searched your farm."

After several minutes of silence, Serena asked, "Did you get any more information from the cold-case box?"

"There was a sex offender named Randall Davis who lived west of Little Falls. His alibi that night was from a woman he was abusive to, so I'd like to revisit him."

"What was her name?"

"Let me think for a second."

"You didn't write it down?"

"I didn't need to. I've used stories to remember things since I was a kid."

Serena softly asked, "What was going on in your life when you started doing that?"

She was keeping me off task, but it was a question I'd never been asked. I thought about it and answered, "It started when Victor was about thirteen and struggling with auditory hallucinations. I think my parents assumed Victor stopped being crazy when he went to bed. We shared a bedroom, and it got scary when he'd talk about the devil, so I started playing number games in my head to ignore him. To completely shut him out, I'd challenge myself to find a way to remember the numbers later. Now it just happens automatically. It was a depressing time for me. "

Serena hesitated before asking, "Is it possible your dad could have killed Mandy? Your mom made it sound like he went DEFCON One on you after Victor urinated on his military stuff."

"Dad was losing a farm that had been in his family for three generations. Victor was having hallucinations of the devil, my sister Theresa was out running around, and my mom responded by going into religious rants. It was crazy-making. But then, Victor's medication began working, Theresa fell in love, and Dad finally accepted that bankruptcy didn't mean he had completely failed as a man. Mom calmed down, and we ended up okay." I thought a moment. "Dad's a good man. After graduation, he asked me to stay away from the farm because he worried about me every minute I was there. I think he sensed how unhappy it made me. All that work, and we walked away with nothing."

"How do you forgive a brutal beating?"

"He changed, years before Mandy came into the picture. My dad was just a child who got old. He had a big heart and a short fuse. When Mom threatened to leave, he tantrummed for a bit, but then grew up." Serena had a way of helping me assess my circumstances that led me to insights I'd never reach on my own. I said, "When people honestly change, they stop frantically making excuses. You sense the guilt, but they're not looking for self-pity. They're honest and matter-of-fact. If Dad had killed Mandy, he would have confessed and gone to jail." With all the tenderness I could muster, I said, "I should be mad at you for not telling me you were with Mandy. But your smile and those perfectly smooth bare shoulders are really unfair. Logic escapes me, and I feel the same raw emotions I had about you when we were teenagers."

Serena laughed. "So, at this moment, I'm dangling in your brain with all those numbers."

I grimaced, realizing my words were not very poetic, and offered, "You'd be a prime number."

Serena rested her head on my shoulder, and we sat in silence for a moment before she said, "This isn't exactly *manja*."

I kissed the top of her head. "I have a lot to think about."

She kissed my cheek and in a barely audible voice, said, "Let me help you shut it off for one night. Staying fixated on a task is a poor way to problem-solve. Tomorrow, you can come back to it with fresh insight." She rubbed her bare shoulder and, with her head down, sighed, "I'm sorry for not telling you I was with Mandy that evening. I can apologize for it all night if you'd like. It's tormented me for a decade. But I have nothing more to tell you, so it would be a big relief to me if we could just take a break from talking about it and hold each other. I almost lost you."

Sensing the depth of her remorse, I offered, "Maybe you're right."

"Not maybe. I can feel you're mad at me, even if you don't say it. I never intended to hurt you." Serena cautiously leaned into me and brushed her lips against mine. "Are you feeling okay?"

No, but good enough for some manja, I thought, which came out as, "Yes." *Hell, who am I to treat anyone poorly on the basis of suspicion?*

I decided to just put it out there. "Through all this, I still desire you more than I've ever desired anyone, and the attempt on my life has greatly diminished my desire to postpone positive events." If anybody could shut off my obsessive thoughts, it was Serena. Evil temptation or amazing kindness?

She kissed me.

I took my time and savored kissing her full lips, her neck, and her bare shoulders. She tugged at the bottom of my t-shirt, and as I removed it, she helped me carefully pull it over my bandaged arm.

I slid her blouse down her shoulders, revealing her bare breasts.

She timidly asked, "What are you smiling about?"

"You're beautiful." Her long, dark hair flowing down to her breasts was sensuous, fine art. Loving Serena felt so right.

With the pleasant warmth of our chests skin to skin, we held each other close and kissed. Her tenderness and affection had the intensity of tangible gravity.

Serena whispered, "Mindfulness—focusing on the immediate moment. Isn't it nice?"

Concerned about the recent attempt on my life, and of keeping her safe, I suggested, "We could do this behind bolted, solid oak doors in my bedroom."

Serena picked up her shirt and held it in front of her chest. "Do you mean the vault your dad made for you?"

Without saying a word, she headed to my bedroom, tossing a seductive look at me over her shoulder. I admired her lovely dark curls dangling down her bare back before silently following.

Chapter Thirteen

Jon Frederick
Evening
Friday, April 4
Birmingham Apartments, Minneapolis

Maurice officially instructed me on Wednesday to stay away from the investigation for a week to heal. I was frustrated, but Serena had made the last couple days the best I'd lived. I worked out in the morning, then picked up the ingredients needed to have a gourmet meal ready when she was done with her work day.

One benefit to my obsessiveness was that, when I finally convinced myself to shut off work, it was off. So, I focused on making my environment Serena-friendly—a red wine blend she loved, fresh fruit, and a great dinner. After our meal, we went for a walk, shared back rubs, and she stayed the night to "assist with my recovery." It was so peaceful to finally lie in bed and not have numbers churning through my head. I had never experienced that tranquility with anyone else. I still had a headache from my wound and the pain in my hand, but I slept.

A little after 6:00 p.m., Sean Reynolds paid a brief visit to my apartment to make sure I was doing okay. The gesture felt genuinely benevolent. He had returned to the BCA headquarters in St. Paul to pick up forensic reports.

The reports indicated Brittany hadn't been shot. Even though it had the appearance of a bullet aperture, the wound was made with a long tool, probably an awl. The awl had been run completely through her leg from the front, then pulled back out, leaving large blood stains on both the front and back of her sweatpants. This explained why no one heard a gunshot.

Sean rubbed the top of his head as he constructed a new theory. "The entrance and exit wounds in Brittany's leg would be the perfect angle if she was a passenger sitting in the front seat, and Jeff stabbed down on her leg from the driver's seat." Sean slowly imitated a stabbing motion that could have been taken from *Psycho*. He added, "She had to be struck hard."

I pointed out, "But there was no blood in his vehicle."

"Yeah, it had to happen outside," Sean said. "Maybe in the ditch."

Sean's short intrusion brought me back to thinking about work periodically throughout the evening.

At midnight, Serena was lying prone on my couch with her bare backside presenting a pleasant, natural horizon. Her smooth skin was lit by the city lights shining from below through the open curtain. She still had a glow in her eyes from making love. I delivered a bowl of vanilla bean frozen yogurt topped off with malt, dark chocolate, and my home-roasted almonds, which I had prepared for our late-night dessert.

Serena demurred, "You're spoiling me."

She lifted her feet as I sat on the couch, then, feeling comfort in the contact, rested them in my lap. I told her, "I need to return to Little Falls tomorrow. Even if I can't work on the case, I want to be brought up to speed."

Serena's tone became serious. "How is Victor doing?"

"Okay." I massaged the backs of her calves with my good hand while she enjoyed a spoonful of dessert.

Serena silently enjoyed the massage for a moment. "I always liked Victor. He introduced me once by saying, 'She invented flowers.'"

I started massaging a foot. "He obviously likes you. Victor associates positive events with positive people."

"Like you associate numbers with stories?"

"I guess we're both a little crazy."

Serena lifted her other foot to my good hand, suggesting I rub that one, too, while she playfully contradicted her unspoken request. "You don't have to rub my feet. I feel like I've been spending my evenings at a love spa."

I kissed her foot. "Then it's working."

Serena turned over, sat up, and stilled my hands with her own. "I hate to even ask this, but do you think it's possible that Victor killed Mandy? You said he used to wander around the farm at night, and Mandy was just down the road. I think she walked to your house that night."

I told her, "Victor wouldn't have killed Mandy. At that time, his meds had finally stabilized, and he was doing well. Victor never hurt anybody, even when he was struggling. He was an easy target for bullies because he didn't have the self-preservation to stand up for himself."

Serena was careful to not bump my injured arm as she slid her arms around my waist. "I'm sorry I brought this up," she said. "I want to work through this with you, so it helps me to know what you're thinking."

Anticipating more questions about my family, I said, "Theresa was living out of state at the time, and my mom just wouldn't have done it." I hoped that put to rest any suspicions.

Saturday, April 5
Little Falls

After Serena left, I found a crumpled piece of paper with what appeared to be a list of suspects she had compiled in Mandy's disappearance. The list included my brother, my dad, Clay, Randall Davis, Whitey, and most concerning, Serena herself.

As I drove to Little Falls, uneasiness started to stir inside me. I began to envision a scenario where an argument between

Serena and Mandy resulted in Mandy getting out of the vehicle and Serena taking off. The worst part of being obsessive was that a slight discrepancy could become a disturbing snag that must be addressed. Investigators are taught to pay special attention to the last person who was with the victim. In Mandy's case, it was Serena.

Last night, Serena had asked me if I'd ever consider walking away from this investigation. She appeared to ask out of fear for my well-being. When I was with her, I was one-hundred percent convinced of her innocence, but now that I looked at the evidence, doubt crept back in. Despite my concerns, I was progressively falling harder for Serena. I wanted her, and there was no doubt she reciprocated my affection. It would be just my luck that the only person with whom I could get a good night's sleep was a killer.

AS I APPROACHED LITTLE FALLS, my phone buzzed with a text from Serena, saying, "Thank you for the last few days. Hope to see you tonight. *Han-xu*." I reached out again to my friend at the BCA, who shared that *han-xu* is pronounced "han-she" and is Mandarin Chinese. He stated that, even though the Internet suggests it means "reserved," in China it generally refers to when a woman loves a man, but is unable to properly express it to him. I simply texted back, "I love you," because it was honest. I didn't know how to proceed with the investigation of Mandy's disappearance, and I wasn't even sure I wanted to.

I DECIDED TO STOP at the AmericInn. Someone had tried to shoot me, and I wanted to see if my room had been disturbed.

It was a cool, sunny morning. A hard-looking young woman paced outside the hotel smoking a cigarette with intensity, as if it would be her last. Her pale skin had a tinge of purple, and she was underweight. At first glance, I thought, *A history of methamphetamine abuse, but clean now.* I guessed her to be in her mid-twenties. She was tall—maybe five-foot-ten—and all angles, with bony shoulders, elbows, and knees. She wore her hair short and dyed an unnatural red. The piercing in her nose seemed to accent the knob in the middle of it, rather than to highlight any beauty. Her burgundy lipstick was out of place with her tattered jeans and gray hoodie. Yet, underneath her tough exterior, she was pretty, once.

When I stepped out of my car, she marched up to me and nervously asked, "Are you Jon Frederick?"

I hesitated, then nodded. "I am."

Throwing her cigarette on the ground and crushing it under her Converse tennis shoe, she spoke quickly. "If you want to find out about Jeff Lemor, follow me."

She didn't wait for an answer, just jumped into a dented and dusty, gray Grand Am, and lit another cigarette as she started her car. I was curious enough that I dropped back into my car to see what this was about. I called the sheriff's dispatcher and asked her to run the license plate, while I followed the young woman east on Highway 25, toward Pierz. For my own protection, I left Maurice a message indicating where I was headed.

The dispatcher called back soon after with information. The Grand Am belonged to a Vicki Ament, whose criminal history included a charge for possession of a controlled substance, methamphetamine, two years ago. Her physical description on the arrest report matched the woman I was following, adding that she had a tattoo of a hummingbird on her shoulder, and tattoos of a pair of hands on her buttocks. The dispatcher added in a low voice, "Now, how do you suppose those hands stick out of a bikini bottom? Oh, here it is, like someone's holding her from behind. Now, isn't that Godly?" She added with disdain, "Her grandparents must be very proud of her."

I followowed Vicki to a farm in the Pierz area, grimacing as I watched her discard cigarette butts out the window along the way.

When I exited my car, the air felt pleasant and calm. "Halcyon" would be the perfect word for it. The farm had a long, narrow gravel driveway splitting large, black banner-like fields. I saw an old barn with aged gray wood showing beneath chipped white paint. Not far from the barn was a faded white, two-story box-like farmhouse, with a few narrow windows. A dim light glowed inside, giving it a sense of warmth. A large, dark, barren oak tree shadowed the farmhouse with its long, twisting branches. Beneath it sat a small child's swing and a larger wooden swing, which looked big enough for two adults to share. A small flurry of wind set the swings in motion. The chains rattled, and there was an eerie screech of metal scraping against metal. In a matter of seconds, the feeling changed from tranquility to a scene reminiscent of a Stephen King movie. Being shot heightened my awareness of sounds and movement around me. I unbuttoned my jacket enough to allow easy access to my gun in its shoulder harness beneath.

Vicki ran a package of diapers into the house, and then came back outside to greet me. She motioned toward the wooden swing, and I followed.

Vicki patted the space next to her on the swing. "Have a seat."

The wooden seat was small enough that our legs were close to touching. I was uncomfortable with the close proximity, but reasoned that if she was okay with sitting this close to me, she wasn't setting me up to be shot.

Vicki showed no discomfort with the closeness. She gave me a strained smile, and said in a voice bruised from smoking cigarettes and, most likely, hard use of meth, "I wanted to talk to you because my grandparents know your parents, and they trust you. They told me that the only reason people accused you when Mandy Baker disappeared was because your family is poor. It's easy to accuse poor people, because nobody's gonna help them."

I appreciated her sincerity, but I had no desire to probe into my past with her. "Tell me about Jeff."

She looked out at the fields. "If you check my record, you'll see I have drug charges. I want you to know I've been clean and sober for two years. I got pregnant, and I didn't want to be a pump and dump mom."

"Pump and dump?"

"You know, one of those breastfeeding mothers who goes out and gets wasted, and then has to pump and dump all of her milk the next day so she doesn't totally mess up her kid. My sperm donor liked the idea of having a kid, but when I started getting fat, he just moved on."

"What can you tell me about Jeff Lemor?"

Vicki pushed a stray strand of hair off her forehead with the back of her hand. "I was with Jeff at his trailer at one o'clock last Sunday, on the day Brittany Brennan disappeared. I know everybody wants him locked up because he's a so-called 'sex offender,' but he didn't have anything to do with Brittany."

"How long were you there?"

Vicki rested her chin on her fist as she thought. "About an hour. We got into an argument and I took off."

It would have taken Jeff about twenty minutes to get home, driving fast, from where Brittany disappeared. He still could have abducted her, but he wouldn't have had the time to submerge her body. "What was the argument about?"

Vicki muttered, "Acceptance."

"Acceptance of what?"

She scrutinized me. "Acceptance of your life. I can't drink. I can't do drugs. If I use, I'm picking using over living with my daughter. I've accepted that. If social services told me I couldn't wear red in order to keep my daughter, I wouldn't wear red. When you mess up, they put rules on you. Your opinion of the rules doesn't matter. He was trying to tell me there's nothing wrong with having a few beers on a Saturday night, and I told him, 'You just don't get it. You took innocence away from a fifteen-year-old girl, so the judge took things from you. Nobody gives a shit that you don't like it. Just accept the deal you got, and go on.'"

"That's good." I had miscalculated Vicki's wisdom at first glance. "Can you tell me exactly when Jeff arrived home on Sunday?"

"He was home when I got there." Vicki scrunched her forehead in thought. "Why don't you just see when he called in?"

"The phone surveillance system wasn't working that day." I didn't bother to tell Vicki this wasn't the first time the county's sex offender call-in system had failed. "What was Jeff's mood like? Was he angry?"

Vicki responded with a long, drawn out, "Noooo." She pulled her feet up onto the swing, further narrowing the gap between the two of us. "He was trying to find an excuse for drinking, but he knew there wasn't any, so he started saying things about his mom dying, over and over again."

I considered this. "Like a man who had just been involved in something traumatic?"

"No. I've seen this a hundred times with guys who were hungover. Kinda sad, and still kind of drunk."

Vicki had given me the information we needed to keep Jeff in custody. He had violated probation by drinking alcohol. I challenged her to convince me Jeff was innocent. She suggested we visit Jeff's trailer, as he had a place where he hid items of value inside his home. She thought viewing the items would give me a better understanding of his "good nature."

I warned her that the BCA had already obtained a search warrant for Jeff's trailer, so we might have company.

We drove together to Lemor's. On the way, Vicki gave me an adolescent grin. "I was once with your friend Clay at a party."

The comment caught me by surprise. I asked her to convince me Jeff wasn't the killer, and she brings up Clay? I looked at her in confusion, but patiently waited to see where she was going with this.

Vickie continued. "I know you used to hang around in school with him. In junior high, you notice the cute older guys."

It shouldn't have surprised me that Vicki knew Clay. Pierz is a town of only a thousand people. I remained silent, aware Vicki would fill the void.

"I know Al and Mary Brennan, too," she said. "When I was about fourteen, I talked to them at parties."

Needing to get her focused, I asked, "So, what's at Jeff's?"

If she had an answer, it was lost with her sharp gasp of breath as Jeff's trailer came into view. The molding was torn loose from the bottom, and there was a large pile of cobweb-infested straw nearby, which had been pulled from underneath the dwelling. Sherriff's deputies were hauling items through the doorway of Lemor's home, under Sean Reynolds's direction.

I stepped over the carelessly discarded *Sports Illustrated Swimsuit Edition* and *Automobile Trader* magazines as I approached.

In a moment, Vicki's mood changed from concern over Jeff's trailer being trashed to her asking, "Who's the cute black guy?"

Sean turned and called into the trailer, "Paula, Jon brought a visitor."

Vicki gave him a flirtatious smile and led us to the kitchen. She opened a drawer, sharing that she believed the drawer had a false bottom.

Paula Fineday looked like someone had dragged her down a gravel road on her back. She was obviously the one who had been under the trailer. She removed the contents of the drawer while Sean took a knife off the counter and carefully peeled back the bottom. Beneath it were about thirty pictures of Lemor's hippie-like mother and himself at various ages. Sean carefully sifted through the pictures while leaving them all in their exact location.

I noticed an item which would be of particular interest to Vicki, so I stepped back and motioned for her to peer inside.

Vicki's eyes welled up at an image of her and Jeff, both in their early teens, sitting on the hood of a car together, their faces bright with the uninhibited laughter only kids share. Vicki asked, "Can I have that picture?"

Without looking at her, Sean answered sternly, "Not at this time."

I politely asked Vicki to wait outside, as Sean, Paula, and I had noticed something intriguing about the way the pictures were placed in the drawer. They were pushed to the side, leaving a triangular space. An imprint where a handgun once rested, which looked very similar in size to a nine-millimeter, was etched into the felt on the bottom of the drawer. The false bottom was tight enough to press the handgun into the felt. Even though we now knew Brittany wasn't shot, I had been. This was an incredible break, as it put a gun into Lemor's possession.

Sean commented, "Vicki doesn't have a clue, does she?"

I shook my head and added, "I feel like I've underestimated Jeff Lemor."

Sean continued to study the drawer. "This is an incredible piece of work. It had to take considerable time. Where did he get the tools?" Sean ran his finger across the groove in the drawer where the false bottom had rested. "He needed a router for this. I haven't seen anything like that here."

Paula brushed some flecks of straw from her thick hair and added, "Perhaps there was an awl among those tools, too."

I told Sean and Paula, "I know this looks bad for Jeff, but I'm not convinced he's the one who assaulted Brittany."

Paula's dark eyebrows furrowed as she skeptically responded, "Tony told me a meth whore had contacted him about being Lemor's alibi. Tony didn't buy it, so now she's here with you. We have a suspect with a criminal history, with a weapon, and witnesses who put him at the scene. Have you ever heard of Occam's razor?"

I nodded. William Ockham was a fourteenth-century Franciscan friar who produced works in logic. Occam's razor—spelled differently than his name, as a result of a conversion to Latin—is a theory in science that you need to shave away the long shots and focus on what's obvious.

Paula warned, "It's simple. Don't be distracted."

I had an argument, but couldn't pull it to consciousness. I'd struggled with retrieving thoughts since I was shot.

Paula went back to work, suggesting, "We're going to want to take a picture of this drawer from the top before we remove the photos."

Sean nodded his approval at me. "Good work. Ask Vicki if she knows of any other hiding places, then get her out of here. We'll need to do a very thorough examination of the inside of this trailer."

I asked, "Should I put some of that straw back under the trailer? If the temps dip below freezing again, his pipes might freeze and he'll have a big mess here."

Sean flatly said as he walked away, "He isn't coming back."

That wasn't an acceptable answer for me. "Are you done underneath the trailer?"

Surprised, Sean gave a bewildered nod. "Yeah. Have at it."

Once outside, Vicki watched as I got on the ground and, with my one good hand, began pushing the straw back underneath the trailer. I made sure I had it packed around the pipes. If the pipes froze and broke, it would be an expensive repair bill for a young man who was barely getting by. I don't like destroying people's property. I know all too well how long it takes impoverished people to pay things off. When I was done, Vicki helped me push the molding back into place as best we could.

Surprised by my efforts, Vicki stepped to me and hugged me. "Thank you. That was really nice of you."

I decided to spend the night at the AmericInn. My head was pounding and pain pulsated through my left hand. I had pushed myself a little too hard today, and now I just wanted sleep. I was told I could observe Jeff's interrogation tomorrow morning, if I stuck around.

Despite having found additional evidence to add to Jeff's prosecution, I had a problem that complicated this case. The sequence of events didn't make sense if you knew the geography of the area. Consider the BCA's theory: Jeff Lemor first drove by the Brennans' south field, and then headed north down the gravel road, where he found Brittany. He then continued north for a half a mile further, sexually assaulted her, and buried her in a culvert. The Bosers stated that after the truck went by, it never returned. So, why would he shoot at me for looking for evidence in the south field? Nothing in the south field could connect Jeff to Brittany, because he drove by that field before he encountered her. And another problem? Vicki honestly believed Jeff didn't assault Brittany, and I believed Vicki. Even though she was rough cut, Vicki wasn't wearing love-struck blinders. She viewed Jeff with pensive eyes.

Chapter Fourteen

Serena Bell
Morning
Sunday, April 6
Pierz

Jon stayed in Little Falls last night, so I got up early and drove to Pierz. Jon needed to find some balance. When he was with me, he was completely present and so attentive. It was wonderful. But when he was gone, he was completely gone, leaving a void. I knew it would be better if we were married, but I had to believe God was okay with two lonely single people loving each other.

I had volunteered to help his mother with her painting, so this was the perfect day to follow through. I even went to church with Bill and Camille in the morning.

Camille Frederick was a slender, strong woman. It was obvious where Jon got his handsomeness and lean frame. Even dressed casually, she was still a classic beauty.

Camille and I spent about two hours looking over new colors for her kitchen. She had first suggested burnt orange and, after considering a variety of oranges and greens, we came back to a light orange.

After Camille and I had finished, Victor wandered into the room, giggling at his own private joke, and asked if I wanted to go for a walk with him. Victor had inherited his mother's lean frame, too, and stood at about five-foot-ten. Unlike the rest of the family,

Victor had long, disheveled blond hair. His brown moustache suggested his hair was dyed. Victor had bright-blue eyes like Jon, but his thoughts were so random that he seemed a polar opposite of his brother. Their commonality made sense, if you understood how the frontal lobe worked. Victor and Jon both struggled with the same issue—regulating focus. Victor struggled with remaining focused, while Jon struggled with letting go.

I pulled my coat tight around my neck as the cool air crept in. I breathed in the musty dampness of the barren field as we walked alongside it.

Victor wore an insulated jean jacket and a white bomber hat with ear flaps and a visor. The hat looked a little goofy, but his obliviousness to it warmed my heart.

I asked, "How are you, Victor?"

He stopped and sadly dropped his head down. "Dang it."

"What's the matter?"

"Last night, I made a list of questions that people might ask me today. I had that one written down, but then I thought, no, and crossed it out. So I don't have an answer."

I put my hand on his shoulder. "It's okay."

Troubled, he looked back up at me. "Why did you even ask that?"

Before I could respond, he smiled with a sudden insight.

"Wait a minute. You were just trying to break the ice, weren't you?"

I grinned. "Yes, I was."

"Okay." Feeling reassured, he started walking again. Victor said, "Jon likes you."

"He does?"

"Uh-huh. Did you know Alfred Hitchcock once used a three-foot teacup in a scene in *Notorious*, so he could hold both the cup and Audrey Hepburn in focus on camera at the same time? On film, it looked like the cup was sitting way out in front of her. That's crazy."

"I didn't know that. That is crazy."

"I'm crazy. Did you know that?"

"I always thought you were nice."

Victor smiled. "Well, I'm crazy." He started laughing, pointing toward his temple and making loops with his finger. "Crazy as a loon."

I had to ask. "Do you still walk at night?"

"Yeah. We have a barn owl and a screech owl. Some people think they're the same thing, but they're not. They don't even look anything alike. Barn owls look like their edges were smoothed on a lathe and screech owls look like they were torn out of cloth."

I smiled and said, "That's a creative description." I hadn't come here to interrogate Victor, but I had an opportunity to clear my lingering concerns that he had a role in Mandy's disappearance, so I asked, "Did you ever see Mandy Baker when you were out walking at night?"

He initially didn't respond, but he did seem to be considering the question. After a few more steps, he cautiously looked around, and as if he was revealing a great conspiracy, softly confided, "You can only see Mandy Baker when it rains."

His comment caught me by surprise. "What do you mean?"

Victor wiped the mucus off his nose, and then reached out and took my hand.

I cringed inwardly, but not wanting to hurt his feelings, I took his hand as he led me to the edge of a field. Scattered rocks protruded here and there in the charcoal-black dirt, and I could see a couple of large rock piles on the other side of the field.

Victor pointed across the field and said, "There."

I looked around, "What? All I see is rocks."

"That's my point."

Confused, I said, "I'm sorry, I don't understand."

Victor started singing, "Blue eyes cryin' in the rain . . ." and then drifted into word salad. People who suffer from schizophrenia often speak in "word salad," which involves sentences that make sense independently, but don't combine to form coherent paragraphs.

Personality testing on schizophrenics looks the same as if they were randomly responding, due to their disjointed thoughts. I never managed to get him back to talking about Mandy Baker.

On my way back to St. Paul, I reviewed my list of suspects in Mandy's disappearance:

Victor Frederick
Bill Frederick
Randall Davis
Clay Roberts
Whitey
me

I had a feeling this would all come back to me. It honestly should.

Chapter Fifteen

Jon Frederick
Morning
Sunday, April 6
Little Falls

Tony and I sat on the other side of the mirrored glass and watched the interrogation of Jeff Lemor. Incarceration has a way of making men look guilty, and Lemor looked like your typical redneck criminal, with his unshaven face and scraggly, unwashed hair. He was adorned in bright orange jail attire with green cloth slippers. His handcuffs and leg shackles had been removed. He attempted to sit in a laidback manner on his molded plastic chair.

Sean had started the conversation unobtrusively, and the plan was for Paula to jump in like a bucking bronco to get Jeff to reveal more than he planned in the heat of their argument. Sean casually sat at the end of the table, commenting, "So, I hear you've found Jesus." Jeff gave him a thousand-yard stare, so Sean shrugged. "Well he's bound to be somewhere. I guess this is as good of a place as any."

Jeff calmly said, "I know a lot of guys say they've found religion in here. But it's different for me."

Sean casually mused, "Jailhouse Christians." He scratched his cheek. "Do you feel that Jesus will forgive you for your sins?"

"I have accepted Jesus in my heart. I can't keep living the way I was—like everyone should just make me instantly happy. Vicki was right. I don't have to like the rules. I just have to live by them." After a pause, he continued. "I'd like to believe people can be forgiven for their sins as long as they don't repeat them."

Sean agreed with a simple, "Okay."

Paula leaned over the table toward Jeff as she snarled, "Can you be forgiven for sins that you lie about every time you're questioned on them."

Jeff thought long and hard before replying to Paula. "I think you have to be honest about things that hurt people. I don't think I'm going to hell for possession." Jeff stopped himself.

Sean tilted his head to one side, sizing Jeff up. "So you're just sort of a Christian. Because if you can't be honest, you're only a Christian when it doesn't involve any persecution or pain."

Jeff seemed lost in his own head for a minute, but finally he responded with an edge. "I am honest—about everything that matters. I could have lawyered up, but here I am, answering your questions. Jesus didn't ask for an attorney."

Tony leaned toward me in the observation room and muttered, "Jesus could have used an attorney."

Paula sneered at Lemor. "I think you won't tell us who you were drinking with because you spent the night thinking about a young girl walking down the road all alone. Brittany made that walk every Sunday, and this wasn't the first Sunday morning you made that drive home."

Jeff stared straight ahead at the wall and calmly responded, "I didn't abduct that girl. Vicki said there was a dead skunk in my mailbox when she drove out to check my mail. I still had to go through my bills and get them paid. The guys in here tell me that if they ever catch me alone, I'm dead. They call me 'chomo,' which in here means child molester. Don't tell me I'm avoiding persecution." Jeff's bravado was fading fast as he added, "But, if they don't kill me, I'm coming out stronger."

I turned to Tony. "I'm not a big fan of Friederick Nietzche. Nietzche had a concept of the 'overman,' which suggested that man has an intrinsic will to power, sometimes expressed in violent or sexual behavior. Nietzche admired Napoleon."

Tony glanced at Lemor and, chagrined, told me, "I don't see this hombre as that deep. I think everybody uses the quote 'What doesn't kill me makes me stronger' at one time or another."

We watched another twenty minutes of useless banter before Tony turned to me and asked, "Do you want to watch any more of this?"

I shook my head. "No. Do you figure Jeff was out drinking with someone else who was also on probation?"

Tony smirked. "My bet is he was cheating on Vicki."

Tony was probably right. There's very little honor among thieves. Jeff would give up another parolee to have a reduced probation violation, but he wouldn't risk losing Vicki, since she was now his only friend.

Before leaving Little Falls, I drove to St. Gabriel's Hospital. As I strolled down the sky-blue hall, I spotted a police officer sitting on a chair outside of Brittany's hospital room, paging through the *Morrison County Record.* After some small talk, the officer shared that Mary was inside with Brittany, but there hadn't been any other visitors.

My heart sank upon seeing Brittany's thin little body covered up to her shoulders in a pink blanket. She was such a small girl. Mary was awkwardly settled in a chair next to Brittany; both were asleep. Brittany was breathing on her own. I went to the window to pull the shades. I briefly looked out at the sky and said a silent prayer before closing them. *God, we need some help. I know we're all a bunch of irresponsible mutts, but I'd really appreciate it if you'd help this kid out.*

As I was leaving, I met Alban in the hallway. Al was wild-eyed, unshaven, and his thick hair protruded out in a variety of unruly directions. He was agitated, and walked directly toward me. "Your name didn't register the first time we spoke. You're Jon Frederick—

the same guy who was accused of killing a girl, here, ten years ago. How does a killer get a job as an investigator?"

I responded to his attack with a simple, "He doesn't."

Al pointed a finger at me. "My daughter was raped by a sex offender you guys had in jail, but let out, and then you have the gall to harass Mary."

Mary must have shared her feelings about our visit to their home. I was a little taken aback, but, trying to be professional, I told him, "I'm sorry. We were desperate for information, because at that point, we hadn't found Brittany."

Al sensed my apprehension, and it seemed to escalate his attack. "Your family couldn't even run a farm. How are *you* gonna get a conviction?"

I didn't respond. After being accused of being a killer for years, being a bad farm manager didn't seem like a great insult.

I simply said, "I'm praying for Brittany," and departed.

VERBAL ATTACKS AREN'T UNCOMMON in investigative work. People want every case to be solved in an hour, as they are on TV. I called Tony and recounted my run-in with Al.

Tony gave me credit for walking away without making a scene, and eventually got around to asking, "Do you have anything new on Mandy Baker's disappearance?"

"I do." I wasn't sure how he was going to take this. "Serena Bell drove the white car that picked Mandy up on the night she disappeared. They hung out at Serena's home and drank a little. When Serena woke up, Mandy was gone."

Surprised, Tony said, "I didn't see that coming. Maybe you've never been able to solve this because you've always refused to consider that Serena was involved in Mandy's disappearance."

"I don't believe Serena killed Mandy. You know as well as I do that ninety-two percent of violent crimes committed against women are committed by men." Additionally, sixty percent of men who abduct and murder women they don't know well are employed in construction, but I didn't say that to Tony.

Tony paused a beat before responding. "Most crimes are also solved within forty-eight hours. Maybe the remainder of them aren't solved because they don't fit into the statistics. Why didn't she come forward? And why didn't you tell us ten years ago that you had another girlfriend? We could have made the connection back then."

"Serena and I didn't date. We were just friends."

Tony dismissed this. "I get the impression it was more than that. It's time to gather information on Serena. Maybe some of your old friends have something they've never told you."

"I'm not a guy who has a lot of friends." I considered Serena as a suspect from a physics perspective and said, "We both know dead weight is a real phenomenon. Bodies are heavy. How did Serena get rid of the body?"

Tony chuckled. "Hell hath no fury like that of a scorned woman. You better let me handle investigating her. You're too close to have the proper perspective." He added sardonically, "You're sleeping with the prime suspect." I heard him laughing as I ended the call.

I headed back to the hotel to pack up. On my way there, I called Clay. I wanted to hear what he had to say about Vicki. She might have brought up her encounter with Clay as a teaser to a longer story.

Without hesitation, Clay responded in a gruff voice, "What's she saying?"

His failure to take any time to offer any information convinced me he had sex with her. "She told me she was with you at a party right after we graduated." She would have been fourteen, and he would have been eighteen.

"Are you recording this?"

"Clay, someone's trying to kill me. I've got bigger things to worry about than your indiscretions. I just want to know how much of what she's telling me is the truth."

Clay begrudgingly said, "Just promise me you'll never bring this up again. It's not something I'm proud of."

"Have I ever embarrassed you before?"

"Just that one time, when you killed your girlfriend."

I responded, deadpan, "I guess there's that."

"Okay, Vicki was at a graduation party. Pretty, young girl. Kinda skinny, reddish hair, cute freckles, but a lost soul. She was hanging around with a bunch of stoners who were burning something illegal that she wasn't into."

"Ultimately, she got into meth and ended up pregnant," I said. "Claims she's clean now."

"Good." Clay paused, and then added, "Vicki was a mess and looking for someone to cling to."

"*Tabula rasa.*"

Clay growled in irritation, "What the hell is that?"

"It's Latin for 'blank slate.' I know this isn't my business, but Vicki insinuated something happened between the two of you, and I want to know if she's being honest or if she's a drama queen."

"We didn't do anything she didn't eagerly go along with. I felt like I had a lot of leeway to do whatever, but it was all normal, vanilla sex. I feel bad about the way it ended. She wanted to hang around the fire with me and my friends, but I told her I needed to go. She was fourteen, and I really didn't want anyone to see me with her. She said she'd go with me, but she had to go tell her ride she was leaving. It took her a while, so I chilled and drank some more. By the time she returned, I had just convinced our classmates I wasn't with her, so I just kind of ignored her. She didn't make a scene. Just took the hint and left." Clay added, "What a dick, huh?"

I groaned. "You're a jerk."

Clay thought out loud, "You're right, but it was the right thing. I didn't respect Vicki. If I would've stayed with her, I would've just used her. She would've hung around. I can pat myself on the back for ending it that night. One more good choice that might send me to heaven."

"I'm not sure how the scoring works in heaven, but it seems like you shouldn't get any points for using a fourteen-year-old girl and then ignoring her."

"I heard Vicki got a tattoo on her hips, of someone holding her doggy style, and guys used to bark at her at parties. Drunks can really be pricks."

It was time to switch gears. "I have some interesting news about Mandy Baker. Serena was the one who picked Mandy up on the night she disappeared."

Clay immediately went into a furious rant. "Are you kidding me? Serena puts on that act like she's a saint and instead, she was just saving her own ass. What have I always told you about her? She just uses you. I think she loved being with you when you got attention in sports, but as soon as you were in trouble, she turned her back."

I laughed. "Let's not rewrite history, here. First of all, I wasn't a standout, and she was too busy to even go to my games. Serena didn't care about any of that. She just wanted to be alone with me. I made the mistake of taking it as an insult, when it was a tremendous compliment."

Clay hesitated for a moment, then said, "Okay, you want to know about the real Serena? Here it is. Your sweet little Serena has come knockin' on my door, late at night, and I didn't turn her away. Has she told you about that?"

It was a punch in the stomach. "I doubt it."

"That's rich. After she's lied to you for a decade, you don't believe me."

I thought out loud, "If you honestly believed she killed Mandy, why would you sleep with her?"

Clay slowly said, "Why does a wolf chase a rabbit? Because that's what wolves do." We endured a painfully long silence before Clay tried smoothing it over. "Look, I'm sorry I even said anything. You're just so blind when it comes to her."

I was struggling to keep my breathing even. He wasn't sorry for doing it. He was sorry for telling me.

Oblivious to my misery, Clay continued on. "It's sort of a compliment, when you think about it. Think of it this way—I found someone you liked attractive. I'm not going to punish you with details. Use your imagination."

Unfortunately, I could imagine a lot, and like most obsessive people, my imagination was my worst enemy. I closed my eyes and said in a low warning, "That's enough." I couldn't stand to listen anymore. When he started talking again, I hung up.

My obsessive, jealous thoughts were stuck in an endless loop, forming ruts that threatened my stability. I called Serena. She told me she had to finish what she was doing, but would call me back in ten minutes. I paced back and forth while my imagination tormented me with a wicked carnal brew for what ended up being thirty minutes before she finally called back.

Sounding relaxed, Serena purred, "Right now I'm stretched out on my old high school bed just down the road from your farm, with a smile on my face, thinking about our last night together."

I paused, but I couldn't hold it back. "You slept with Clay?"

She took a deep breath. "Once. It was a mistake."

I seethed in silence, waiting for her to continue my torment.

Serena softly said, "You're not saying anything. You're really mad. What?"

I tried to keep my voice quiet and steady. "You and Clay?" I paused and tried to explain. "You're entitled to be with whomever you want. I get that. But it bothers me that the information I get about you doesn't come from you."

"I carry a ton of shame over not telling investigators I picked Mandy up that night. For years, I thought I'd rather we didn't talk at all, than to have you hate me." It was quiet for a minute before Serena continued. "I didn't think I'd ever see you again when I was with Clay. I was a single college student at the time. He and I got together a few times, and I realized it was a mistake and that was it."

"So, now it's a few times. I can't do this." I felt physical pain in my heart as we spoke.

Serena sounded dumbfounded. "We only slept together once, but we went out with friends a few times. What have I done that I can't be forgiven for?"

"I guess that's a question only you can answer." I agonized over the possibility that Tony was right. I was being taken for a fool.

"What's that supposed to mean?"

"First you dropped the bombshell on me that you were with Mandy on the night she disappeared, and you just left me hanging out there to be ridiculed by everybody. And now tonight, I find out you've slept with my best friend, and your response is you didn't want me to be mad at you?" I paused, trying to keep myself in check, then asked, "Do you think I'm happy, now? Because this is how dishonesty feels."

She softly said, "I'm sorry."

"I'm done," I said flatly.

"Whoa, Jon—wait. That's not fair. Where are you? I can come to you."

I didn't want to talk to her tonight. It was too painful.

When I didn't respond, Serena continued. "We can work through this, Jon. I'll stay at my parents' tonight. Just come to me. I know I should have said something, but I wanted to give you time to get to know me again first. For what it's worth, I've been just sick about it. Clay told me if I said anything, you would never forgive me."

"It's nice that you can be so open with Clay. Right now I feel like a jagged piece of metal is cutting through my heart. I can forgive a lot, but I can't stand being lied to."

"It was a mistake I'll never make again. It's in the past, and I wanted to leave it there."

I ranted on, "I feel like you dragged me back into that incestuous small-town bullshit we both hate, where if one person cheats, it's probably with someone who is a friend or related to the other."

Serena softly said, "This is going to get worse before it gets better, isn't it?"

"I think you're being optimistic."

Serena was silent.

"Goodbye, Serena. I wish you well." I waited for thirty seconds, thinking of the song lyrics, "Say something, I'm giving up on you." When she didn't respond, I hung up and shut my phone off. I'd never hung up on anyone prior to that night, and I'd done it twice in a half hour. I needed to find a way to stop being a prick. I just couldn't shut it off.

I didn't have a logical explanation for turning back and driving to the hotel in Little Falls, other than being angry and self-destructive. I wasn't convinced the person who shot me was in custody. But I did know that, if the shooter came after me tonight, he'd have more than he bargained for. I could have stayed under armed guard with my parents, or behind secure locks at home, or even with a lover who wanted to console me. But instead, I was lying in a hotel next to a loaded gun, thinking, *Bring it on.*

Chapter Sixteen

Panthera
2:15 a.m.
Monday, April 7
Pierz

In the cover of night, I remove my gloves and press my bare hands against the siding of the old Bell farmhouse. Serena lies in her nightwear, inches away, on the other side of this wall. Her reading light has gone out, and now the two of us are sharing a moment. At some level, she senses my presence. I feel it.

Friedrich Nietzche wrote that the greatest aspiration of a woman should be to give birth to an Ubermensch—a man who would reign supreme over others. If I impregnated her, she'd have my child. Even if she didn't appreciate the prince she was carrying, she would never give him up. But it's not my favorite way to have sex, and I'd be better off rid of her. Still, imagine the power of walking into a teenager's life and telling him, "I'm your father. Do you want to know me? We don't have to tell anyone."

The light comes back on. "I dare you to step outside for a breath of fresh air . . ."

Chapter Seventeen

Jon Frederick
4:00 a.m.
Monday, April 7
Little Falls

At four in the morning, there was a knock on my hotel room door. A light sleeper, I quickly threw my jeans on and went to the door, gun in hand. It could have been Jada, who was sleeping just down the hall, or better yet, Serena, but friendly faces didn't find investigators at four in the morning—only bad news did. I roughly rubbed the sleep out of my face and looked through the peephole. Tony was standing outside my door, dressed for work.

When I opened the door, Tony looked at the gun at my side. "You're actually here. What the hell are you doing here?"

"I didn't feel like driving back to Minneapolis last night."

"Get dressed. I've got to go to a fire on your side of the county."

The glow of the fire was visible from miles away in the darkness. The black silhouettes of trees in front of the bright orange fire looked disturbingly eerie. The only person on the scene was the state trooper who had spotted the flames. It wasn't surprising that we beat the fire department there, since it was a voluntary force. Thick, black smoke billowed from Lemor's burning trailer as Tony and I approached it. We stepped into the muddy sludge surrounding it. Alban Brennan's van was stuck in the mud next to the trailer.

It, too, was engulfed in flames. Seeing the van burning gave me an uneasy feeling. It didn't help that the scene stunk like burning plastic and all things toxic. The CSI team had gone through Al's truck, but when Jeff became the prime suspect, we moved on, and the CSI team never got to the van. It wasn't a priority because we'd been told it wasn't drivable. Yet here it was, and the tire tracks indicated it had, in fact, been driven here. If Jeff Lemor was guilty, it wouldn't matter that the CSI team hadn't gone through it. Still, the burning van ate at me.

Tony immediately contacted Paula. He turned away and, in that moment, I realized Tony had been with Paula at the hotel. I considered the times Tony showed up to my room with hair unaffected by the blustery April winds and realized this likely wasn't the first time. He turned slightly toward me, and I could hear him say, "Did he leave it here to make a statement that he's coming for Lemor, or did he just leave it because he got stuck?" Tony hesitated as the fire trucks rolled in. He commented to Paula, "We're going to have a dead suspect if we continue to allow Al's anger toward Lemor to escalate."

Although I couldn't hear it, Paula must have offered a dissenting view, as Tony argued, "He's interfering with the investigation. Our ability to match fibers from the blanket Brittany was wrapped in to the inside of Jeff's trailer is gone. The gun drawer is gone. Al's stupidity is making our case more difficult. Get that message through his thick skull."

After Tony ended the call, he joined me watching the burning van. He said, "Paula seems to think that if we arrest Al for this, there will be an outcry of support for him, and people would be even angrier at Lemor. If we don't arrest him, people will begin to question Al's behavior, and this could help de-escalate the community's anger toward Lemor."

Paula was right. The best play would be to let the public begin to question Al's behavior. I pointed out, "If Al planned on torching the trailer, why did he park so close to it?"

Tony wearily responded, "Okay, so he torched the van. It didn't run most of the time, anyway. I could certainly envision him doing it out of anger because it wouldn't start back up. And Al would revel in the opportunity to confront Lemor man to man. Maybe he's thinking he'd do it in jail."

After two and a half hours at the site, Tony and I concluded there was nothing further to see and left. Both the van and the trailer were trashed.

Paula called and said Al was refusing to talk, beyond stating, "My daughter lies there like she's dead." Mary suggested, "Maybe our van was stolen." Jason said he slept through it all. They didn't arrest Al.

Morning was now only a couple hours away. We headed back to the hotel, and I tried to find sleep.

3:45 p.m.
Sheriff's office, Little Falls

Jeff Lemor and a fifty-something, gray-haired polygraph examiner sat in an investigation room at the sheriff's office. Jeff was noticeably nervous. His dark hair was unkempt, and he was still in his orange jumpsuit. He was generally worse for wear since yesterday's interrogation. He was unshaven and had a bruise on his cheek, which I was told was from being struck by another inmate.

Jeff was going to be asked four questions during his polygraph examination:

1. Is your name Jeff Lemor?
2. Did you shoot at Investigator Jon Frederick?
3. Did you ever sexually abuse Brittany Brennan?
4. Did you have any involvement in Brittany Brennan's disappearance?

Polygraph examiners prefer that the respondents are anxious, as their charts will then display greater discrepancy between honesty and dishonesty. Paula had spoken to Jeff ahead of time, to make certain he was adequately primed.

Tony and I sat in an observation room watching the examination through mirrored glass. The polygraph examiner wrapped the pneumo tubes around Jeff's chest and stomach to measure his breathing. Two small metal cups were wrapped around the tips of his fingers with Velcro. The metal measured galvanic skin response, or sweat. A blood pressure cuff was wrapped around Jeff's left arm.

Tony had positioned the examiner so we could see the charts on the computer. We patiently watched the green, yellow and red wavy lines on the computer screen as a stable pattern of breathing, blood pressure, and sweat was established. We both knew how the charts would deviate from the normal path when a person was lying. When someone claimed they passed a lie detector test with "flying colors," it wasn't true. They passed with consistent, unremarkable colors.

Jeff sat with his feet flat on the floor, staring at a blank wall.

The polygraph examiner glanced at Jeff over his reading glasses and told him, "I want you to focus on a number between one and ten. I'm going to ask you, 'Is it one?' and I want you to say 'no.' I am going to ask you, 'Is it two?' and I want you to say 'no.' I am going to ask you, 'Is it three?' and I want you to say 'no.' I want you to say 'no' to every number through ten. This will give me the opportunity to show you how this polygraph examination works."

The examiner asked, "Are you ready?"

Jeff nervously nodded his understanding.

The examiner stated, "You will need to say 'yes' or 'no.'"

Jeff stated, "Yeah."

The examiner reminded him, "Not yeah—yes or no."

Jeff said, "Yes."

The examiner began the instruction. "I want you to think of a number between one and ten." He hesitated for a moment, giving Jeff a chance to choose a number. "Is it number one?"

Jeff responded, "No." The examiner turned the charts slightly toward Jeff to show a relatively stable pattern of breathing, blood pressure, and galvanic skin response.

The examiner asked, "Is it two?"

Jeff responded, "No." The polygraph charts remained the same.

The examiner asked, "Is it three?"

Jeff responded, "No." The polygraph charts remained stable.

The polygraph examiner asked, "Is it four?"

Jeff responded, "No." The polygraph charts spiked in all three measures.

The polygraph examiner smiled toward Jeff. "The number was four, correct?"

With some surprise, Jeff responded, "Yeah."

The examiner pointed to the graphs and told Jeff, "This is what it's going to look like every time you lie to me. I wanted you to see this, so there won't be any question when this polygraph examination is done. Is there anything you want to tell me before we begin?"

Jeff responded, "No." The charts remained stable.

The examiner turned the screen directly toward us, and asked, "Is your name Jeff Lemor?"

Jeff responded, "Yes." The polygraph charts remained stable.

The examiner asked, "Did you shoot at Investigator Jon Frederick?"

Jeff responded, "No." The charts remained stable.

Tony matter-of-factly stated, "I'm going to drug-test him when he's done, to make sure he didn't get ahold of a central nervous system depressant."

We both knew the odds of that weren't very good. Inmates were generally taken off their medication during their incarceration unless the meds were for a health issue, like diabetes, or if they were taking an antipsychotic medication. More likely, he simply wasn't the one who shot at me.

The examiner continued. "Did you ever sexually abuse Brittany Brennan?"

Jeff Lemor hesitated, and then said, "No." All three of the graph lines remained stable.

The examiner asked, "Do you have information regarding Brittany Brennan's disappearance?" The polygraph examiner paused, realizing he had asked the question incorrectly, but then added, "that you haven't shared with investigators?"

Jeff responded, "No." The lines spiked significantly, reflecting dishonesty.

The polygraph examiner looked at the mirrored glass toward us, realizing he had messed up. He quickly picked up a pen and wrote down his new question. In a polygraph examination, the same questions are repeated three times. The examiner was now committed to asking a question other than the one we had given him.

Tony tightened his fist and mumbled, "He asked the wrong damn question! He was supposed to ask if Jeff had any involvement in Brittany's disappearance! So we're still not going to know."

"The suggestion that he didn't sexually abuse her takes away his motive," I said. "But he also knows something he's not sharing."

Tony pointed out, "It's possible that Brittany was sexually assaulted by someone else at a different time and Jeff picked her up to abuse her, but she resisted, so he tried to kill her."

I stared straight ahead. "The examiner recovered pretty well. I was afraid he was going to stop at, 'Do you have any information regarding Brittany Brennan's disappearance?' Everybody in the state has information regarding Brittany's disappearance. He was smart to add the part about his having information he hasn't shared with investigators."

When Jeff was informed he failed the polygraph examination, specifically with regard to having information on Brittany's disappearance that he hadn't shared, he refused to say anything further.

It appeared that Lemor wasn't the person who shot at me. This brought me a strange sense of satisfaction, because him shooting me wasn't logical. Dad suggested it might have been some crazy redneck from the past who still believed I was guilty of killing

Mandy, but I doubted it. If that was the case, they'd have shot me ten years ago. This was somehow all related—I just wasn't seeing the connections yet.

I glanced at my phone and noticed a number of text messages from Serena and a voicemail from Jada. Jada offered to buy me lunch for giving her the Brittany Brennan story. Aware that my feelings for Serena had become so discombobulated, I concluded this was the worst time for me to talk to Jada. Jada also suggested we have an exit interview regarding our relationship, but I felt it was unnecessary. The lines had been drawn. I wanted children and she didn't. I didn't need to meet with her to be reminded of my misgivings. My obsessive ruminations were tormenting me at this very moment. I sent her a text saying, "I consider myself blessed to have enjoyed part of my life with you. I love your insight and genuine concern for the suffering in the world. We're on different paths now. No time to meet—send a letter if you wish, and I will give heed to it. Best wishes."

I needed to take some time before I responded to Serena, as I felt like I had been rubbed raw, and my nerves were hyper-reactive. But I wasn't a vengeful person, and I wasn't going to disrespect Serena by talking about this with Jada. For God's sake, I had blamed Serena for everything that happens in small towns, when the truth was she really hadn't done anything wrong. The problem was my incessant ruminations. I couldn't let go of the thought of her being with Clay, in every way imaginable, and if I couldn't let go of it, I shouldn't be with her. It wouldn't be fair to continue to punish her because of my obsessiveness. Right now, I needed to work. If I couldn't work on Brittany's case, I'd work on Mandy's. I called the sheriff's office for Randall Davis's address. I decided to visit the most violent offender identified in Mandy Baker's murder book.

I quickly drove west through Little Falls to Flensburg, a rural town of about one hundred people. From the middle of town, I could see the edge of town in every direction. I didn't even know if it was fair to call Flensburg a town. It was more like a few houses close together. I knew making this visit without backup was a bad idea, but I convinced myself it was somehow necessary. Someone had tried to kill me, and I no longer had any friends I trusted. I felt I didn't have anything to lose. The address took me to a small, dilapidated one-story house, its white paint crackled with age and neglect, its windows boarded up rather than replaced.

Randall Davis answered the door wearing tight jeans and a clean white "wife-beater" undershirt. His angular face had hawk-like features. He had a thick, dark crew cut and thick eyebrows that seemed a little too close to his dark eyes. Randall was a weight trainer with a solid five-foot-eight frame. A blue tattoo of a dragon was inked on his right bicep, while "Fight or Die" was tattooed on his left. Randall looked like a man spoiling for a fight. Standing in the background of the small, dark home was a heavyset woman with straight, raven-black hair. Her enflamed, battered face was obviously the result of recent bruising. She seemed to fade into the darkness of the home in her deep-red blouse and dark jeans. This was a crisis situation, and I decided right then I wasn't leaving without her.

The woman in the background timidly inched closer.

Over his shoulder, I asked the woman, "Are you Anna Hutchins?"

Randall spit out, "I haven't had anything to do with that dumb bitch for years." He yelled to the woman, "Misty, you called the cops again, didn't you?" Misty quickly cowered and slunk away.

"Actually, she didn't," I interjected. "She's not why I'm here. I'm working a cold case, and I need a few questions answered about your relationship with Mandy Baker."

"I don't even know who the hell you're talking about." Randall's meaty fists were bunched tight with suppressed rage.

"Mandy Baker disappeared about a decade ago, and you were dragged in and interrogated by Investigator Tony Shileto. I imagine you remember."

His jaw clenched and unclenched as he processed what I had said. "Oh, I remember. That asshole Shileto kept me handcuffed to a chair for close to two hours, even though he had no cause. And I'll tell you the same thing today: I never met the girl. Every time something happens in Little Falls, they drag me back in. I'm sick of it. It's bullshit." He raised his arms and gripped the doorframe on both sides, effectively blocking my way into the home. "You need to leave."

I cracked my neck and stood straighter. "That's not going to happen, Randall." The horrific amount of violence perpetrated by abusive men against women infuriated me.

Randall pounded his fist into his hand, like a schoolyard bully. "I should probably tell you, I'm training to be an ultimate fighter."

"With Misty?"

"Go to hell." He took a step toward me.

I considered telling him the "go to hell" suggestion was what brought me to Flensburg, but as angry as I was, I decided to take it down a notch. I have to admit, the idea of a brawl to vent my frustration had appeal. But, my job is to de-escalate these situations, regardless of my personal feelings. Putting my hands up defensively, I said, "As much as I enjoy standing here arguing with you, we're not going to fight."

Randall smiled. "I think your decision to leave is a good choice."

I turned toward my car and dialed 911 and muted my phone. I hesitated, turned back and asked, "What drug is Misty on?"

"I never said she was using."

I smiled. "There's a reason she doesn't have family or friends out here. She's alienated the people who once came to her rescue. It's not meth."

Randall nodded in agreement. "She's too fat. Cocaine."

I had meant that she didn't have the facial skin damage you see in meth addicts, but not wanting to argue, I asked, "Why don't you just leave her?"

"I ask myself that all the time. Look at me," he said, gesturing to his steroid-pumped physique. "I can do better." Randall went on about his talents and accomplishments.

I needed to keep him engaged for a few more minutes, as I knew I would soon have backup. I decided to try to placate him with some drug trivia. "Cocaine is a beast. They did a study with monkeys, and a monkey will push a bar over ten thousand times for one hit of cocaine. This means pushing the bar over and over again for hours, nonstop, until its arms are so sore he can barely move them."

"No shit?" I had his attention.

"If animals are given access to cocaine whenever they want it, over ninety percent are dead within thirty days. Misty's going to need some detox."

Randall dismissed it. "Ain't nothing they can do that I can't do right here."

The problem was, Randall might kill her in the process, because he couldn't regulate his own emotions. I could hear the sirens closing in.

Randall was initially surprised and, as his face darkened, he seethed, "She called the cops."

I quickly corrected him. "I did. I can't leave here without making sure Misty's okay. It's just something about the way I was raised." The reality was that Randall would likely only be in jail for the night, if Misty refused to press charges against him. But in that time, the police would get an advocate to talk to her and she would receive medical attention. She was given an exit, but it was up to her whether she'd take it.

Randall glared and was about to strike me, but held back as a squad car sped into the yard. He pointed a finger directly at me and said, "You'll get yours."

"I know Misty needs help, Randall, but so do you. You need an anger management program and maybe a shot of Inderal." I once helped on a case where a violent man's anger had finally come under control after he was placed on Inderal, which was actually a heart medication. It was ironic when you realized that women were with Randall because they were on drugs, while Randall was with them because he wasn't. The horns in his head fit perfectly into the holes in theirs.

When I returned to the investigative center, Maurice gave me an intense lecture over the stupidity of confronting a dangerous man without backup. Dangerousness was relative. People living in the south Halsted neighborhood in Chicago last year had a one in seven chance of being a victim of a violent crime before the year ended. Most small towns only have one cop, so they're out there alone every day. Still, I was smart enough to keep my mouth shut and apologize. I didn't regret intervening, for Misty's sake, but I should have followed BCA protocol.

Maurice had basked in the glory of Jeff Lemor's arrest, but was now being questioned as to why Lemor hadn't been formally charged. We were holding Jeff on a probation violation—drinking alcohol. The BCA had a major problem in its efforts to convict him. We couldn't prove the gun found in the woods belonged to him. The gun apparently had been stolen from a home in Hillman four years earlier, and there were no fingerprints on it. Jeff knew what he was doing when he ran that gun to the property line and threw it. No one clearly saw him carrying a gun, and his attorney would point out that the gun was not even found on his land. The imprint in the drawer in the trailer was now burned up, and we couldn't use his failed polygraph examination in court. For whatever it's worth, Sean did discover where the drawer had been modified. Along with milking cows, Jeff performed a variety of construction chores for his employer, and his employer sang praises of Jeff's handiwork. Jeff had access to all sorts of tools on the farm, as the farmer he worked for was a former cabinetmaker.

Brittany's doctors were saying her brain was active, and she should be talking, but she wasn't. They felt that her failure to talk was trauma-related.

I returned to the hotel. I had a series of messages from Serena in my email inbox. She said she was driving back to Pierz again tonight, so it would be convenient for me to visit her at her parents' old home. The last email warned that, if I didn't respond, I would need to grant her some latitude, as she would resolve this in her own way.

I considered how much I was like my schizophrenic brother. I was losing a relationship with a real person to an obsessive thought. It was delusional. It wasn't about forgiveness. Serena hadn't done anything that warranted forgiveness. It felt so petulant, but I couldn't let go of the idea of Clay's hands having been on her. Any conversation I had with Serena at this moment would be painful for her, and if seeing me would only bring pain, she'd eventually leave me. I needed to resolve this before I spoke to her, if I wanted to have a future with her.

Chapter Eighteen

Serena Bell
7:45 a.m.
Tuesday April 8
Minneapolis

I didn't get a lot of sleep last night. When I did fall asleep, I had nightmares, so I looked like hell. To compensate, I tried to dress especially nice for work, in a mid-length black skirt and matching jacket.

Jon had amazing problem-solving skills, but his logic could paint him into a corner, where he was trapped until he found a fresh perspective. I loved to problem solve with him. I just needed to create an opportunity to talk with him. I heard a vehicle near the farm last night. Had he come to talk to me and then turned back?

It was a cool morning, but there wasn't much of a wind. As I walked to the Fairview office, I took in the landscaping. I'd walked by it every workday, giving it little consideration. When I approached the door, I noticed some of the rocks in the flower bed were still wet with dew, revealing their true rose quartz color. The dry rocks looked as colorless as the sidewalk. I immediately understood what Victor had said to me on our walk: "You can only see Mandy when it rains." The colors of the rocks became vibrant when they were wet. Victor had walked me to a rock pile, and when I told him I didn't see anything, he said, "That's my point." Was it possible that Mandy was in that rock pile? I felt queasy. Reporting this could be the final straw that would break my already strained relationship with Jon. If I was right, Mandy's death fell on either Victor or me. Jon's family would be furious with me, but I couldn't think about that. This time, I needed to do the right thing, and right away.

After trying to contact Jon again, without success, I left work and drove to Little Falls. I sat at the government center, waiting for him to return.

Tony Shileto found me sitting outside the investigation center office and invited me in. Tony could be very intimidating. He told me Jon had shared with him that I was the last one with Mandy Baker. After answering his questions, it didn't take long before I revealed my theory about the rocks to him. It all happened so fast, I felt like I hadn't had a moment to think. By the time I left, I was wearing a wire, on my way to engage in a conversation with Victor. The trick was that I needed to have the conversation outside. While Bill and Camille still owned the home, the land it sat on had been lost in bankruptcy. Tony would receive permission from the land owner to record a conversation on his property, which meant he could put his plan in place without a search warrant.

I was jittery with nerves when I approached Bill and Camille's farmhouse. The deputies assured me this was the right thing to do, but I knew I was betraying people who had cared for me—people who'd opened their home to me. I kept telling myself Tony was someone Jon trusted. Tony had told me if I called Jon, he would surely interfere, and that would cost him his job. And I knew he was right. I steeled myself and rang the doorbell.

Camille greeted me warmly and hugged me. Her red sweatshirt had smears of orange paint on the sleeves. She explained she was starting the trim work, so the task would go quicker when the two of us painted together. Her smile froze in place and left her eyes as I told her I needed to speak to Victor. I remained outside.

Bill stepped out to join me, followed by Camille. There was sadness and resignation in his eyes, which made me realize he knew what I was there for. In his worn, blue flannel shirt and patched jeans, he looked old and tired. The wrinkles around his eyes, which most times reflected well-earned happiness, now simply aged him. He asked, "Is this about the rock pile?"

I was a bit taken aback, but he had just made it a little easier for me. "Yeah, it is." I could feel Camille's eyes begging me not to say another word, but I continued. "I think Victor was trying to show me where Mandy Baker's buried." I felt sick to my stomach.

"I guess I should be surprised Victor kept it quiet for ten years." There was an honest despair in Bill's voice that broke my heart. "After we lost the farm to bankruptcy, I agreed to stay on and care for the fields for the new owner. I couldn't leave. To protect my family, I had accepted the role of sexton for one teen body, for the rest of my life. When I saw Victor walk you toward the rock pile, I had a sinking feeling he had found someone he felt he could trust." Bill opened the door and yelled into the house, "Victor!"

Camille stepped inside to find her son.

I silently prayed, *Bill, please stop talking to me.* I wanted to tear the wire off and run away.

Camille and Victor soon joined us outside, and the four of us walked toward the rock piles. We were led by Victor, in his white bomber hat and a thick, white, fur-lined parka. Camille had obviously chastised Victor about telling me about Mandy, as he avoided eye contact with me. I didn't want Bill to say anything further so I stared at the ground, ignoring him. We silently marched along through the brown, lifeless brush, like death row inmates headed to the gallows. I couldn't help but think Tony and his officers could step in any time, now.

Victor broke the silence, telling me, "You really shouldn't throw stones at people who live in glass houses."

If I wasn't feeling like Judas, it would have been a funny misinterpretation of the old saying, "People who live in glass houses shouldn't cast stones." But he was right. You shouldn't throw stones at people who live in glass houses, either.

Victor begrudgingly said to Bill, "I thought you said it was okay that I just buried her body." He suddenly stopped in his tracks and nonchalantly asked me, "Are you wearing a wire?"

My face suddenly felt on fire. I frantically nodded, trying to discourage anyone from saying anything further. Sirens howled from the squad cars, which had been hiding just out of sight, as they rushed into the farmyard. I tried to tell the Fredericks I was sorry, but I panicked and couldn't get any words out.

Victor started to run, but Bill was ready for it and after a few quick steps he dragged Victor to the ground from behind. Victor wildly flailed as he tried to escape. Bill yelled, "No! You can't run, Victor. They'll shoot you."

I wanted to help, but I was pretty sure my assistance wasn't welcomed. In my anxious state, I felt paralyzed.

Deputies were now running toward us.

To my horror, Victor managed to escape Bill's grasp by slipping out of his jacket. An officer pulled out his gun and aimed it at Victor. I yelled, "No!"

After only two steps, a second officer shot Victor with a taser. His body convulsed as the current pulsated through him, and he fell to the ground. Saliva dripped from the side of his mouth, and he had wet himself.

Camille ran to him, and when his seizures ended, she dropped to his side and started to smooth his hair off his forehead. She attempted to reassure him. "Just breathe. You're going to be okay, Victor. Just breathe."

Roughly shoving Camille aside, an officer quickly pulled Victor's arms behind his back and cuffed him. Victor's eyes looked wild, and there was little doubt the shock had sent him into a psychotic state.

Camille was shouting, "Victor, Victor!" but his mind was now in another place.

I turned away, only to see an officer reading Bill Frederick his rights as he cuffed him.

I stood in the midst of it all, seemingly invisible. This was not what I had imagined would happen. Tony had told me that, after

Victor led us to the general location of the body, I would be guided away. In my mind, this was all going to occur in a calm and orderly manner. They had promised me a professional who specialized in working with mental illness would intervene and work with Victor. That was obviously just said to placate me. Instead, Victor was cuffed and forcibly marched by two officers to a squad car.

Trench coat flapping, Tony came running to the rock piles with two officers with water canisters strapped to their backs. Tony directed the officers to begin spraying the rocks in the first pile.

As long as I was being ignored, I stepped closer to observe. I couldn't see anything out of the ordinary as the rocks revealed their colors, and I prayed to God I was wrong. I watched officers set some rocks to the side, to no avail. Tony finally told the officers to move to the second pile, and again, they started with similar results. Toward the side of the second pile, I anxiously watched as a line formed in the dark gray feldspar. An outline of a cross was revealed when they sprayed the entire area. One officer removed half a dozen rocks, peered down and yelled, "We have a body!"

I turned to the farmyard to see Bill being pushed into the back of a squad car. Victor was staring blankly out of the back of another squad car's window as it pulled away. Camille was completely distraught and being held back from the squad cars by a police officer. I asked into the wind, "Victor, what did you do?"

Jon pulled into the driveway, so I ran to him to tell him what had transpired with his family.

Jon was incredulous. "Why didn't you call me?" he asked.

"I tried to, but you weren't returning my calls." It sounded like a sorry excuse even to me, but Tony had insisted it would be better for Jon if I kept him out of it.

"Really? Because my phone hasn't buzzed for hours." Betrayal was etched into Jon's face.

"I wanted to do the right thing this time," I implored. "What can I do to help?"

"I think you've done enough. What the hell, Serena? I wouldn't have left Mandy's body out here, not even to protect my family."

I cringed as he turned away from me, shaking his head. I reached for Jon, trying to get him to look at me. "I'll pay Bill's bail," I offered. "I know they're not going to release Victor, but they'll release Bill, right?"

"No. Absolutely don't."

I sighed and pleaded, "Jon."

"If Victor's in jail, we need Dad in jail, too. We need someone in there who can help Victor calm down. Just leave us alone."

"Call me."

Jon glared back with penetrating hatred. "Don't you get it, Serena? If you would have called me, we could have brought this to the police. Instead, I look complicit in a cover-up. Victor's going to be charged, Dad's going to be charged for withholding evidence, and I'm going to lose my job. A dead girl was found on land I was living on when she went missing. I'm going to need to find a way to come up with some money for bail, and fast."

"I'm sorry." It sounded weak.

"Yeah, that doesn't change anything."

And he was gone. Jon was right. He was going to lose his job. I should have seen that coming, but I was too overwhelmed to think clearly. I stood helpless in the driveway, debating if I should try to comfort Camille. I decided I should just leave. I had tried to handle things right this time, and it all blew up in my face. Defeated, I returned to my car.

I needed to talk to Jon. I'd sit outside his apartment door and wait for him if I knew he was going home, but I doubted he'd go back there with everything happening here. He'd probably stay with Camille. But if I went there, Camille might tear me apart.

I looked at my list of suspects. I decided to find out more about Randall and Whitey. Bill and Victor would be scrutinized enough by the investigators.

Chapter Nineteen

Jon Frederick
Wednesday, April 9
Morrison County

The discovery of Mandy Baker's body was big news, even though her disappearance hadn't received any attention outside of Morrison County ten years ago. It was a nightmare. Victor was in a psychotic state, spending the day rocking back and forth in his cell, the picture of madness in orange jail attire. He was sweating like an addict going through withdrawal, with his stringy, dirty-blond hair now matted to his head. Each psychotic state took twice as long to recover from than the last, and required additional medication. More meds meant more side effects, like dry mouth, poor balance, and fatigue. Victor was charged with murder and, subsequently, would not be getting out of jail to see a psychiatrist. It had been arranged, however, for a psychiatrist to see Victor at the jail. Fortunately, Dad was there, and the guards were kindly letting him assist in calming his son down. This would only last for a few days before my father would be released. Dad was facing a charge for having concealed evidence.

I had progressively become more obsessed with thinking Serena loved me the same as I loved her. I had to remind myself that, just because I felt something so intensely, didn't mean normal people felt the same. The self-loathing that came with obsessive thinking was unbearable at moments like this. My insistence that Mandy's case be reopened had hurt my family and broken my heart. But like all obsessive people, my solution was to amp up my obsessive behavior. I would focus on helping Victor.

Fortunately, Morrison County had a history of offering bail, even in murder cases. They typically made the bail high enough where they believed the defendant wouldn't be able to come up with it, however. I'd been told Victor's bail would be set at one million dollars. I would have to come up with ten percent of this to get him released, standard for bail cases. Victor wasn't resilient enough to endure the bullying he'd receive in jail, so I had to find the bail money.

Dad and Mom were just surviving; they didn't have any financial reserves. With cashing in the little I paid in so far in my 401k, taking out a loan on my car—which I had paid off—selling my couch, recliner, big screen TV, kitchen table and chair set, and utilizing the money I'd saved, I'd be able to come up with half of that amount. Unfortunately, my extended family was like most rural Catholic families, and had no financial resources. My generation was the first on my dad's side to go to college. My mom's side had some college-educated members of the clergy and Peace Corps workers, who, of course, had no money to assist. A person didn't get rich helping poor people.

WITH DAD AND VICTOR IN JAIL, I stayed with Mom again last night to help her maintain her sanity. After breakfast, I prepared for a meeting at the investigation center. My work as an investigator couldn't be saved, but I wanted to make an argument for Victor's innocence before I was terminated.

I wore a white dress shirt, black tie, and black slacks, trying to look as professional as possible. I needed to convince the investigators to consider suspects other than Victor. My brother couldn't defend himself, so I needed to, as I'd always done.

Sean, Paula, Tony, and I sat around a table in the investigation center. I launched my defense even before Maurice arrived. "Victor didn't kill Mandy Baker," I began. "He has no history of aggressively acting out. He went for his usual night walk, found her dead body, and buried her. He thought it was the right thing to do. People are going to hear his story and say it's crazy, but he *is* crazy. Victor isn't violent—just mentally ill."

Sean sat back, tie hanging loose in an uncharacteristic state of disarray, and calmly asked, "Did you know about this?"

"No. Believe me, if I'd have known Mandy's body was there, I would have reported it. Mom just filled me in on what happened." I had to be careful how I worded everything. Mom had indeed filled me in, and had given me much greater detail than I could reveal to my coworkers.

Dad had sensed that something wasn't right with Victor, so he immediately hired an attorney for him. He told investigators Victor was schizophrenic, and he was concerned Victor could unwittingly say something to implicate himself.

Dad questioned Victor about that night from a variety of angles for months before he finally got Victor to disclose that he had found a teenage girl's body and buried it. However, Victor couldn't remember where he had buried her body, and when Dad searched the farm, he found nothing. Dad wasn't sure if he could believe Victor, and he didn't want to get him arrested for one of his bizarre thoughts.

Only years later, when Dad was out in the rain on the farm, that he noticed the cross formed by rocks on the rock pile. After finding Mandy's body, Dad did some research and discovered that both of her parents were dead and she had no siblings. Dad assumed Mandy had frozen to death. He decided it was better to keep it quiet, both to keep Victor out of trouble and to avoid desecrating Mandy's body. Victor had told Dad he carefully buried the girl, and then prayed over her. Dad thought Mandy wouldn't get a more respectful burial elsewhere. It had to have crossed his mind that turning the body over to the authorities would have also made people more suspicious of me. My parents believed Victor was honest when he told them he never killed the girl, and they eventually allowed him to resume walking again. They made Victor swear never to talk to me about it, because they knew I'd report it. They thought they were safe, but Victor trusted Serena enough to tell her, and now Victor was looking at serious prison time.

Paula looked comfortable in her usual sweatshirt and jeans. Her hair was somewhat mussed from being in the cold, windy weather earlier. She asked, "How did Mandy's body get on your land?"

I shrugged. "I honestly don't know."

Tony interjected, "Mandy had been just down the road at Serena Bell's home. Serena was the last person who was with an alive Mandy Baker and, coincidentally, Serena has recently found her way back into Jon's life. Serena knows a lot about psychology, Jon. Certainly enough to manipulate you. Vicki did."

Surprised, I asked, "How so?"

"She wasn't with Lemor at 1:00 p.m. on the day Brittany disappeared. I checked her cell phone records, and she had made a call from the Little Falls area at twelve fifty-eight."

I began questioning if there was any aspect of my life that I was handling well at the moment.

Paula smiled slightly and added, "I have some additional information on Lemor. I couldn't get his therapist to give me any information, so I went to probation and asked for a list of sex offenders who had group treatment the same time as Jeff. I've been tracking them down, one by one, and found out through interviews that March thirtieth wasn't the first time Jeff had spotted Brittany walking down that gravel road. This makes the offense premeditated."

I realized Jeff might have failed the polygraph simply because he never revealed that he had seen Brittany make that walk on other occasions. This still didn't mean he was guilty, but it did make him look dishonest. And now he no longer had Vicki's alibi.

Sean said, "It's my sense that the abductor cleaned up the scene. We didn't find anything."

Tony stewed as he quietly tapped on the table with his pen. "I've never heard of a stranger abduction case where the scene was cleaned up, and Lemor was a stranger to Brittany."

Sean interrupted, asking, "Have you gotten the DNA report on the leather jacket yet?"

Tony shrugged it off. "No."

Sean leaned back, rotating his shoulders. "It really seems a long shot that the same person would commit both of these crimes."

Tony conveyed his uncertainty by saying, "It's not as much of a stretch as you might think. These crimes happened about eight miles apart, which is nothing in rural Minnesota. Most people in this area drive thirty miles to work every day. But the jacket theory has taken me nowhere. So, I agree, I think we're looking at two different perpetrators."

Sean started gathering his paperwork in frustration. "I'm not going to sit and wait for Maurice any longer. We've got something to check out." He turned to me and said, "It's been nice working with you, Jon."

Paula reminded him, "He's not gone yet."

Sean nodded and sarcastically said, "Right."

After Paula and Sean left, Tony turned to me and wearily said, "I think Serena set Victor up, and I think you're being played. You need to be careful."

Not needing a lecture from Tony, I put my hand up as if to say, "I don't want to hear it."

Tony sat back and, respecting my wish, asked, "Did you get anything out of your interview with Randall Davis?"

I considered this. "I don't think Randall knew Mandy. He made derogatory comments about every other woman we spoke of, so my gut feeling is that if he would have known Mandy he would have talked trash about her, too."

"You're lucky you weren't shot again." Tony held up his hands in retreat before I could argue. "I understand you need to find Mandy's killer. Just don't be stupid about it."

Maurice entered in his gray suit and stared hard at me, as if I was the only one in the room. His white hair was ruffled. He pushed his glasses up his nose as he spoke. "I think you know what I'm going to say," he began. "You're done for now. I'm going to put you on paid leave, and tell people you're still recovering from being shot. That'll buy us a couple weeks. Hopefully, we'll have some answers by then."

I had no union protection, as I was on probationary status for my first ninety days as an investigator, and could be terminated or suspended for any, or no, reason. I thanked Maurice for giving me a little time. He didn't have to do that.

When Brittany's investigation first started, things happened so quickly it was like stepping into a whirlwind. Now I was being tossed back out.

Chapter Twenty

Serena Bell
Thursday, April 10
Minneapolis

Jon still didn't get it. I could end up in prison for manslaughter before this was over. Still, I went to the police immediately with the information I had, like I should have done ten years ago. Seeing what they did to Victor broke my heart. Before I gave myself up, I first needed to consider other possible explanations.

I was going to start with exploring Randall Davis's alibi, Anna Hutchins. Back when we were still talking, Jon had mentioned her name in connection with Randall. The investigators hadn't been able to track her down, but I had resources they didn't. While Anna might have had an outdated address on her driver's license, and might not show up in the correctional system, she wouldn't stop showing up in the medical system. Medical records were well protected in our system, so only the patient's consulting nurse and doctor had access to them. While I didn't have access to Anna's medical records, as a supervisor in billing, I had access to the addresses of anyone who had been seen in our hospital and any of our adjoining clinics. Nervously, I accessed the database, and it didn't take long to find her. Even though I tried to rationalize that I wasn't hurting anyone, I knew I could lose my job over this.

After work, I drove to the Pines apartment complex in Brooklyn Center. Anna Hutchins lived in a three-story brown-brick complex, with black iron-railing patios.

I told myself, *Act confident and composed,* then knocked on the door. I prayed to God that Tony wasn't tailing me. Anna answered in a tattered gray pullover. The odor wafting off of her indicated she'd been doing some kind of sweaty job not long before I arrived. Her short, dark hair was thick and beginning to gray. Anna was slightly overweight, wore no make-up, and was rather plain-looking. She was a woman who could easily be lost in a crowd and likely planned it that way. Anna studied my professional attire cautiously.

I had violated ethics at work and was about to commit a lie of omission by letting Anna believe I had some legitimate role in investigating Mandy's murder, but I forged ahead. Before she asked for a badge, I appeased Anna by telling her, "You're not in any trouble. The disappearance of Mandy Baker back in 2004 is being reopened, and I'm only here to ask you questions about Randall Davis. From the differences in your current addresses, I assume you and Randall are no longer together."

Alarmed, Anna closed the door until it was open only a few inches, her eyes frantically scanning the hallway behind me. "I left that nightmare over nine years ago. He doesn't know where I live, does he?"

"I have no information that would suggest that," I assured her. "I'm only here because you provided an alibi for him on the night Mandy disappeared. I know Randall had been abusive to you, and I was wondering if this led you to make a statement on his behalf."

Anna studied me. "What ever happened to that girl?"

"Her body was found buried on a farm by Pierz."

There was an incredible sadness in her eyes. Anna looked past me at something, or nothing, lost in thought. She opened the door further. "I remember that night because Randall was hauled in and interrogated the next day. Randall was a piece of work, but that was one crime he wasn't guilty of. Part of me would like to say he didn't have an alibi, just to cause him some of the misery he caused me. But the truth is, he was home with me that night."

I wanted to hug the sadness out of Anna, but I managed to maintain my composure. "Are you okay, Anna?"

"Yeah. People don't really understand. I can't hate him without hating part of myself. I wasn't that fifteen-year-old girl he raped. I chose Randall. He did help me off of drugs, but he was ridiculously brutal about it."

I met her gaze sadly, and all I could think of to say was, "Well, I'm not beyond doing stupid things for a man."

This elicited a low, guttural laugh from Anna. She said, "I like your honesty. Even if it makes us both sound a little pathetic. There aren't too many investigators who'd have the guts to say that." She started to close the door, but stopped and said, "Thank you for talking to me like I'm a real person. Most investigators look at me with a combination of 'I know your type' and pity. It's refreshing to know they're not all like that."

I smiled in return and said, "Thank you for clearing this up. Have a nice evening, Anna." As she quietly shut the door, I heard the bolt snick shut, and I was filled with regret for having to remind her of a time she was clearly trying to put behind her.

When I returned to my car, I opened up my notebook and crossed out Randall Davis's name. I decided I was going to write to Say Hey Ray Benson, to see if I could get on his visitors' list at the prison in Florida.

7:30 P.M.
EDINA

I HAD AGREED TO MEET Clay at Broder's Italian Bistro in Edina, as it was a safe, public environment with a great calzone.

Clay looked good, with tanned skin and muscular features, highlighted by the trim fit of his black button-down shirt. His appearance was the trap. He was most appealing dessert you'd ever seen, but the taste was rancid.

Clay had obviously had a few drinks after work, breaking down the few defenses he possessed. He studied me curiously. "So, what brings you back to me?"

The comment made the hairs on the back of my neck stand on end. I gave him a warning look and said, "Jon's not talking to me. You asked me not to tell him about us, and then you told him anyway. Why?"

Clay gave me an impish grin as he said, "I just did." He took a long pull from his bottle of Heineken before saying, "Sorry about that. I was angry, and it just slipped out. And you know how Jon is. If he told you it's over, you're done."

My anxiety sky-rocketed, and I reminded myself to take slow, even breaths. Clay hit on everybody I knew, so he must have hit on Mandy. She was sensual and seductive. Clay wouldn't have been able to resist her.

I no longer felt like eating, so I just said it. "Mandy came to Pierz for you on the night she disappeared. She told me she wanted to be in Pierz when the bus returned. You were on the bus."

Clay set down his fork and said, "This isn't about Mandy. What is this, buyer's remorse? You were the one who drove to my house to be with me. It doesn't get any easier than that."

I took a chance and stammered, "I was with Mandy the night she disappeared, and you were, too." I kept all expression off my face and just looked at him.

Clay's voice was getting thicker with alcohol. "Are you wearing a wire again?"

He attempted to peer down my shirt, and I quickly raised my hand and said, "No."

Clay scrubbed his hand over his mouth and pushed his plate to the side, laughing, "Nothing I haven't seen before. You tell me what you think happened, and I'll tell you the truth. If you're not comfortable talking about it here, we can go someplace more private. Don't ask me to talk about it if you don't have the nerve to say it yourself, in detail." Elbows now on the table, he rested his hard jaw on clasped hands, waiting.

"Here is fine, Clay." I lowered my voice and shared a tale of Mandy being the coquettish siren, and Clay being the brazen bull who would teach her a lesson. When I had finished, Clay's face flushed red, embarrassed by his arousal.

"I like that story a lot. Is this a fantasy of yours?"

I shook my head. "Not mine. How close was it to the truth?"

Clay put his hand on mine and said, "We both know why you're here. Let's just do this."

Feeling repulsed, I pulled my hand back. "You promised me the truth, so tell me."

Clay turned to me and said with a sneer, "It's a little too late for you to just be a tease. I was with Mandy, but it wasn't on the night she disappeared." Clay raised his voice and his bottle, for the sole purpose of embarrassing me. "I didn't have sex with her—just with you. So don't be too quick to judge everyone else, whore."

The two young women working the counter stared at us for a moment, then looked at each other, uncertain if they should intervene, while the middle-aged couple next to us pretended they didn't hear him.

Furious and mortified, I fought the urge to throw my Diet Coke in his face. Instead, I let my expression go flat, and with quiet anger, asked, "Do you feel better now? You seem to think we have this love/hate thing going, but I don't give a damn about you. You're just a pretty boy who can't seem to see beyond the end of his dick, and you're one year of drinking away from losing your business." I stood and flipped cash onto the table for our meal. "So here, have one more drink on me." I left before I started crying over my ineptness. I had never been this obnoxious to anyone, and I felt anxious and ashamed. My face was burning. I got no satisfaction out of being mean, no matter how justified it was.

I HAD A LOT TO SAY to Jon, so I was pleasantly surprised to find an email from him when I returned to my parents' home in St. Paul. It was less enticing after I read it:

> *Serena,*
> *I hate to ask you this, but I'm out of options. I was wondering if you could lend me some money. I'm afraid jail could be the death of Victor; the bullying will tear him up. I need to come up with $100,000 to bail Victor out, and I'm about halfway there. Any amount you could offer would be greatly appreciated. I promise to pay you back with interest. I'm sorry I was so rude to you last time we spoke, and I'd certainly understand if you can't help. It's a lot to ask.*
> *Sincerely,*
> *Jon*

I decided to wait until we spoke face to face to tell Jon about my encounter with Clay. It had to torment Jon to ask me for money. It wasn't his nature to ask for help from anyone. I was good with money, though, and with what I'd been saving to buy a house, I would be able to meet him halfway. I had a feeling I was going to need to pay for an attorney before this was over, but I was going to give him my money, anyway, in a last-ditch effort to mend my breaking heart. I hoped someday he would appreciate how much I loved him.

I sat staring at my computer screen in my bedroom, searching for words. I pulled the blanket wrapped around my shoulders a little tighter to fight the chill in the room. I'd loan Jon the money, under the condition he would sit down and talk to me. I couldn't let "us" end, tormented by the thought of being misunderstood.

Chapter Twenty-One

Panthera
9:30 p.m.
Thursday, April 10

The wonderful thing about smokers is that no matter how secure their home is, they've got to step out for that cigarette. If she's stressed, she steps out a little earlier. If it's a typical day, she'll come out of the house in about ten minutes. I slide into the dark shadows against her house and wait. She sneaks out the side door, into the darkness, probably because she hasn't told family members she's smoking.

As anticipated, she passes by me. She's nine minutes ahead of schedule. She's shivering, because it's cold and she isn't wearing a jacket—probably afraid it'll smell like smoke and give her secret away.

The pretty young thing blocks the wind with her cupped hand to light her smoke, and then cautiously looks around. I'm right behind her, in the shadows, but she still hasn't noticed me. She's looking for movement, and I'm not moving. I can feel her fear. I love this game. I want her so bad, I'm prepared to defile her to her death. I need this, and she deserves it. It's such a rush to stalk at night, because so much of the darkness is unknown.

Now, she's cautiously craning her neck and looking around. She senses my presence, but hasn't found me. She's looking in every direction but mine. I'll let her have most of her smoke. Bring her anxiety down a little before I engage her. But I do have to take hold of her before she turns back in my direction. She inhales a deep drag and closes her eyes while she exhales.

Perfect. I step in and wrap my hand around her mouth. I can feel her warm breath in my bare hand, and she can feel the gun in her back. "We're going to go for a little walk."

Rigid with fear, she mindlessly moves with me as I walk her to the darkness alongside her garage. She's too afraid to make a decision. It's funny how people can sense when it won't faze you to take their lives. I whisper into her ear, "If you want to live through this, you'll go along with everything I say. Remove your pants and underwear."

I free her to let her undress, and she pleads, "Please don't kill me. I'll do anything." She kicks off her shoes and with trembling hands, does as she's told.

I feel an endorphin rush as she complies. This is the best drug on earth. "Now bare your top."

She turns her back to me to remove her shirt, and as she's pulling it over her head, I knock her down and pin her to the ground, facedown. Her arms are tangled in her shirt, so without them to break her fall, she lands hard. She lies there lifeless, but she's not fooling me. I shake her, say, "You're not dead," and then taunt her. "Don't act like you are."

Through her whimpers she softly pleads, "I'm not going to fight you."

I grab a handful of hair and push her face into the cold, hard dirt. It has to feel like rough sandpaper against her body. I feel so strong. She coughs hard in response and tries to spit out the dirt she's just inhaled.

I undo my pants and then grind hard into her. "I like it rough."

She bites her hand as she tries to bear the pain, but true to her word, she doesn't fight . . .

She slowly gets up and dresses, like this was simply a bad date she now regrets. She's accepted humiliating defeat. She straightens her shirt and through her tears tells me, "I won't tell anyone."

"I'll kill your family if you do."

With a blank stare, she concedes. "I know."

"If anybody asks, tell them Jon Frederick did it."

She glances down for a moment, and I sense despair when she tells me, "No one will ask."

She's right. I'm her master and her compliance makes her someone I can return to. A port in a storm. I was prepared to kill her if necessary, but I think I'll keep her around for the time being.

Without another word between us, she limps back to the house.

A rush of power washes through me, and I feel good over granting her the right to live, for the time being.

Chapter Twenty-Two

Jon Frederick
7:30 a.m.
Friday, April 11
Pierz

I woke up to a car pulling into the driveway. Tony parked his rusty Chevy and walked to the rock pile. I quickly dressed and met him there. The rock pile had been carefully disassembled by the CSI team, and Tony solemnly reflected on the scene. "Mandy's body was pretty decomposed, but covering it with rocks kept the animals from getting to it. Her neck was broken. I think it's safe to say that it happened in a struggle. Whoever did this didn't break any bones, other than her neck. She probably didn't intend to kill her."

I told Tony, "Sometimes I wonder if Mandy called my name that night. I woke up to something, but I didn't hear any more after that. Maybe it's my brain trying to fill in, after the fact."

"A false memory." Tony looked out into the field. "I know you think all these attacks are related, but I don't believe that. I think Mandy's death, ten years ago, is separate from the assault of Brittany, as well as the attempt on your life."

"I feel like I'm missing something obvious, so I keep recounting everything that happened ten years ago," I said. "My parents were going through bankruptcy. What if my parents owed money to whoever killed Mandy, and he threw her on our land just to create misery for our family?"

Tony thought hard for a few long minutes. "I doubt it. This murder was about Mandy."

"I think the murder was about Mandy, too. But maybe there's a separate reason she ended up on our land. She didn't walk there—she was too afraid of the absolute darkness out here. Someone picked her up and drove her to our farm from the Bell home."

Tony looked straight at me. "Open your eyes! Serena is the reason Mandy Baker ended up on your land. She was with her. She resented her. She led the police to her body. What more do you need? Wouldn't it be more likely Serena struck her in the heat of an argument, than Serena just fell asleep? Your friend Clay probably helped her move the body, and maybe she slept with him because she owed him."

Tony could be a jerk. Instead of responding, I silently walked back to my parents' house.

Mom was standing propped against the kitchen counter, looking older than I remembered. Wrinkles gathered around the pain in her eyes, and I could see some white at the roots of her auburn hair. She wore a white cotton undershirt, covered by one of Dad's red flannel shirts.

She had made me some eggs and toast, which were too done for my liking, but out of consideration for her effort, I thanked her and ate it.

Mom turned to me and, rather unemotionally, stated, "With his paranoia, Victor will never live through all those guys picking on him for entertainment."

As Mom went on and on with her dire prophesy, I felt brick upon brick piling up on my back. It was shameful for me to take money from Serena, but I had to swallow my pride to keep Victor alive. I told Mom, "I need you to help me. What can you tell me about the state of Mandy's body?" Mom was the one person Victor would have shared details with. I stilled her shaking hands with my own.

Mom thought for a moment. She knew from my work that the state of the body spoke volumes. "The straps were torn from her tank top, and her jeans were undone and partially down." Mom laughed softly to herself. "You know how naïve Victor is. He said, 'Maybe she died in her underwear so somebody dressed her.' I just agreed. Mandy wasn't wearing a jacket, and it was well below freezing."

"How was her body positioned?" Mom looked confused, so I explained, "Was she curled up, or lying on her stomach?"

"She was lying on her back. Victor said she looked like she had been laid to rest." A small shudder rippled through her shoulders.

5:30 p.m.
Birmingham Apartments, Minneapolis

The bail money was accepted, but Victor wasn't going to be released until Monday, when the paperwork went through. During murder cases, counties were deliberately slow at processing paperwork on Fridays so they had the weekend to gather further evidence.

Tonight would be my moment of reckoning with Serena. I took the money, so now I had to face her. I wasn't upset with her. Serena was a lover—maybe a little overindulgent at times, but a lover, nonetheless. I was an obsessive jerk who ruminated over imperfections, and I hated myself for that. That had to end, if I was going to maintain a loving relationship. I hadn't always been like this. Before Victor's psychosis kicked in when he was about twelve, I was a fun-loving kid. I needed to find peace again. I had tethered my life to my past with Mandy Baker, and I yearned to be free.

As I had sold all my furniture for bail money, Serena sat on the only place left to sit, the edge of my bed. She was in a lovely sundress, and nervously but matter-of-factly shared her past interactions with Clay, up to the present. It was easy for me to get lost in her green eyes and long dark curls. Serena told me, "Before I bare my soul any further, I want you to know that I like small towns, and I like Pierz. The same crap happens in houses across the nation. The only difference is that in the country, the houses are farther apart. And no matter where you live, the haters are always the loudest. You still have a lot of people who believe in you."

I accepted this with a simple, "Thank you." It was nice, but I needed answers. "Why are you on your own list of suspects?"

Serena swallowed hard and looked down. "I'm responsible for Mandy's death. I brought her to my home. I didn't stop her from drinking—hell, I drank with her. She must have tried walking to your farm and froze to death. She was heartbroken and drunk, and had nobody. Your parents claim Victor found Mandy's dead body and buried her, and I believe them. This is my fault. It was never my intention to hurt your family. I just needed you to hear the truth from me before I turn myself in. I love you, and I swear, if I had known Victor had buried her body ten years ago, I would have turned myself in then. I am so sorry—"

"Shhh." I felt bad for Serena. I took her hand and told her, "Mandy didn't freeze to death. I talked to Tony. They don't have the forensic pathologist's report yet, but it appears that her neck was broken from a severe blow just below her skull. Victor is incarcerated because Mandy was murdered." I could see a weary sense of relief and sadness wash over Serena as I continued. "She didn't walk to our farm. She was deathly afraid of the complete darkness of the country at night. Mandy was struck hard by someone who was probably on top of her while she was lying prone. From what Mom managed to get out of Victor, her body was found lying face up. The straps were torn on her tank top, and she wasn't wearing a jacket. Her body was dumped on our land. So you can cross your name off the list."

Serena wrapped her arms around me in a fierce hug and said, "Thank you for telling me that. I can't decide whether to be sad or happy to hear it. It helps me, but not Victor, and poor, poor Mandy." I held the embrace out of fear that this was all we had left. She pulled back and searched my eyes intently, and finally asked, "Jon, what have I done that I can't be forgiven for?"

"I'm miserable, and I want you to be happy, but I don't think you can be happy with me," I said. I tried to think of a way to explain it. "This is how I envision boundaries. When I choose an intimate partner, that person is on the top floor of the house with me. My family and close friends are important, so they're on a floor just below us. And everyone else is outside. You were sexual with someone in my house, and when I think of you with Clay, it makes me crazy, and being crazy is very painful. It makes me unstable, and having an unstable foundation makes me subordinate to you. I feel like the only way I'm ever going to have peace again is to empty the house, except for family, and start over."

Deep in thought, Serena silently studied me before she softly said, "I've seen you resolve difficult things." Nothing was said for three long minutes before Serena tentatively rested her hand on mine and broke the silence. "Jon, if this is the only way, go ahead and clear out the house." She softly stroked my cheek and searched my eyes. "Is it empty?"

I didn't want to, but I didn't have another solution. So, I closed my eyes for a moment before I sadly told her, "Yes. It's empty—except for my crazy family." I took a weary, deep breath.

Serena smiled cautiously. "Then, I'd like to step in from outside and introduce myself. I'm Serena Bell, and I'd like to date you. If it makes it easier, I'm already in love with you."

One of the problems with picturing abstract ideas is that the image can be an obstacle. It takes someone who is patient and creative, like Serena, to help me out. We would start anew, as she suggested, with Clay removed from friend status. He was now on the outside, and overall, I felt good about it. I wouldn't choose to be friends today with someone with whom Serena had a past relationship. Situation resolved.

I told her, "I love you, Serena. I'd like to start over. It's too hard not to."

Chapter Twenty-Three

Serena Bell
11:00 p.m.
Saturday, April 12
Birmingham Apartments, Minneapolis

Jon's breathing was slow and relaxed. He and I had a long night of honest, nonjudgmental sharing. It lifted a heaviness off my heart. When my emotional rollercoaster finally crashed, I slept for ten hours straight. After sleeping in, we worked out together, showered, ate at Café Ena, and went for a long walk before returning to bed. My body was a little sore, but it was the kind of soreness that brought a smile to my face. Quite a start for a couple who claimed to have just met. This wasn't going to help Clay's opinion of me, but I didn't care.

I lifted my head off Jon's chest and asked, "What do you think of the possibility that Mandy was waiting for Clay?"

Jon ran his fingers tenderly through my hair. "It's better than any theories I have. My mind's been racing, and I've struggled with sleep since we've been apart. Stay away from Clay."

I was startled by his vehemence.

His bright-blue eyes pleaded with mine. "Clay's been drinking more lately, and it concerns me that he publicly embarrassed you."

"I embarrassed myself. I never should have been there. I hope you know that I'd give anything for a lifetime full of days like I've had with you."

Jon scratched lightly along the top of my spine. "It's only been a day."

I closed my eyes and enjoyed a nice, long scratch. I may have purred. When he finished, I told him, "If it wasn't your dad or Victor who murdered Mandy, I'm down to two suspects—Clay Roberts or this Whitey person." I propped myself up on an elbow and suggested, "Fly with me to Florida. We could visit Ray Benson together."

Jon smiled. "You should be a detective. Say Hey Ray is the one person who can identify Whitey. I wish I could go with you. But I need to get Victor free, and make sure he's in a mental state my parents can handle. I'm not wild about the idea of you going alone, though."

I rested my head on his chest once again and listened to his heart. "Are we okay now? I don't want to leave if we're not good. I'm afraid if we don't solve this, I'm going to end up in jail. Tony hasn't made it a secret that I'm his prime suspect."

"Leave Tony to me. He can be obnoxious, but he eventually listens to logic. I'm not letting you take the blame for this." He tightened his arms around me and kissed the top of my head.

I slid my body up to kiss him. "Let's go to church together tomorrow. I'd like to sit with my parents. They're worried about me, and I want them to see how happy you make me. We could have lunch together." I looked directly into his blue yes, and it just came out. "I want to have a family—with you."

He didn't hesitate. "Marry me."

I wasn't expecting this. My heart sank and my eyes welled up as I silently shook my head.

Crestfallen, Jon looked away.

I took his chin in my hand and kissed him. "I love you, Jon, but not now. Let's get this taken care of, and then I want you to officially propose to me. Keep in mind, I didn't *say* no."

"I thought I did just propose to you."

I knew he felt badly, so I tried to make light of it. "No, you said 'marry me.' Kind of like a grunt. I want the sweetness I know you're capable of. Woo me off my feet, like you've done before." When he didn't respond, I said, "This is just a postponement. I tell you what, I know you're headed back to Morrison County Monday. How about if I extend the weekend a little by meeting you at my parents' old place Monday night?"

Chapter Twenty-Four

PANTHERA
8:10 P.M.
MONDAY, APRIL 14
MINNEAPOLIS

THE PROSPECT OF PHYSICALLY dominating Serena Bell has played over and over again in my brain since I first saw that cute rump of hers resting in my territory. Serena's always looked like the perky cheerleader type, even though Pierz didn't have cheerleaders. Athletic women played sports. But now, ten years later, she wouldn't be a match for a man who performed hard physical labor every day.

My heart races as I watch her car pull into the driveway. The anticipation of her resistance, and penetrating that shapely ass of hers, is so damn exhilarating. I take a couple hits out of my flask of Captain Morgan just to calm down. The adrenaline rush has already started.

Tonight, I'm fully prepared. I've busted the yard light. I've broken the locking mechanism of a window to allow my entry. I've got an industrial zip tie for her wrists, and a rolled washcloth to shove down her throat. I doubt anyone's close enough to hear her screaming, but I don't like the distraction of it. I just need an opportunity to catch her vulnerable. I'm a patient predator, so I'll find it. It'll be a rush, followed by the satisfaction of a dominant victory. This is the first time I've started an assault knowing my victim will die when it ends. Either I'm maturing as a predator, or

I'm seeing the larger picture better. I need her gone. It's necessary to maintain my right to live as I choose—to roam freely and rule my kingdom. Serena's a loose end, and she needs to be silenced.

Chapter Twenty-Five

Serena Bell
8:15 p.m.
Monday, April 14
Pierz

April is the busiest time of year for clinics in Minnesota. I think the long winters wear people down. When I was finally able to leave work, my brain felt fried from looking at numbers all day. I was exhausted, but I'd promised to be in Pierz tonight, so I made the drive.

It was unusually dark in our driveway. I made a mental note to tell my parents the yard light had burned out. The wind made it difficult to hear, which, combined with the darkness, felt terribly unsettling. Maybe Jon's warning to be extra careful was making me paranoid. Maybe not. My skin crawled with an eerie feeling of having eyes on me. Before exiting my car, I reached into my purse for the comfort of my cell phone. I took out my car keys and pressed the panic button to sound my car's emergency horn, not caring if it proved to be embarrassing. With the horn's shrieks piercing the night, I ran from my vehicle and slipped inside the house. I didn't care if I looked crazy. It worked, and I was safe.

My cell phone started ringing as I raced through door, so I rushed to free my hands. When I was finally able to answer, Jon had already hung up. I decided to settle in before I called him back.

I returned to the back door, to ensure I had bolted it. I pulled hard on it, making certain it was locked. It was all good. There was an odd odor in the air, a little sweet and musty. For some reason, it reminded me of college. I inspected my clothes, thinking maybe I'd spilled something on myself at work, but the smell wasn't coming from me. Giving up, I decided to snack on something, then take a nap. I was bone tired, but would have a glass of red wine as a consolation for my trying day.

I got into my pajamas and, glass of wine in hand, sat on the bed and pulled my knees up to my chin, thinking Jon and I were finally starting to work out. Then I froze. I was certain I heard faint footsteps in the living room. It didn't seem like the usual groans of the house settling—it was too rhythmic. Then it was quiet again. I sat rigid, not breathing for another minute, but heard nothing. Jon's warning about Clay intruded on my thoughts.

I decided this was a good time to call Jon, so I grabbed my cell phone off my nightstand. After we said our hellos, Jon shared that Victor was paranoid and looking for an opportunity to run, so he wouldn't be able to leave his parents' home until Victor fell asleep.

I sighed, "I'm afraid."

Jon could tell I was shaky and asked, "Did you make sure all the doors are locked?"

"Yeah, it's just . . ." I thought I heard another step, so I sat perfectly still, straining to focus on the sound. Aside from my quickening pulse thundering in my ears, the house was silent. It had sounded so real.

"What's on your mind?" Jon prodded.

"I'm tired, and I'm becoming paranoid. I need to take a nap. I miss you. It's only Monday, so it's going to be a long week of work for me, if you're gone. But I know you need to be there to help with Victor." I nervously plucked at some fuzz on my bedspread.

Jon said, "I want to thank you for sticking it out with me. I get lost in that labyrinth in my brain, and it was nice of you to take my hand and walk me out of it."

"That's why you need to keep talking to me. The best times in my life were when we were helping each other."

He paused for a moment before saying, "I'm sorry for proposing and making it awkward between us. I should have realized this is too soon for you."

"Please don't apologize. It isn't too soon. It's just not the right time. We both know there'll be no peace for your family until Mandy's case is solved." I sighed and told him, "I wish you were here right now. I have never told any man I wanted to have a family with him before . . ."

I settled into bed, feeling like a child with the covers pulled up to my chin. I tried to fall asleep on my back, so I could still open my eyes and see around the room, but it wasn't working. I finally resigned to flipping onto my stomach, as this is how I slept best. My long day of work started to take its toll, and soon I was drifting in and out of a light sleep. Again, I heard the creak of floorboards, and I tried to tell myself it was an old house, and old houses creak. Listening intently, I smelled something that was both unpleasant and familiar at the same time. Then I tensed as the realization came to me. It was the stench of stale booze on a man after he had been out drinking. Adrenaline coursed through me like electricity. I started to lift my head, but instantly, a strong hand grabbed a handful of my hair and pushed me face-first into my pillow. Before I could move, his weight crushed down on me. I attempted to scream, but something fabric was shoved roughly into my mouth.

His body pressed heavily into my back, and his toxic breath was in my ear. "Do you feel that? That's what my life's like," he growled. "Suffocating pressure."

It felt like my hair was being ripped from the roots, but I had no intention of giving up. I elbowed him in the ribs, then swung my arms, hoping to rock him off of me. I tried to say, "Go to hell," but my voice was muffled by the cloth gag. It had quickly absorbed any moisture I had in my mouth and felt glued to my tongue. It was too hard to work on spitting it out and fighting at the same time, so I focused on fighting.

My thin night pants tore as he yanked them and my underwear down.

I managed to keep them at my knees by twisting my hips. I prepared to fight any attempts to turn me over. It was stifling, and I couldn't get out from underneath him. This wasn't only a fight to avoid the brutal rape of my body. This was a fight for my life.

He punched me between my shoulder blades with a crushing thud that rocked my body. As I gasped, he whispered in my ear, "I like it rough, so keep on fighting."

With adrenaline-fueled rage, I swung my arms back.

Unfortunately, he had anticipated this. In one quick motion, he grabbed both of my wrists behind my back and bound them together with some sort of plastic that bit into my skin.

With his full weight on top of me, he drove me face-first into the bed. My hands were effectively cuffed. I tried to scream, "No!" but this just forced the cloth further down my throat, and I began to choke. Using my tongue, and aided by my gag reflex, I managed to dislodge it from my throat and back into my mouth. With my arms now immobilized, I could only use my abdominal muscles to wriggle back and forth. I had to be more calculated in my effort to escape. I attempted to work my way to the side of the bed, but he was so heavy and so strong. Still, I kept inching toward the side of the bed, like a caterpillar, a little at a time. It was my only chance.

He breathed heavily against my cheek from behind, filling my nostrils with the nauseating stench of sour alcohol.

The cell phone on my night stand began ringing, but I couldn't move my arms to reach it. I knew it was Jon. If I could just touch it, he would know I was in trouble. I'd hit it with my face if I had to. I amped up my efforts, urgently straining toward it, ring after painstaking ring. The phone was now fewer than two feet away from me, but it could have just as well been on the moon. It must have rung ten times, but ultimately, it went silent.

Once the phone stopped ringing, my attacker let up on the pressure for a second as he pulled his pants off. I had managed to work my head off the side of the bed. I dug my foot into the mattress and used it to pry hard enough to push our bodies over the edge of the bed, rocking him off as we fell. I heard the satisfying crack of his head against the nightstand. Thank God for sharp hardwood corners. The gag in my mouth came loose with the fall and I was able to spit it out. I had a fleeting moment of victory and screamed as I slid away and rocked myself to my feet.

I had walls both behind me and to my right, and my bed was on my left. The silhouette of a man rose to block my exit. As my hands were still tied behind my back, I was afraid to risk rolling across the bed. I shouted, "Clay, why are you doing this?" Before he could respond, I kicked into his groin as hard as I could, driving his bare testicles into his body. A hard right punch blasted my jaw as my kick landed. I crashed backwards, and the back of my head smacked hard against the bedframe.

I was nauseated at this point, and lying on my back on the floor. My hands were pinned to the floor beneath my hips. My legs were spread and when I attempted to will them back together, they didn't move. I wasn't completely unconscious, but felt woozy, and no longer had the strength to fight or cry out. I was now a silent observer of the unfolding scene. An odd memory of my psychology coursework reminded me that my cerebellum had been jolted. It took time for the muscle control to come back. I was done. The fight was all out of me, and it wouldn't come back in time to help me. I was defeated.

The monster-like man loomed over me in the darkness like a prize fighter who had KO'd his opponent. He hesitated for a moment and then took advantage of my stunned state. He staggered as he reached down and pulled my pajama pants and underwear the rest of the way off and kicked my feet further apart. He held his hand against his head, then looked at it. He must have been bleeding from the wound. I could hear low, guttural swearing and groans of pain. He seemed to be in a similar state of disorientation. After steadying himself, he reached down, then pulled my night shirt over my face, baring my breasts.

I thought it was just as well. I didn't want to see him, anyway. And then my stomach heaved. I began to vomit violently into my shirt. I shook my head, trying to get my shirt off my face so I wouldn't choke in my own vomit. My body convulsed as I threw up, turning me on my side.

The dark shadow was still looming over me. For God's sake, how could he still be aroused? I could feel him ogling my body. Tears scorched paths down my cheeks. It took all my energy to simply weep, "No."

With his foot, he rolled me over on my stomach, grumbling, "You can choke in your own puke." He put his foot to the back of my head and ground my face into it, gagging me. Finally, the pressure lifted from the back of my head, and he stepped away. I pulled my filthy face up, gasping for air.

Involuntarily, I curled into a fetal position. I could only envision the skull-faced monster from my nightmares. He was rubbing his groin. I couldn't tell if it was because of the pain or if he was getting ready for an attack. My eyelids were getting heavy, so I closed my eyes, anticipating rape would occur at any moment. Instead, I heard his departing footsteps, and, with relief, heard the door as he left the house.

I wasn't sure how long I'd been lying in the darkness, but the next thing I remember was a harsh blast of light as the room was illuminated.

Chapter Twenty-Six

PANTHERA
8:50 P.M.
MONDAY, APRIL 14
PIERZ

FUCKING FUCK, FUCK, FUCK. I had to get out of that damn house just to stop oozing DNA all over. I run through the woods to the ravine where I hid my vehicle. The steep sides of the gorge surrounding my vehicle prevent anyone from seeing me, but also make it impossible to see toward the farmhouse. My balls feel like they were squeezed in a vice, and I need to stop this bleeding. Okay, think. I should have found a cloth wrap in the house, but I couldn't afford to take the chance I'd pass out.

I need to collect my thoughts for a minute. I was too excited about tonight. I thought with the zip tie, I could take care of Serena with my bare hands. The shots I took to calm down were a mistake. It slowed my reaction time. I should have brought the gun just in case. She got so damn lucky—the phone buzzing when she had almost given up, the fall stunning me long enough to give her a free kick. Fucking bitch. I should have killed her the last time I was with her. I close my eyes and lean my head against the driver's side window. This is bad . . .

It hurts to smile, but I can't help myself when the answer finally comes to me. Serena was about to pass out when I left. She's still tied, so she can't call anyone. And she's still alone in the middle of nowhere. I have a solution for the DNA. I have a canister of gas in the back of the truck. I'll torch the fucking place, starting with her body and her bedroom. Now I'm feeling a bit of a rush. The predator circles back on his prey. Victory stolen from the hands of defeat! If I'm too sore to perform, I could still shove something up her, just for the fun of it. A great predator is never out of the game.

9:15 P.M.

The bedroom light is on when I return to the house. Serena's car is still the only car in the driveway. I can hear sirens in the distance. She must have found a way to call 911, so I have to work fast. I carry the five-gallon gas can up to her bedroom, but she is nowhere to be found. I don't have time to search, so I douse the bed and anything I touched with gas, and light it. The huff of gas fumes ignite the bedroom, and it is soon dancing with flames. I make my way downstairs, pouring the accelerant in a trail all the way to the door, and then empty the contents in front of the exits. Go ahead and hide, Serena. The flames will still find you, and being barbecued is a hellish way to go.

Chapter Twenty-Seven

Jon Frederick
8:52 p.m.
Monday, April 14
Pierz

I arrived at the Bells' home a little before nine o'clock, and seeing the door banging open in the wind, sprinted into the house to Serena's room. I bent down and hastily cut the industrial zip tie holding Serena's wrists together. I imagined this same type of tie being used in Clay's work. I gently laid a blanket over her, then picked her up and carefully set her on the bed. My tears joined hers when she wrapped her arms around me. I slid out my phone and dialed 911.

Serena was now curled up in bed with a blanket snaked around her mostly bare body. Her eyes looked empty as she stared off at nothing. Her stained night shirt still hung loosely around her neck. I wanted to investigate the scene, but only Serena was deserving of my attention right now.

I slowly unraveled the blanket from her shoulders and soothed her. "I'm going to help you take your shirt off because you threw up on it." I went to her closet and retrieved a hooded sweatshirt. I carefully pulled her night shirt off, slipped the sweatshirt on, and found a pair of her cotton socks. "I'll bring you a warm washcloth to wipe off your face, and a glass of water to rinse your mouth. You can just spit back into the glass. They won't want you to wash too much because they'll be collecting DNA."

After preparing the washcloth, I lightly brushed some of her matted hair out of her face and gently wiped it clean. I ended up holding her head and pouring some water in her mouth. She managed to cooperate enough to rinse. Serena breathed slowly and heavily and the dazed look in her eyes stayed, as if everything she was experiencing was now playing only on the inside.

I decided not to touch her underwear or pajama pants, which were lying on the floor beside the bed. "I want to help you dress before the police arrive and start taking pictures, okay?" She nodded her acceptance. "Do you want jeans or sweatpants?"

When she didn't respond, I found a pair of underwear and sweatpants in her dresser and carefully slid them on her. She momentarily shook herself out of her shock. She frantically looked about the room, and pleaded, "Please, Jon, just get me out of here!"

I didn't have the callousness to deny her, even though it generally went against protocol. I helped her to her feet, and she leaned on me as I helped her to my car.

WHEN WE ARRIVED AT THE HOSPITAL, I provided the necessary information to the nurses. Serena was in shock, but she refused to take a sedative. Shortly after 10:00 p.m., a police officer called me and told me the Bell home was burning when law enforcement arrived. I wouldn't have minded being there to confront the arsonist, but I was damn glad I had gotten Serena out of there.

It was past midnight after all her testing and her statement were completed. Serena was released to my care and fell asleep in my car as we left the hospital parking lot. As long as she was sleeping, I decided to drive her back to my apartment, so she wouldn't have to deal with her parents or mine tonight. I did call her parents, and told them Serena had been assaulted, but that she was released from the hospital and I would keep her safe tonight. It was a heartbreaking conversation to have with them.

At my apartment, Serena mumbled something about a shower, so I gently led her into the bathroom. I started the water for her, placing a clean towel and washcloth on the vanity, then helped her undress and step under the spray of water. I stood outside the tub and spoke to Serena as she showered. I told her the deadbolts were locked and she was safe. I was going to stay with her and take care of her. Her lack of response concerned me, so I cautiously slid the curtain open and asked if I could help her.

Serena was sitting with her knees up, staring at the marks on her wrists as the shower behind her relentlessly sprayed her hair across her face. She looked at me with glazed-over eyes, clearly needing help, but unable to find a way to make the words audible. I considered my options and then removed my clothes. I grabbed a washcloth and soap and joined her, quickly depressing the shower plunger so the bath would fill directly from the tap.

I knelt in front of her, took her face in my hands, and as I gently pushed the hair out of her eyes, I softly explained, "I'm going to start with your feet and make certain any trace of him is completely gone, and then we'll rinse off, so you can go to bed absolutely clean tonight. If you feel like I need to clean any area a little more intensely, or a little longer, just nod your head."

Accepting my offer, she nodded and I went to work. Inch by inch, I soaped and cleaned her body, telling her which part I was going to wash, to warn her, as I didn't want her to be surprised by any of my contact. It was a somber, nonsexual event, and I couldn't stop the tears from streaming down my face. At one point, Serena tilted my head up and looked at my face, and then reassuringly patted my shoulder as if to indicate it was okay. I wanted to tell her that she didn't need to comfort me, but instead I continued to bathe her in silence.

Fortunately, Serena had left an overnight bag at my apartment. By the time I had her dried off and ready for bed, she was more lucid and ready to talk.

Once in bed, she curled up on her side, turning her back to me, as she said, "It bothers me that they have rape kits at hospitals. That rape is so common they have a kit ready for the next victim." Her speech was sluggish, and her voice sounded like she'd swallowed sand.

I agreed. "I am so sorry you had to go through this. If there's anything I can do for you, please let me know." I felt tremendously guilty for not protecting her.

Serena rasped, "Set the alarm for six thirty. I have to go to work tomorrow."

I gently placed my hand on her shoulder. She initially flinched, but then held it there when I attempted to pull it away. "Serena, I'm sure they'll understand."

With little emotion, Serena told me, "I'm going in to do my job. I have to finish turning in data for an audit tomorrow. I'm not going to let this jerk interfere with that. I'm going to need you to drive me, though, since my car is still in Pierz."

I pressed the issue, saying, "I still haven't returned to work, so I can stay home with you."

"I'm going in. If I can finish the audit, I can take some time off. I won't be able to deal with this until I finish my work. Do I need to set the alarm?"

"No," I sighed. "I'll take you to work." Then, I had to ask, "Do you think it was Clay?"

She took a deep, shaky breath. "I don't know. I thought it was at first, but it didn't seem like it at the end. It was dark. I'm not a hundred percent certain. Who else would it be?"

I smoothed her hair from her cheek. "I wish I knew. Let's try to sleep."

We were still for a moment, before Serena quietly asked, "You're not going to go after Clay after I fall asleep, are you?"

I assured her, "No, I'll be with you every second. You're all that matters to me."

"Thank you." She pulled the blanket tight. "I'm sorry I'm not nicer. I don't feel like being nice. I'm angry and I'm really tired. I feel terrible for my parents. They could have used the money from the sale of that house."

"You don't have to be nice, and I'll do anything you ask," I said. "Your parents feel bad for you. They're just glad you're alive. Your dad said the insurance is probably worth more than the house was, anyway." I doubted it was true, but it was nice of him to say.

She quietly spoke into the sheet she was now holding up to her mouth. "I fought as hard as I could. If I wouldn't have kicked him in the groin, I think he would have killed me—raped me, for sure." Her voice was thick, as if she was on the verge of tears.

I leaned over and kissed her forehead. "Serena, you're amazing. You fought a killer for your life, and won. Bob Marley once said, 'You never know how strong you are until being strong is your only choice.' You are strong. If you want to talk, talk. If you want to close your eyes and go to sleep, go ahead. I'll be here all night."

Serena snuggled back against me. "I'm so tired. I just want to sleep. Talk to me while I'm falling asleep. It helps to hear your voice."

"Okay. Is there anything you want me to talk about?"

She was silent long enough that I thought she may have drifted off, but then she asked, "Why didn't you marry? You once told me that more than any career, you wanted a family."

"Because I work all the time. I have dated, all serial monogamy. I'm not a player. But I never felt like it was the right person—until now. Plus, there's the whole bit where I say, 'I enjoyed talking to you, but now I'm going to work a stakeout for the next three weeks, so I won't have time to see you. And by the way, if you haven't heard, I was once accused of murder. But don't worry, they never found the body.'"

"Now you can tell them they found the body on your parents' farm."

I appreciated her attempt at humor. Her spunk gave me hope she'd eventually be okay.

She murmured, "Why do you work all the time?"

"I need to know what happened to Mandy." I hurried to keep talking, so she didn't have to keep asking questions. "But it's not just that. You know how my family struggled. At times, my parents would send me to the store and ask me to put things on credit, only to find our credit wasn't any good anymore. That's pretty embarrassing for a thirteen-year-old boy in a small town. All of our vehicles barely worked. We missed out on events sometimes, simply because we didn't have a trustworthy vehicle to get us there, and my dad didn't want to ask anybody for help. I still receive some satisfaction at actually arriving at my destination. I hate to complain, because my parents are good people. They were just trying to make it farming, during a time that no longer supported the family farm. So I decided my life wasn't going to be like that. When I marry, I want to be financially set. And now I am." I paused. "Or at least I was, until I had to come up with bail money."

I could hear that her breathing pattern had changed, and when I leaned into her, I could see she had drifted off into a light sleep. I whispered, "And the only woman I proposed to turned me down." I prayed, *God, please help heal her wounded soul.*

Chapter
Twenty-Eight

Jon Frederick
10:00 a.m.
Tuesday, April 15
Pierz

Once I dropped Serena safely off at work for the day, I returned to Pierz. I was furious, and the last place I wanted to be was in a church, which convinced me it was exactly where I needed to go. A special prayer vigil was being held at St. Joseph's Catholic Church for Brittany Brennan, which I decided to attend. The assault on Serena angered me much more than the attempt on my own life. I prayed for God's guidance to keep from overreacting.

St. Joseph's was packed with Christians praying for the revival of the girl who was left for dead. The choir performed a heartfelt version of "Angels Among Us" in front of the altar, leaving the choir loft empty. The loft was above and behind the congregation. I thought this was the perfect place for me to pray, undistracted, so I made my way up there. Tony must have spotted me, as he joined me within minutes.

Tony was already aware of the brutal assault on Serena, so I shared that she had an argument with Clay only four days prior. Serena had asked me this morning if it was common for a rapist to forcibly sodomize his victims. Her assailant had never attempted to turn her from the prone position. According to Tony's notes, he believed Mandy died facedown, though she wasn't found that way. A man who beats and anally rapes a woman is getting aroused from her pain. But a sadist isn't going to go ten years without other victims, and Tony wasn't aware of any reported sexual assaults against women in Morrison County that met this description.

Tony suggested the man who shot at me was afraid I had discovered something. If this same man assaulted Serena, was he afraid she knew something? What could Serena have known?

We grew silent again as the service continued. The fact that Tony and I were having a conversation about such brutality in the sacred setting of a church was not lost on me.

After Mass, Al Brennan immediately exited out a side door. Mary headed toward the cameras on the church steps, while Jason remained in the front pew. The elderly priest returned from the sacristy and, after observing Jason alone, sat with him. It made me feel good that someone was reaching out to him, beyond the people looking for a story.

Tony and I made our way down the steps of the choir loft toward Jason and Father Oliver. As we closed the distance, it was clear that Jason was not faring well. He looked disheveled, and the dark circles under his eyes suggested he had been having difficulty sleeping. Jason's decompensation bothered me. His sister was recovering, and the alleged perpetrator was in jail. Shouldn't he be sleeping better?

Father Oliver smiled at us, and we left him to work whatever magic he could on Jason.

As Tony and I exited the church, he shared with me that a rift was forming between the BCA investigators and the Morrison County investigators. The BCA was committed to proving Jeff Lemor assaulted Brittany. I perceived this as a thinking error. Deductive reasoning involved starting with a suspect, and looking for evidence to convict him or her. Great detectives used inductive reasoning, which allowed the evidence to lead them to the perpetrator. So why is Sherlock Holmes known for his powers of deduction? Because the author, Sir Conan Doyle, used the term incorrectly. "Deduction" is still used incorrectly in the Robert Downey Jr. portrayals of Sherlock Holmes. Sherlock's powers were of *induction.* Sorry for the tangent.

Tony suspected Brittany was assaulted by Jason. Jason's alibi at the time Brittany disappeared was that he was installing a new stereo in their vehicle, but even though the van was burned, the lab crew was able to determine that the original stereo had never been removed. In addition, the front seats had been completely torched, particularly the passenger seat. Tony intended to continue initiating conversations with Jason until Jason finally gave up some incriminating evidence.

Tony was returning to the investigation center, so I called Serena to make sure she was doing okay. The swollen bruise on the back of her head was making her head pound, but she was determined to complete her work for the audit.

Serena's voice sounded hollow, like someone who could burst into tears at any moment, when she told me, "After I fell asleep last night I had that nightmare again, where that creepy man is looking down at me, staring in my face."

"Did you recognize him?"

"No. I get a chill down my spine just talking about it. I hope it doesn't come back every night, now. I keep telling myself that God doesn't give us any more than we can handle."

I didn't want her to try to resolve this all on her own, so I responded, "I think God gives me more than I can handle every day, with the expectation that I won't be too proud to ask for help. You've taught me that I certainly do better with your guidance."

Serena's coworker lived near my apartment and had offered her a ride when they were finished. Serena expected it to be a later day than usual, but when it was finished, she would be able to take a couple weeks off. Serena promised to let me know when she was on her way, and I promised to be at my apartment when she arrived.

5:00 p.m.
Edina

I drove to Clay's steel-sided house in Edina. The house was dark, so I guessed he was still at work. I'd seen him enter his security code in the past, and of course, I had no difficulty remembering it. I searched his garage and found some zip ties, but there was no exact match for the one used on Serena.

A careful search through his laundry, garbage, and house offered a shirt in the laundry with a dried bloodstain on the sleeve, and a significant number of empty Grey Goose vodka bottles in the recycling.

About ten minutes later, I heard Clay's truck pulling into the driveway. I anticipated this situation was going to end poorly, but I couldn't walk away from it. Maybe I hadn't learned anything since I'd beaten up that bully on the playground.

I turned the kitchen light on and waited for him at the table to give the illusion of composure. Showtime.

When Clay entered, he wasn't surprised to see me. His long-sleeved undershirt and jeans bore the signs of a hard, dirty day's work. Appearing exhausted, he ran a hand through his hair as he told me, "I was expecting you."

As I sat, the picture of calm, cool, and collected fury raged maniacally through my veins. I was certain I could beat Clay to death with my bare hands. In Pierz, we were taught to take care of our own, and Serena was closer to me than anyone. I forced myself to remain seated as I confronted him, to keep this from immediately becoming a brawl. "What's wrong with you? What could possibly make attacking Serena okay in your brain?"

In typical Clay fashion, he responded in anger. "What are you doing here? You broke into my house. I could shoot you and have no legal consequences for it." Clay went to a drawer and opened it.

Not knowing what he was retrieving, I unbuttoned my jacket and reached for the gun in my shoulder holster.

Clay pulled out a pack of cigarettes and a lighter. He shook one out and lit it, holding the nicotine in for a beat before exhaling angrily through his nostrils. If he had noticed me going for my gun, he ignored it as he continued. "I never assaulted Serena. I didn't have to."

Unable to contain my frustration, I abruptly stood up, slamming my palms on his sleek tabletop. "You always overreact out of your own damn hubris." My composure huffed out of me like Clay's cigarette smoke.

Clay looked for something to flick his ashes into. He finally stalked back to the drawer and retrieved a glossy black ashtray. In between deep pulls from his cigarette and dragon-like exhales, he continued. "You should be thanking me. I didn't tell the police this, but I believe that crazy bitch killed Mandy Baker. I think Serena's been leading you around on a puppy collar, and you're so excited to be with her the chain never gets tight." He stubbed out his cigarette and, with his hands in the air, backed away. "You're right. I used to overreact. But I'm not like that anymore. Owning my own business has made me realize you never get even. You just move on with minimal damage." Clay studied me for a moment and gestured to where I'd been sitting. "Grab a chair and let's reason through this. It's what you're good at."

I was still smoldering, and reluctantly returned to my seat at the table.

Clay leaned in and looked directly at me. "You're my best friend, Jon, and even though I don't trust Serena, I wouldn't hurt her." Clay gathered his thoughts for a moment. "What do you want to know? Ask."

"Do you have an alibi?"

"No. I was a little hungover, so I worked part of the day, and went home to sleep it off. The crew and I had finished a multimillion dollar home in Eden Prairie the night before, so we celebrated."

"Can I look at your head?" I stood up and challenged him to deny me.

"Have at it. The police did the same thing. What's that about?"

A closer look at his head indicated there were no cuts. "Whoever assaulted Serena should have a nasty cut on his head."

Vindicated, Clay smirked. "Okay. Do you want to see my balls, too? The police looked at them."

I couldn't resist a barb. "No, even if they're swollen, they'd only be average size."

Clay smiled at the insult and said, "Fuck you."

I noticed a padded area under his left shirt sleeve that appeared to be a bandage, so I asked, "Can I see the injury on your left arm?"

Clay was losing patience. "My arm got pinched in some of our metal scaffolding at work." He pulled his sleeve up over his forearm and then pulled the bandage away, revealing a deep half circle of a cut, obviously made by the end of metal piping.

It occurred to me that maybe Clay didn't hit his head, as Serena thought. Maybe he put his arm out to break the fall and reopened a wound. I sat back down. "Tell me about Mandy. You told Serena that you were with Mandy."

Clay re-covered his forearm as he appeared to consider his story.

I interrupted his train of thought. "Honesty is easy to recall."

Clay purposely hesitated before suggesting, "I was just thinking that you could apologize for being such a dick."

I stared hard at him. "When I'm convinced, I'll apologize." I firmly said, "The truth."

"All right. But don't go bat-shit crazy if you don't like what I'm saying. I was with Mandy a couple nights before she disappeared. She called me to ask if there was anything she could do to save her relationship with you. So I took her for a ride, and I told her you were dumping her for Serena. I took her to Devil's Canyon. You remember how the pitch in that road increases—you can't see more than ten feet in front of your car driving into it. I thought if anything could scare the pants off a girl, that place would. It was an overcast night, so she couldn't see anything but the dash lights. I was thinking fear and arousal sometimes work together . . ." he stopped, shrugging at his logic.

I summarized his statement. "So you tried making out with her."

"She was a better match for me, anyway. You can't argue with that. But her exact words were, 'Mandy's whorehouse is shut down.' I tried kissing her, and she slapped me, so I gave her a ride home. I don't need to force women. I guess something about being with you makes women not want to have sex. She turned into a raging tomcat in a flash, and I hadn't done anything but try to kiss her. If she was like that with the wrong guy . . ." he turned his wrist palm up and didn't finish his statement.

"You didn't see Mandy the night she was killed?"

"Absolutely not. I never saw her or heard from her again."

"What did you do after you dropped me off at home on the night Mandy disappeared?"

"Are you kidding? We lived in Pierz. There was nothing to do. I cruised up the main drag a few times and headed home. I wasn't feeling too good that night. If you remember, we beat Mora, but we didn't play well. That game made me realize we weren't going anywhere. Our conference was so physical, and we dominated it, because that was our game. But when we had out-of-conference refs like we had in Mora, who called everything, we were in trouble. We couldn't adjust. What did we have, four guys foul out? And unfortunately, our playoff games were going to be all nonconference teams. The writing was on the wall, but it was too late to change it." He looked away, lost in a decade-old memory.

Without realizing it, Clay had just convinced me he hadn't killed Mandy. He was talking about something that happened on the night of Mandy's murder that bothered him, which was completely separate from the murder. This is something innocent people do, but guilty people seldom do. The game bothered him, because nothing more significant happened to him that night.

I told Clay, "Our friendship is done. I can't be a friend to a guy who had sex with the woman I want to marry. And, by the way, why did you tell me to use my imagination? You knew it would torment me."

"I figured if you're going to be a prick, think whatever you want. I know you think I just use women, but it's not like that." I gave him a doubtful look, and he quickly added, "Okay, it's like that *sometimes.* But it wasn't like that with Serena. There are so many times when I start talking to a woman I convince myself she's exactly what I need. But by the next day, I look at her and realize she isn't anything special, so I just keep looking."

"It bothers me that you pursue women who are in relationships. Who do you think has ruined more relationships, you or your mom?"

Clay's eyes flashed with anger. "I could hit you so hard, you'd starve to death bouncing."

"No, you can't, because I've been your only friend. And I'm going to miss insulting you."

Clay quietly considered what was lost, before saying, "Me, too."

There's an irony about Clay I found perplexing. The same women who criticize men for pursuing ladies with movie-star bodies are the ones who pursue Clay for the exact same reason. It was all too easy for Clay, and it ruined him. Great lovers aren't easy, and easy lovers aren't great, and that's why love never lasted for him.

Clay asked, "So do you finally believe I didn't assault Serena?"

I thought for a moment and answered, "I believe you didn't kill Mandy. I'm going to let the investigators handle Serena's assault." I warned him, "I know you're angry at Serena, but stay away from her. She's been through a terrible trauma, and I'll do whatever I can to protect her. I have no vendetta against you. I just want the guy who assaulted her locked up."

"I'll stay away," he conceded. "But remember this—maybe Serena was that sweet girl back in high school, but that all ended when you chose Mandy over her."

It was time for me to leave. As I started my car, a text from Serena announced that she'd be at my apartment in a half hour. It was perfect timing, so I made my way home.

10:30 A.M.
Wednesday, April 16
Pierz

Serena came north with me, so she could collect her car and meet with her parents' home insurance investigators in Pierz. When we arrived at the burned-out shell of her parents' home, we sat in reverent silence at the loss for a moment. Then Serena straightened herself up, kissed me goodbye, and climbed into her car. Even though the snow had all but disappeared, warnings of a major blizzard lit up the news. I asked Serena to stay close until we decided where we'd spend the night. I needed to meet with Tony.

Since I didn't want Victor to see Tony, and I was no longer welcome at the investigation center, I met Tony on the dirt road by the Brennan farm. The sky was overcast, and the cold seeped into my bones. Tony's relationship with Paula had cleaned him up. He looked rested and ready to go, and wore a crisp white shirt and khaki pants with his tan work boots.

I told him everything, because I needed as much help as I could get.

Tony asked, "So now you're okay with Serena having been with Clay?"

"It was before we got together. And in the greater scheme of things, who cares?" I loved her more than I thought I was capable of loving.

Tony thought it over, then reluctantly agreed. "I think when you get older, that kind of stuff matters less. When you're young, it's easy to get emotional about the wrong things."

"I feel bad for Serena. She had a brutal fight with whoever attacked her."

Tony still wasn't ready to express sympathy for Serena, so he changed the subject and flatly told me, "Vicki's disappeared."

Concerned, I asked, "Did they issue an APB?"

Tony dismissed the all-points bulletin suggestion. "Hell, no. Why? Rumor has it she's burning out in a meth house on the west side of Little Falls. And don't go after her. The DEA has a drug sting involving that house, and we've been directed to stay away."

"Is her daughter with her?" I was overcome with sadness. I felt like no one ever took her seriously, which had to be hard on a person. What had happened to her?

Tony shook his head. "Vicki's daughter is with her grandparents. In other news, the CSI crew found porn on the Brennan home computer. Sites like Barely Legal. And the ballistics test proved the gun we found by Jeff Lemor's home didn't fire the shots into your car. But just so you know, the BCA team still believes Lemor is the guy."

I was becoming even more convinced that the crimes were connected. I thought the perpetrator burned both the van and Serena's home in an effort to destroy evidence. I turned to see Sean Reynolds's silver Crown Victoria approaching.

Tony muttered, "Sorry, kid. You're going to be interrogated about the assault on Serena and, indirectly, about Mandy's murder. Both Serena and Mandy were dating you, and you were in close proximity to both at the time of the assaults. Your cell phone pinged off a tower close to Serena's home at the time she was assaulted."

I didn't like the familiar feeling of having my innocence questioned. "I was at my parents'. They'll vouch for me."

Tony nodded. "Their credibility is not real good at the present time," he reminded me. "Serena reported her attacker was bleeding. The blood could have easily come from your injured hand. Just don't cover up for anyone and you'll be fine. You need to get free of the web you've let Serena spin around you."

I had already considered that I was an obvious suspect in both assaults, so I was a bit surprised it took this long before I was brought in. Tony was right about one thing: I was caught in a web, and it was tightening around everyone close to me.

Chapter Twenty-Nine

Serena Bell
2:30 p.m.
Wednesday, April 16
Pierz

It was starting to snow, and I had no plans to drive back to the Cities tonight. I absolutely didn't want to be snowed in without Jon, either. I was finished with the insurance investigators and now without a place to stay. I couldn't presume to stay with the Fredericks' until I had a chance to apologize to Camille and Bill for the whole wire incident. I prayed we could get past it.

I spent some time on the phone with my parents, who were dreadfully worried about me. I considered myself incredibly fortunate to be the benefactor of their love and kindness, but I needed the comfort only Jon could provide. I was too afraid to be alone, so I stopped at Red's, a small-town gas station that served food and was a hub of activity in town, to grab a sandwich. While I was eating, an old high school friend stopped in with her daughters and invited me over to spend the afternoon with them. I thanked God for the rescue. I found out later that being Pierz, everyone already knew about the assault, and the owner of Red's had called someone who knew me when she saw me eating in the booth alone. My good fortune was more small-town kindness than coincidence.

4:45 p.m.
Pierz

It had begun snowing in earnest, and I needed to decide where I was going to spend the night. To my relief, Jon was finally finished, so I agreed to meet him at his parents' house. Bill and Camille had taken Victor for a follow-up psychiatric appointment in St. Cloud and had yet to return, so I would have a little time to acclimate myself to the environment before I faced them.

When I arrived, Jon hugged me and then leaned back against the cupboard in his untucked button-down shirt and blue jeans. Camille had baked bread, and the heavenly scent permeated the air. I studied Jon's lean, muscular frame before focusing on his blue eyes. I set my overnight bag down, and he handed me a warm slice of buttered bread. He had warmed a dipping sauce made from homegrown tomatoes, peppers, and onions that his mother had canned. For the moment, I felt completely safe and at peace as we feasted on our comfort food and shared our day's events.

After over an hour of laughing about stories of growing up naïve Catholics in Pierz, Jon stood up with an obvious purpose. He pulled me close for a long, heart-warming kiss. He smiled as he slowly pulled away. "I'm going to shovel a path so my parents won't have to trudge through the snow," he said. He went to the entryway and pulled on a parka and gloves. There were already six inches of snow on the ground. He opened the door, waved, and said, "*Nivatus!*"

I smiled at the familiar word, remembering how his mom would use it when she'd occasionally threaten to lock Bill out of the house on winter days for being grumpy. *Nivatus* is a Latin word that means "cooled by snow." I didn't know anyone other than old Catholics who used it.

The phone started ringing, creating an unwanted and eerie reminder of my assault. I hesitated, but then decided I should answer in case Bill and Camille had an accident trying to drive home in the storm. Bill Frederick was surprised to hear me answer, and his initial response was rather cold. He reported, "We're finally going to leave St. Cloud."

I forgot for a moment that I still needed to deal with Jon's parents. Feeling very humble, I decided to just put it out there. "Bill, listen. I'm so sorry for wearing that wire and bringing you so much grief. I have the greatest respect for you and Camille. I was just doing what I was told by the investigators. I wish I would have stopped and thought about it. It all happened so fast."

Bill grunted, "Camille's still a little upset. But I pointed out to her that I'd be disappointed if our daughter didn't handle the situation in a similar manner. You cooperated with the authorities."

As long as he was being forgiving, I added, "I was hoping to stay over tonight, if it's okay. I can sleep on the couch. But if you'd rather I leave before you get home, I can get a room at the hotel in town. The last thing I want to do is cause more distress for you and Camille."

Bill laughed, "The Hillbilly Haven?" He said, "No. I'd rather you stayed with Jon. When I see Jon with you, it's a pleasant reminder that there is someone normal in our family."

I smiled at his unspoken reference to Victor, and to his ongoing concerns about Jon's older sister. Theresa had left home and married young, but it had taken some time for her and her husband to let go of youthful indiscretions.

Bill paused, then said, "You know, Camille would prefer we stayed in St. Cloud, and I'm thinking that with this storm, it might be wise. They're talking about over a foot of snow in this part of the state."

"Thank you," I breathed, then was embarrassed I had said it out loud. I wanted to say, "That's not what I meant!" but it was.

Bill's voice was gruff. "I honestly don't care where you sleep. Just don't make it obvious tomorrow."

Good old Bill. I said with relief, "Take care, Bill, and travel safely tomorrow."

When Jon came back inside, his cheeks were red and he was out of breath. After putting away his winter wear, he approached me in the kitchen.

I put my hands on his cold cheeks and kissed him hard. He picked me up, and I was in such good spirits that I was ready to go with him wherever he wanted to take me. I thought he was going to carry me upstairs, but he carried me toward the door.

"What are you doing?" I said, realizing we had different intentions.

"I was going to toss you in the snow—*manja*." He quickly retreated. "Maybe it's a bad idea. I wasn't thinking about everything you've been through."

I grabbed his face in my hands and made him look directly into my eyes as I told him, "Hey, I'm not going to live my life as a victim."

He kicked open the door, and snowflakes fell on us. I taunted him, saying, "I dare you . . ." My face was quickly spattered with snow as he carried me out the door and into the blizzard. I still didn't believe he'd actually throw me in a snow bank, but he did, sort of. Instead of tossing me, he carefully set me down into a three-foot-high mound of snow. I quickly sank into a frozen bath. I felt the snow trickling into my shirt and sliding into the back of my jeans. Both laughing and surprised, I pulled Jon down and I rolled over on top of him in the snow. I threw snow in his face and quickly escaped back into the house. I locked him out and made him say the magic word before I let him back in.

After offering "abracadabra" and "freeze," he finally said, "Please." Grinning like a little kid, Jon came traipsing inside.

The snow had managed to seep into everything—my shirt, jeans, socks—everything. I began peeling away my snow-covered clothes, right there in the kitchen.

Jon glanced in the direction of the driveway, checking for his parents. Wide-eyed, he asked, "What are you doing?"

I was now down to my underwear and trying for seductive as I peeled away the final layer—as seductive as a girl can be covered in rapidly melting snow. Between bursts of shivers that probably resembled mild seizures, I teased, "You're always telling me how bad you want me. If you want me that bad, let's make love right here, right now." I nonchalantly leaned on the kitchen table and patted the top of it. "Right here." Another chill shot through my shoulders, but I held his gaze.

It only took him seconds before he said in a rush, "Okay!" He yanked his shirt off.

I stopped him short. "Jon, I was just kidding! Geez, for all you know, your parents could be walking in the door any minute—which they aren't, by the way. They called while you were out shoveling." I was laughing in earnest at this point, and stepped in to wrap my arms around his bare waist. "I wouldn't have stripped if I thought there was any chance they'd be walking through the door. I stripped because I thought it would be better if I didn't track snow all over their house." I gave him a quick kiss, then pulled back. "And for God's sake, the kitchen table? I would think of it every time I ate dinner with your parents."

Jon quipped, "Once you've tasted how dry my mom's Thanksgiving turkey gets, you might welcome the distraction. Turkey jerky."

I reached up and ran my nails slowly from his shoulders down his back, and lowered my voice. "As soon as I get my clothes in the dryer, I'm running upstairs and sliding under your blankets. You're more than welcome to join me."

His eyes lost focus for a second. "I'll start the fireplace in the living room, and be right up to warm you up."

His skin was pleasantly warm from the fireplace when he joined me. The heat from his body was gratifying, and for a time, all thoughts of murder and assault were forgotten. I eventually drifted off to sleep in Jon's arms.

When I awoke, the room was dark. Jon's warm body next to mine was comforting, but it took me a moment to remember where I was.

The only light in the room was moonlight, filtered by the falling snow through a partially opened curtain. My overnight bag was on the floor, but I decided to go with one of his t-shirts. After I pulled the t-shirt over my head, I found myself facing a painting of Jesus. A metal plate below it, which glimmered in the moonlight, read, "Bert Faust Electric." Bert Faust was a stoic, portly, local German electrician, who had quietly worked in the area for decades. I turned back to Jon, who had been watching me dress.

Jon said, "I've always thought highly of Bert Faust's work."

As I lifted the painting, I couldn't contain my laughter. Camille had hung the picture of Jesus over the breaker box in the room, but it didn't quite cover it, leaving Bert's insignia on the bottom.

Jon and I made our way downstairs to the living room. The crackling fire he'd made cast shadows dancing eerily across the wall, but I felt safe in Jon's arms. He had laid out a number of blankets in front of the fireplace to give us extra cushion on top of the carpeted floor. Jon disappeared into the kitchen, and soon returned with a large bowl of popcorn and two mugs of hot chocolate.

He looked at me sadly and said, "I need you to leave, Serena."

My heart sank. "What? Why?"

"Not now, but by tomorrow night." There was so much regret in his eyes as he gazed into mine. "Because I can't solve this and protect you at the same time." We sat in front of the fireplace, and he pulled me close. "Someone's trying to hurt us. And if Tony finds you, he's going to interrogate you, and that's not going to help you right now. I need to get you out of here, so I can rattle cages until I shake something loose."

This was scary. Jon was the one who typically calmed me down. I closed my eyes and leaned against him. His warmth felt so comforting. I said, "You don't think it was Clay, do you?"

"Clay doesn't have a cut on his head, and I'm convinced he didn't kill Mandy."

I whispered, "Let me help. I need to help."

Jon gazed into my eyes. "You could be a great help by talking to Ray Benson. The more I think about it, the more I'm convinced

Say Hey Ray knows who killed Mandy. She called someone to pick her up that night. It probably wasn't the first time she needed a ride when Ray and her mom weren't available. Ray would know who Mandy would call. Since you're already on his visitor's list at the prison, this could be our best move. I hate sending you off to do this alone," he finished as his fingertips grazed my cheek.

I tried to muster some confidence as I told him, "Jon, I planned on doing this anyway. I had kind of hoped I wouldn't need to, but of course I'll go."

Jon slumped sadly. "You know you can refuse. You've been through a lot, and I honestly don't know what's best for you. It's better for me to keep working this, but I don't know if that's right for you."

I didn't want to go to Florida alone, but I had to get us out of this mess. I told him, "I'll go and see Say Hey Ray. What are you going to do when I'm gone?"

"I'm going back to where I was shot. I need to find out if being at that location was a factor in the shooting," Jon said. "And I'm going to find Vicki Ament. Vicki convinced me she knew with certainty that Jeff Lemor was innocent, yet she lied about being his alibi. I think I haven't given enough attention to the fact that this is rural Minnesota, and everyone involved in these cases seems to know each other. I also need to talk to my dad about people who might have been angry about his bankruptcy. Alban Brennan made an odd comment to me, that someone may have hurt Brittany over a debt."

I had become mesmerized by the fire, but this surprised me out of my reverie. "Be extra careful, Jon." I paused. "Alban. That's kind of an unusual name," I mused. "Any idea what it means?"

Jon shook his head.

I picked up a mug of hot chocolate, which was now cool enough for me to take a large swallow. It was rich and comforting. The whipped cream gave my lips a sweet coating, and I kissed Jon to share it with him. I put my mug back down and stretched out on the blanket, facing the fireplace.

I could feel his loving eyes on me as he smiled and whispered, "You're beautiful. I'm sorry for not talking to you more. The mistake I made was thinking our relationship is much more fragile than it is. I've always been afraid that if I said something wrong, I'd never be able to repair it."

I turned on my back and looked up at him. "I can handle it. We're better together." I pulled him on top of me and caressed him.

His warm body brushed against mine, and he lightly kissed my cheek, as if admiring a precious gift. I found his tone comforting when assured me, "We're snowed in, just the two of us, in front of a nice, warm fireplace. Thirteen inches of snow tonight has everyone grounded. You can't even see this house from fifty feet away. The two of us are our entire world, tonight. No one else, nothing else, matters . . ."

Chapter Thirty

Jon Frederick
10:00 A.M.
Thursday, April 17
Pierz

When my parents finally returned home with Victor, Serena and my mom disappeared into the living room and had a long talk. They seemed to be in a better place, and ultimately, Serena and Mom packed up some homemade bread and jam and left to go on some "Christian mission." Dad, Victor, and I were left home. Victor had moments where I could converse with him, but was still lost in another dimension most of the time. He finally retreated to his room, instructing us to leave him alone.

I sat down with Dad at the kitchen table and asked him if there was anyone who may have been especially upset about debts he owed. He rested both elbows on the table as he told me, "Years ago, I went to everyone I couldn't pay back and apologized. They weren't happy, but they understood. Half the farmers in Pierz lost their farms. You couldn't get a small-farm loan, unless you took a big chance. The problem with going big is that I was still just one person, with one son who wanted to go to college in Minneapolis, and another son who was a liability." Dad looked out the window, trying to think of a way to soften what he had just said about his mentally ill son. "I don't blame Victor. His battle is worse than ours. I was constantly worried about him getting hurt."

"Still, someone could have been angry."

Bill explained, "They pitied me. I'd rather be hated. Camille said even if we didn't have any money, we were going to volunteer to help others every time the opportunity presented itself, because we still knew how to work. So, that's what we do. And somehow, during this time, Victor became more manageable. It was a much appreciated gift of grace." He hung his head and solemnly added, "One I never deserved."

Dad swore under his breath when he saw Tony pull into the driveway. Dad was wise enough to leave me alone to deal with him.

Tony's salt-and-pepper hair was combed, and he wore a crisp burgundy dress shirt with his jeans and hiking boots.

I raised an eyebrow and teased, "Is Tony in love?"

Tony shot me a warning look. "I'm a bloodhound who's just got a sniff of the suspect, so I've only got a few minutes. Mary Brennan called me and told me Jason took off during the night. He's on the run."

It didn't surprise me that Mary called Tony rather than anyone else on the case. Being married to Al, she probably felt a stronger connection to an investigator who was obnoxious. A person with little self-esteem only trusts someone who recognizes the ineptness in others.

Tony shared, "Jason unintentionally made a comment to me about an awl being in the van."

"So, we need to find Jason."

Tony tapped me on the chest as he replied, "*I* need to find Jason. You're still not back on the case. I have a bad feeling that Jason was sexually abusing his sister, and he tried to kill her to keep her from talking. And Al covered up for him by torching the van. But your BCA friends are still convinced it's Lemor."

I rubbed the back of my neck, frustrated. "Jeff's in a bad spot. I know what it's like to be falsely accused. I wouldn't wish that on anybody."

Tony dryly retorted, "Keep in mind, being persecuted doesn't make him innocent."

"If the absence of innocence alone makes someone guilty, then I guess I'm guilty myself," I said, challenging him.

Tony chuckled. "Yeah, me too. I think this line of work does that to you."

I said, "I think the attack on Serena is somehow related to this. Someone wants me off this case. I'm going to go back to where I was shot. I feel like there was something there I missed."

"Fine," Tony said with a grimace. "But call me when you get there, and call me when you leave."

Chapter Thirty-One

Serena Bell
11:00 a.m.
Thursday, April 17
West side of Little Falls

After throwing myself at her mercy, Camille had accepted my apology. She even reluctantly thanked me for helping bail Victor out of jail. It wasn't in her nature to sit with anger.

I couldn't let go of the fact that, at this very moment, a young mother was wasting away in a meth house and nobody was doing anything about it. I got the feeling that Jon was actually more afraid of the possibility that Vicki wasn't there, because if she had been abducted, no one was looking for her.

I agreed with Jon that the man who assaulted me had raped before. He knew how I'd respond. While I didn't know Vicki, Jon explained that she'd be an easy target, maybe a probable target, as he believed she had information related to the case. So while Jon and Bill sat in the other room discussing the case against Victor, I recruited Camille to pack some of her homemade bread and raspberry jam and join me on what I was calling a "Christian mission."

Once we were out of earshot from the guys, I gave Camille a rundown of the situation and my intention to try to save Vicki, including the fact that the meth house where we hoped to find her was being observed by the DEA. I explained that we would have to use our real names, if asked, since my license plate would likely be noted and our conversations may be recorded. As we climbed into my car, I turned to her and said, "If you don't want to go in, I understand."

Camille buckled her seatbelt immediately, always the law-abiding citizen. She sat primly in the passenger seat in a red wool coat, with a black-and-white plaid scarf wound snugly around her neck. Her hands were clasped tightly together in her lap. As I pulled out of the driveway, Camille asked, "Shouldn't we tell Jon what we're doing?"

I gave her a half-smile. "Not just yet. Jon's been told to stay away from that house, but we both know he's not going to. He's got too big of a heart to leave Vicki wasting away in there. And if he interferes with this DEA investigation, they'll never let Jon work as an investigator again." I reached over and squeezed her arm. "So, we're going to save him from himself, and beat him there."

"How do you know where the house is?" Camille was still trying to wrap her mind around what we were doing.

"I heard Jon and Tony talking about it. Jon told him he wanted the address so he could be sure to avoid the house in question. As soon as he said that, I knew Jon planned to go there. I need to act now, while he's still contemplating how to proceed."

Camille sighed with uncertainty, and I attempted to reassure her. "We're simply going to stop at a couple houses on the block with our gifts, so it's not obvious we targeted that house. When we finally get there, we'll offer them free homemade bread and jam if they're willing to listen to a Bible verse. The mouth-watering smell of this bread will get us in the door. I'm sorry for giving away your bread like this, but it could save Vicki's life."

Camille chuckled softly, shaking her head. "I'm not worried about the bread. You sure you should do this after what you've been through?" I had told her, tearfully, about my attack, and she had been an amazing and comforting support to me in the absence of my own mother.

"Yes." I was much less confident than I let on. The truth was that, since the assault, I was more afraid than ever, so it was hard for me to accurately judge risks. Vicki was once a girl like Mandy and I needed to help her—for my sake as well as hers.

Camille carefully looked me up and down, taking time to study my black blouse with its fine gold design. "That's a nice top," she said, but not with the warmth that typically comes with a compliment.

Feeling unnerved by her tone, I asked, "Why do you say it like that, Camille?"

"Oh, don't get me wrong, you look lovely," she said as she patted my arm. "I'm just thinking if a man answers the door, you should do all the talking while I look for Vicki. I guarantee he won't even notice me."

The first two stops were uneventful. As we approached the drug house, I made a quick call to Jon to let him in on the truth of our mission. Despite his protests, we began our rescue.

Camille and I stood on the steps of a rambler covered by faded blue vinyl siding. The siding was cracked in several spots and appeared to be melted in an area where I imagined a grill had once been. The windows were covered from the inside with ratty-looking quilts. We rang the doorbell, knocked, and waited. It took three tries before an unshaven, shirtless man in his early twenties finally answered the door.

The young man had dark, greasy hair matted to one side of his head, and jutting out in all sorts of disarray on the other. He had a tattoo of a slutty nymph on his chest and wore a pair of stained gray sweatpants that had seen better days. His stare was vacant, and he looked as if he was struggling to stay upright. My dad would say he looked "rode hard and put away wet." The boy was a trainwreck. I was disappointed when his initial reaction was to send us away, but before we moved, he was overtaken by the smell of Camille's bread, so he told us to wait on the porch while he cleared a couple chairs. He finally invited us in after ten chilly minutes.

Once inside, I grabbed the chair at the kitchen table facing the bedrooms, so when the young man sat, he wouldn't be facing that direction. The space was filthy, dark, and dingy. I put my elbow on the table before I noticed the layer of grime on it, then quickly peeled my jacket free of the sticky tabletop, suppressing a shudder. Camille and I introduced ourselves, and he followed suit, telling us his name was Chris. Camille made do with a knife she found on the table, and after wiping it with a tissue she pulled out of her purse, she began to slice some bread. Her pursed lips were the only indication of her distress over the living conditions. Chris asked if I was married, and when I told him I wasn't, he proceeded to share that he had always thought Christians were "epic."

Camille handed Chris a slice of bread slathered with jam, then asked if she could use the bathroom to wash the stickiness off of her hands.

Chris said through a mouthful of bread, "Let me make me sure it's presentable first." We all knew this meant he wanted to make sure there were no drugs or paraphernalia lying around. He quickly stood, swayed, then snatched another piece of bread as he ducked into the bathroom.

Camille and I exchanged uneasy glances. She flashed me the card I'd written for her to place in Vicki's hand, if she didn't get a chance to talk to her. It read, "Your daughter, Hannah, has had an accident. You need to come with me. I will leave and wait for you in a black Ford Fusion, just down the block."

Chris returned and told Camille the bathroom was clear for her use. I thought I saw her cross herself before entering. Chris went into a long diatribe of how he was planning to eventually be a music producer, who recruited "only legit acts." I nodded and smiled, while I watched Camille quietly exit the bathroom and sneak into a bedroom. I was concerned about Camille's ability to get through to Vicki. It wasn't long before she stepped out and returned to us at the table. She met my eyes and gave an almost imperceptible jerk of her head toward the bedroom. I could tell by her expression that she questioned the success of her efforts.

Suddenly, a thin, red-headed woman, who met Jon's description of Vicki, rushed in a t-shirt and underwear to the bathroom, from where we heard her vomiting violently. I immediately offered to check on her.

When I got to Vicki, she was still hunched over the toilet, spitting into it and shivering. She looked up at me with trails of black eye make-up etched on her cheeks. Purple bruises were visible on the back of her neck and her lower back. I remembered what Jon had told me of the forensic pathologist's report on Mandy: severe blunt force trauma, resulting in a broken C4 vertebrae. Vicki had a bruise on the same area of her neck; I also had the same bruise. I found myself speechless and gasping for air as I relived being struck hard and high between the shoulder blades during the assault. That punch knocked the life out of me for a moment.

When it seemed Vicki had depleted her stomach contents, she slowly sat back against the grimy bathroom wall. She looked close to death with her smudged make-up and pale skin. She wiped her mouth with the back of her arm and tonelessly asked, "Did he get Hannah?"

I could see from the fear in her eyes we shared life-threatening trauma. I took some toilet paper off the roll, then bent over Vicki and dabbed the sweat from her forehead. "No, he didn't get Hannah, but he got me."

"You?" Vicki looked me up and down skeptically, as if thinking I didn't seem the type.

I slowly pushed out the words, searching her watery eyes. "Who are you talking about?"

Vicki's eyes narrowed. "Shouldn't you know?" She grabbed a handful of toilet paper and weakly blew her nose.

I turned and lifted up the back of my blouse to show her the bruising that was still on my back. Then I turned back and told her, "It was dark, so I couldn't see him."

Obviously lying, Vicki said, "Same thing with me." Confused, she asked, "What happened to Hannah?"

"There's been an accident on the farm." I crouched down and gently held her shoulders until she met my eyes. "You need to come with me to the hospital. I'll leave and wait for you just down the block. Can you dress yourself?"

It was sad to see that Vicki wasn't sure if I was someone she could trust. Seeing my bruises hadn't comforted her. Instead, she appeared to be considering if I was sent here by a psychopath. She sniffed, "Who are you?"

Knowing we might have had eavesdroppers, I didn't want to say Jon's name. I thought I'd take advantage of the fact that everybody from Pierz knew Camille, due to her involvement in every charitable event. "Camille Frederick asked me to help deliver this message to you. She's here with me in the other room," I ticked my head in the direction of the living room. "Your grandparents called her." Using my gentlest tone, I asked, "Will they let you leave?"

She nodded and I helped her up. Vicki warned me, "I'm going to call my grandparents first, before I leave with you."

I told her, "Okay, good. I'll be waiting for you outside." I signaled Camille when I left the bathroom and she gathered her things, anxious to leave. We quickly said our goodbyes and left Chris with the bread and jam, which he continued to eat absently as he watched us depart.

WHEN CAMILLE AND I WERE safely in the car, I explained to her what had transpired.

Camille said, worried, "Vicki was lying in bed with some guy who was passed out. What if they would have assaulted you?"

Trying to sound tough, I said, "I'm packin'." I reached in my coat pocket and slid out a handgun—my dad's—then slid it back. Camille's concern was obvious, so I added, "Ever since the assault. I don't carry all the time." As a matter of fact, I would be leaving it home when I flew to Jacksonville tomorrow. I knew I'd never get it through security at the airport.

We grew quiet, staring intently at the door of the meth house, willing Vicki to appear. We both sagged in relief when she finally staggered out.

Camille humorously conceded, "You are epic."

I had planned to bring Vicki to the hospital and have her placed in detox. Following my instructions, Jon had called her grandparents as soon as my phone call with him ended, and told them to insist that Vicki go to the hospital. Wanting to get her help, they were eager to go along with the deception.

As we made our way into the hospital, I told Vicki the truth about our visit. She furiously leaned toward me, ready to strike, but Camille quickly intervened. Camille reminded her that even though Hannah was physically okay, her daughter was still hurting. Nothing could be harder on a little girl than being abandoned by her only active parent. Vicki immediately called her grandparents again, and her tone softened as the conversation progressed. When we arrived at the hospital, she reluctantly thanked me and made her way toward the entrance. She glanced back for a moment before entering the building. I saw a mixture of terror and resolve in her eyes. She knew what she was about to go through. She straightened her shoulders and pushed through the doors of the clinic, prepared to begin her battle.

When the door closed behind her, I groaned in relief, looked up and said, "Thank you, God."

Camille was still a bit shaky, but smiled, "Listen now. Just because I forgave you for wearing the wire, young lady, it doesn't mean I want to go all Thelma and Louise with you. My goodness, I feel like I've been holding my breath since we left Pierz!"

I gave her a brief hug and said, "I'm sorry, but I needed your help—and baking—to pull it off."

Camille was feeling good, too, and piously proud of her baking, said, "No apology is necessary."

It felt good to act like a Christian, instead of a victim.

Chapter Thirty-Two

Serena Bell
Friday, April 18
Sanderson, Florida

I had returned to St. Paul and spent last night with my parents, as they needed to be certain I was okay. I was, sort of. I discovered that when my anxiety spiked, focusing on deep, calming breathing helped to bring my heart rate down to something manageable. I was focusing on just that as my rental car approached the Baker Correctional Institution in Sanderson, Florida. I was about to have my first visit with Say Hey Ray. I was still a bit jittery from luring Vicki out of the meth house the day before.

It was warm and sunny when I arrived in Florida. Any other time, I'd be greedily basking in the Florida heat after another long Minnesota winter, but I was too preoccupied to appreciate it. I didn't know that I'd ever felt more alone—there was no one there to greet me or support me. It had to be easier for Jon, because he obsessed on the task. I, on the other hand, obsessed on the potential dangers. In an effort to turn negative thoughts to positive, I indulged myself and obsessed on Jon for just a moment. Two nights ago, lying in front of the fire, tiny beads of sweat forming on our skin . . . that was heaven. I wished we were there right now.

Baker Correctional Institution was generally referred to as the Florida State Prison. It was initially a juvenile facility, which was modified to take medium-security adult offenders. The visitor's area was made up of white, painted cement blocks, with bullet-proof glass between the inmate and visitor and a landline phone mounted on the wall by which to converse. I was thankful for the solid walls, once I saw the outline of Ray's prison-orange clad form filling the doorway. He was six-foot-four, with a shaved head and Fu Manchu moustache. His neck was lost in his bulk, so his head seemed to sit directly on top of straight, muscular shoulders. I was reassured he indeed had a neck when he turned to ask the guard something before he sat down. The word "NOTORIOUS" was tattooed in cheap blue ink on the back of it.

I was wearing a conservative navy-blue blouse and dress jeans, but soon found myself wishing I was in traditional Muslim dress. *What am I doing here?* I asked myself. My skin crawled as he looked me over like a vulture that had just discovered a fresh carcass. It was horrifying to think that at least two women with teenaged daughters had invited this man into their homes—and both had paid a terrible price for that concession. This man oozed malevolence through his pores like yesterday's booze. He picked up the phone and with a booming, bass timbre, simply said, "Hey."

I didn't bother with pleasantries. I jumped right in and nervously stated that I was looking into Mandy Baker's murder, and was trying to understand what had happened to her. I told him I knew he hadn't killed her, but I wanted to know if he had any information that could guide me in the right direction. If I could put up with the unease of sitting across from him, I could likely get some useful information, simply because he desired conversation with a woman. He pressed his hand on the glass in some gesture of friendship, but I couldn't get myself to respond in kind. He scared the hell out of me, and was too much like the rapist who attacked me. I would sooner have put my hand up to a rabid dog. Say Hey Ray carefully studied me, and then referred to me as Investigator Bell. When I told him I wasn't an investigator, he dismissed my truth as insignificant.

Deciding to take advantage of this, I suggested, "The parole board would look favorably on your assisting with this."

Ray grumbled, "I know who killed her. I didn't know when I was first locked up, but I've had a lot of time to think with a clear head. I want a guaranteed release before I give you anything."

Going on the little I knew from TV shows and conversations with Jon, I told him, "That's not how it works. You have to share, and if it's useful, they'll make a deal."

Ray laughed maliciously as he held the phone away from his ear for a moment. "Hey, I've been doing this a lot longer than you have, sister. You look too good to have done this work long. Tell your boss I have information, and see what he offers."

I nervously sputtered, "You have to give me an idea of what you have, or he's not going to offer anything. Remember, we still have to find a way to prosecute Mandy's killer."

Ray stared hard at me, then switched gears. "Ask me a question about Mandy, so I know you're for real."

I bought a little time by saying, "Why else would I visit a prison in Florida? Baker Correctional Facility isn't exactly a great vacation spot. Fine." I racked my brain for a moment. "Who would Mandy call if she needed a ride, and you and Carrie weren't available?"

He rocked back in surprise. I had made a direct hit. I was excited for just a minute, thinking I might be able to go home tonight, until I realized I still had nothing if I didn't have a name.

Ray hesitated and said, "Hey, you're for real. Tell your boss I can give you the answer to that question—and that is the all-important question, isn't it?"

I pried further. "It wasn't Clay Roberts."

Confused, he scowled and asked, "Who the hell is Clay Roberts?"

Trying to recover, I suggested, "I'm just saying it wasn't Clay Roberts. Clay was a friend of Jon Frederick at the time."

Ray laughed, showing a sorely neglected set of teeth. "Jon-boy was in way over his head. Kind of like an altar boy dating a hooker. Mandy just was who she was. And she was like that before I ever met her. She can thank her dear, departed dad for that. Dumb bastard blew his brains out." A ravenous smile slithered across his face as he added, "I miss Mandy. Jon-boy tried to change her, but if you put a prom dress on a pig, she's still a pig."

He made my stomach roil. Out of respect for Mandy, I said, "Mandy Baker was a beautiful young girl."

His disgusting smile remained as his lecherous eyes met mine. "She was."

At that moment, it was clear he'd abused her. He would never be prosecuted for it, and to make things worse, he was trying to work me over for a reduced sentence. I wanted to leave him rotting in prison, but he was better at this game than I was. He'd been using others his whole adult life. My best bet was to be honest and let him assume whatever he wished. After all, honesty had seemed to be my best form of deception so far.

A guard entered indicating they were going to do a count, which meant that if I didn't leave right now, I could be stuck here for hours. I gave Ray a curt nod, and was grateful to get out of there. Most people are more likeable as you get to know them better. It wasn't so with Ray Benson. As I was leaving, Ray requested that I return. I could die happily never setting foot in that place again.

Chapter Thirty-Three

Jon Frederick
Friday, April 18
Field south of the Brennan Farm

Yesterday's snow had crystalized into hoarfrost that sparkled in the sunlight. Even though I stood alone over the shimmering field of snow, I took my gun off of safety. My obsessive brain was telling me I had to walk down to precisely where I was shot before I could leave. I couldn't help thinking that a less obsessive man wouldn't have to walk around with wet feet all day. An insight had occurred to me at that spot, and I'd lost it during the subsequent trauma. Trying to trigger that memory, I traipsed down the snow-covered ditch and across the tundra until I found the site where my car had been parked on the day of the shooting. I felt a pang of anxiety as I remembered the four successive shots. I took in a deep, cool breath. It was just blue sky and me, looking at a blanket of hoar crystals. The bright sun made it almost feel like spring. There was no evidence that a homicide had been attempted just a mile away.

I enjoyed spring—it was the beginning of new life, and I remembered the excitement farm animals would exhibit to get out of the barn after a long winter. I inhaled deeply again, enjoying the earthy scents carried by the fresh air. The composition of the soil would give me an idea of how successful Al's corn crop would be. I bent down and dug through the snow, grabbing a handful of dirt. I rubbed some of it through my hands as I closed my eyes and accepted the kindness of the warm sun. Morrison County wasn't a particularly good part of the state to farm, due to the variations in the soil. Black, muddy dirt was found in some areas, and sandy, dry soil in others. Rocks were all over. I had an odd sensation, then a sudden revelation as the dirt fell through my fingers. I gazed at my hand, where there was no muddy residue. The soil was incredibly sandy, and significantly different in texture than the dirt in the ditches where Brittany's body was found. I simply wiped away the sand and my hands looked clean again. As I walked back to my car and brushed the snow off my pants, I knew who had attempted to kill me and Brittany. The snow was melting, but there was no mud on the cuffs of my pants—only snow and sand.

Tony buzzed on my cell phone and I quickly answered it. He was talking fast. "Jason has offered to come in, if we let him talk to a priest. We also got the lab results from the leather jacket we found at the crime scene. Believe it or not, we got a hit from CODIS."

I was surprised. CODIS, the Combined DNA Index System, connects crime laboratories throughout the United States. This meant that whoever was wearing that jacket had been incarcerated. My immediate thought went to Jeff Lemor, but I had to ask, "Who?"

"It belongs to a man we know wasn't there." He seemed to enjoy leaving me hanging.

Impatient, I prodded, "Are you going to tell me?"

"Good old Say Hey Ray Benson."

I didn't know what to say. How the hell did Ray's coat get to Brittany's crime scene? We knew with certainty that Ray was in prison at the time.

Tony continued. "By the way, my friend from the DEA called and told me Serena Bell showed up at a meth house with your mother."

"Believe me, I'd never send Serena into a meth house."

Tony added, "And yet, there she was . . ." He left the statement hanging, and I thought as fast as I could.

"Vicki's from Pierz. She could have called my mom for help, and Serena was with my mom," I suggested.

Tony continued, "And that's what I told the DEA. Look, I'm not opposed to getting Vicki out of there. But what's the point? She'll be back there next week. Consider yourself lucky that it didn't impact the DEA's investigation."

Wanting to get to my news, I blurted out, "I know who shot me."

Tony was quiet, so I continued. "Al Brennan. Al returned home with muddy pants after Brittany disappeared. Remember, he claimed he had been checking out the south field? The soil in the south field is sandy. The area where Brittany's body was found had heavy clay. If Al saw me at that field, he had to figure that, as a farm kid, I'd discover the error in his alibi. There's no way his clothes would have been muddy if he'd been in the south field like he claimed."

Tony mused, "No wonder Jason ran away from home. I thought he was acting suspicious, but he must have been nervous as hell. If Al tried to kill Brittany, why would Jason be safe?" After a moment of silent reflection, Tony asked, "Was Mandy wearing Ray's jacket when Serena picked her up?"

I nodded into the phone as I said, "Yes."

Tony said, "Whoever had the jacket thought it would implicate Ray. They didn't know Ray was in prison."

I was way ahead of Tony on this, and I wanted to guide him carefully to my conclusion. He would defend it more adamantly if it was his idea. I challenged him, asking, "Why did you ask me if the jacket was mine?"

"Because Mandy was telling everyone she got the jacket from you." Tony was quiet, lost in thought for a moment, and I wasn't about to interrupt. "This was about setting you up."

I patiently waited for the conclusion that followed. *Come on, Tony—find it.*

I could almost hear the wheels in Tony's head turning. Finally, with an intake of breath, it came to him. "If Mandy's killer thought the jacket would set you up, it couldn't have been anyone in your family, or Serena, because they would've known the jacket wasn't yours."

"Exactly."

Chapter Thirty-Four

Jon Frederick
Saturday, April 19
Pierz

Saturday morning, I received a call from Vicki. She was ready to leave detox. When I picked her up, Vicki was dressed in an over-washed black sweatshirt and jeans, looking like she'd been through the wringer—which she probably had, in a sense. Her red hair was pulled back into a stubby ponytail. She was gaunt, and thinner than the last time I'd seen her. Her face was scrubbed clean of make-up.

As we drove away, I eyed her. "How are you holding up?"

Vicki sighed and responded, "That was rough, I'm not gonna lie. I'm so pissed at myself for starting that up again, I deserved the hell of detox. When can I see Hannah? Picturing her sweet face was what got me through the worst of it back there. God, I'm starving! Can we grab some food somewhere?"

Knowing that extreme hunger was a symptom of meth withdrawal, I'd grabbed a burger and fries from the Black and White Café on my way to pick Vicki up. I reached into the backseat to grab it, and plopped it on her lap. She gave a groan of gratitude, then dove greedily into the bag. I drove down County Road 45 toward the Brennan farm.

Vicki started to fidget and asked through a mouthful of fries, "Where we going?"

Ignoring the question, I asked her, "Why did you stop visiting Jeff?"

"I gave up. I had no hope to offer him." She crumpled up the paper from the fries and pulled out her burger.

We drove in silence for a bit while she finished eating. After turning onto the dirt road where we found Brittany, I asked, "Who assaulted you, Vicki?"

Suddenly agitated, Vicki glanced over her shoulder out the rear window, as if to make certain we weren't being followed. "I can't talk to you. Talking to you didn't help Jeff, and now it's bad for me." She was becoming more fearful with each passing breath.

I tried to make her understand. "You have nothing to lose, Vicki. He's not going to stop coming after you until he's locked up. The perfect victim is the one who never goes to the police."

Vicki sat in silence for a moment, folding and refolding the wrapper from her hamburger. She gazed out at the snow-crusted fields as she spoke. "Of course I have something to lose—I have Hannah to think about. He's sent me a message not to talk, and believe me, I got it."

Having reached the culvert, I stopped in the middle of the dirt road and shut the car off.

Vicki couldn't stand the silence. She frantically revealed, "After the last rape, something just broke in me. I had to feel something, and I knew a sure-fire way to do that." She turned to me, eyes brimming with tears. "Next time you're praying, thank God you don't understand the pull of that shit. It never really goes away. It just lies in wait, knowing the time will come when its attraction becomes bigger than anything else. I regret it. I hate myself for what I did to me, and to my daughter. I have to start over with my sobriety now, but I accept that." Her energy was visibly draining.

"He's going to find you again," I said gently. "And after he kills you, maybe Hannah will be next." I went around to the passenger's side to open the door for her. She was hesitant, so I took her hand

and gently coaxed her out of the car. Vicki was going to be cold in her sweatshirt, even though the sun was out, as it was only about forty-five degrees.

Vicki stood facing me in the middle of the road, her hands pulled into her sleeves and her arms wrapped tightly around her torso. She was already shivering; whether this was due to residual withdrawal symptoms or the cold, I couldn't be sure. She asked, "What are you going to do with me?"

"I need you to tell me what you know." I started thinking about the attempted murders of Brittany, me, and Serena. "What's happening here goes far beyond intimidation."

With tears in her eyes, she nodded toward the culvert. "Is this where they found Brittany Brennan?"

"Yes, it is."

"I can feel the evil here." There seemed to be a sudden change in Vicki. She swallowed hard. "God, I'm so stupid! You're right—the perfect victim." She dropped her arms to her sides. "You're just like every other guy. Okay, you know what? Just do whatever you want. I don't care anymore."

I had brought her here to get her to understand that the same man who assaulted her had attempted to kill before. Instead, she assumed I brought her here to abuse her. Sadly, I understood why. When you experience it so often, you can come to believe it's simply what men do.

Vicki begged, "Just please, don't kill me. Hannah needs me. I'm going to do better this time." At that moment, the shadow of a cross slowly drifted over Vicki's body.

I instinctively drew my gun and turned to see a large sand crane gliding overhead. Vicki dropped to her knees and started to cry. I quickly holstered my gun, then lifted her chin so she would look at me. "Who hurt you, Vicki?"

She wrenched her chin out of my grasp and stared at the ground. "I'm so stupid. I trusted you. But that's what addicts do—we put our faith in the wrong people."

Vicki was shaking, but I still needed her to give up her attacker's name. If I said it first, I could be accused of leading the witness. I looked down and spoke to the young woman falling apart in front of me as I considered my next step. "I believed you when you told me Jeff was innocent. When I heard you lied about being his alibi, I thought I was taken for a fool. But now I think you knew Jeff was innocent, because you knew who did it. I think you're the one person who has always known who hurt that little girl. I need to know your story."

Awash with guilt at my methods, I was about to help Vicki up when she finally started talking. She confessed through her tears, "When I was sixteen, I was at a party at the Genola gravel pits. There was something in the pot I was smoking, and I ended up passing out, facedown across the seat in my boyfriend's truck. A couple hours later, someone was yanking my jeans off. I thought it was my boyfriend at first, so I kind of tried to shoo him off. But then I realized it was somebody else. He put his hand over my mouth and asked me if I liked it rough." She shuddered. "Do I really have to go over the rest?"

I squatted down next to her and rested my hand on her shoulder, gently prodding, "I don't need the details of the assault. I need to know who did it."

Vicki swallowed hard and said, "He told me if I ever told anyone, he'd kill me. It was brutal, and there were other times when I was using that he caught me alone. At my grandparents' farm, about a week ago, I had to go through it sober for the first time. He threatened my family, and he will kill me if he thinks I told." Her voice was barely audible. "He said he's killed before. When his daughter was found, I knew what had happened. Brittany must have threatened to tell on him."

I gently helped her up. "He is killing you, Vicki. If Serena hadn't pulled you out of that meth house, you could be dead right now. He's pushed you back into using. He got you to abandon your daughter."

"It's hard to be sober when every day, I wonder, is it going to happen again today? And what's with the forced anal sex? It felt like I was being ripped to shreds from the inside. This last time, he pushed my face so hard into the mud, I couldn't breathe. I used to not care if he killed me. My life wasn't that important, until I was sober. But after last time, my thoughts went right back to that dark place, anyway."

"This ends right now, Vicki. Give me the name, so I can stop him."

Emotionally exhausted, Vicki spoke the name. "Al Brennan."

"You've already survived the worst, so I know you're resilient," I told her. "You're a lot more insightful than you give yourself credit for." I'd never been much for hugging others, but this moment begged for it, so I reached out to her. She was stiff at first, but gradually began to surrender to the embrace. I told her, "Al's a sadistic pig. I think he killed Mandy Baker doing the same thing he did to you. Help me get him out of our community." I felt sadly incompetent for not finding another way to get her to divulge this information. "I'm sorry for taking you here. You didn't deserve this."

Vicki was trembling. She searched my face. "What are you going to do?"

"I'm going to take you home," I said, keeping one arm around her and leading her toward the car. "And you're going to get Hannah, and drive to the women's shelter." I kept talking. "Have you ever toured the Soudan mine in northern Minnesota?

Confused, Vicki shook her head. "No."

"They take you down a half mile below the earth's surface, and for a moment, they turn off the lights. It's a darkness beyond imagination. I know a woman who works for Hands of Hope, who I swear could even find a ray of light there. She talked to Serena after she was assaulted. I'll ask her to talk to you tonight at the shelter. I'll call the police to make sure they keep an eye on the place, and I will do everything I can to get Al Brennan behind bars tonight. Can you promise me you'll go there?"

Vicki nodded. "Yeah, okay. I don't really have a choice now, do I? Now that I've talked."

"No, you don't." I wanted to tell her she never really had a choice, ever since Al first selected her. Like Mandy and Brittany, he would continue to use her until he left her for dead. "I'll call your grandparents and let them know you're coming for Hannah, then I'll let the shelter know you're on your way there. The support will do you some good while you struggle through the rest of your withdrawal symptoms, too." She was leaning heavily against me, growing so weary she could barely nod in agreement. She looked up at me, her eyes reflecting the gratitude she was unable to voice.

Vicki was asleep before I'd even turned the car around.

Chapter Thirty-Five

Serena Bell
Saturday, April 19
Sanderson, Florida

My greatest discovery occurred after I returned to the Travelodge Suites in MacClenney, Florida, last night. It was all the luxury sixty dollars a night would buy. I managed to get a room on the second floor, which I had convinced myself was safer, since it was a floor above the dimly lit parking lot. Spending the night alone in a hotel ten miles away from the Baker prison was disconcerting. It didn't help that the hotel was located thirty-eight miles straight east of Jacksonville, along Interstate Highway 10. I considered whether I was more likely to be murdered by an escaped prisoner or a freeway-traveling serial killer. I attempted to distract myself by surfing the Internet.

After looking up a variety of trivial information, I found myself wondering again about the name "Alban," so I typed it in the search engine to see what came up. When the definition popped up, my jaw dropped. Whoever named Alban Brennan either didn't anticipate he'd have dark hair, or they didn't consider the meaning of the name. Alban was an old German name. Morrison County was full of old German communities, albeit more old-German ten years ago than today. What would old Germans nickname a guy whose name means "white"? My heart rate ratcheted up a notch and I immediately called Jon.

Jon was excited with my discovery, and told me he had additional news regarding the investigation to share with me when I returned. I didn't know why he couldn't just tell me. My sense was he was handling me with kid gloves. It would have irritated me if I wasn't 1,500 miles away from anyone I knew. With this in mind, I decided to trust his judgment. Jon told me my rescue of Vicki worked perfectly, and didn't interfere with the pending investigation. Vicki was now headed to the women's shelter with her daughter. That felt good.

To put me at ease, Jon kindly accepted my calls throughout the night. I never did fall into a sound sleep; I simply decided to stop calling Jon, so he could get some sleep. I did have that horrible nightmare again, where I was just lying there on the couch in my parents' old home, looking at "skull face," with his puppet chin and shaggy hair. Who was he? This time the dream morphed into his pinning down and assaulting me. It was awful, and the nightmare ended with me engulfed in flames in that house.

I was afraid Jon was going to ask me to stay longer, since I hadn't learned anything significant from Ray Benson. Mercifully, he didn't. Jon knew how afraid I was right now. No matter how late he worked, I was going to wait for him at his parents' house tonight. Camille and I would share a toast to our successful rescue mission.

I had to come up with something during my last interview with Say Hey Ray today. Jon had a lot of faith in me, and I didn't like letting people down.

Say Hey Ray was back, looming across the glass from me. His nostrils flared angrily as he looked me over, and with his thick, shaved head and pasty skin, he reminded me of an albino bull. Ray started the conversation by expressing his disappointment that my shirt was buttoned all the way up to my neck, and lewdly suggested there were ways to get him to give up information. This solidified my belief that he should stay exactly where he was, for as long as possible. Ray didn't care if I felt degraded, as long as he got what he wanted. He would likely find my humiliation arousing. Begging him for information was just going to result in his wanting to see me beg more, so I decided to try another tactic. As casually as I could, I told the caged bull, "We've got some new information, so I'm not sure we can use what you have to offer."

His eyes narrowed skeptically. "Hey, you still need something, or you wouldn't be back." He crossed meaty arms over his chest and sat back with a greasy smirk.

Buoyed by the thought of going home after this visit, I confidently told him in my best sing-song voice, "I told you, that's not how this works. My flight leaves tonight, so I thought I'd give you one more chance to help yourself. If you choose not to, so be it. The case will go forward, with or without you."

"You must have had a bad night," he said, sliding lazy eyes over me. "Do you want to talk about it?"

I didn't answer, just kept my gaze leveled on him. Responding either "no" or "yes" would lead to an extended conversation I didn't want to have.

He stroked his Fu Manchu between his thumb and his forefinger, thinking. "So, what do I get if I give him up?"

"I'm still not convinced you know anything," I said confidently, waving the figurative red cape in front of him. I had never received so much satisfaction out of changing the power dynamic in a conversation. I hoped to provoke him enough to charge.

Ray sat stock still, contemplating his next move. He finally nodded, and said, "Okay, what I tell you isn't any good, unless I agree to testify anyway. She called Whitey. Mandy called Whitey anytime she needed a ride. He was married, and even had a couple kids, but he was chasing Mandy. That's the son of a bitch who should be sitting where I am."

I needed to know with certainty that he was talking about Alban Brennan. "Was this the Whitey who was killed in the car accident?"

"No," he snorted. "That's Off-Whitey. That Whitey offed himself driving wasted. So he went from 'Whitey' to 'Off-Whitey.' I had a guy working for cash for me, trimming trees, that the old folks called Whitey. Obvious replacement, right? We didn't even have to learn a new name. Strong farm boy, with big, bushy dark hair, like he thought he was one of the Black Crows. Carrie never liked him, because he was always mackin' on Mandy, but the man could work." Ray continued. "After Carrie started finding Victoria's Secret underwear in the laundry, she confronted Mandy, and whatever had been going on stopped. But hey, I think Mandy got stuck somewhere that night, and since we weren't around, she called Whitey."

Ray was so out of touch with what I was feeling, he had the gall to ask, "Hey, what do I get for it? Besides a break on my sentence, I oughtta see some serious skin." His eyes crawled over me, and I felt pins and needles prickle across my skin in response.

I thought for a moment. "I'm a modest woman," I whispered conspiratorially, "but I could send you a picture."

Ray mulled my proposal over. He wanted immediate gratification, but a seductive picture of a law enforcement employee was of high value in prison, and he still believed I was an investigator. Jon told me that, believe it or not, the prisoners managed to get naked photos from some of the prison staff they professed love to, and some from jilted boyfriends of employees. They shared them for status, or sold them like playing cards. If Ray could get a picture of a female investigator, it would be a big notch in his belt.

Ray leered at me. "Hey, you know what kind of picture I'm talking about, right?"

Against all of my instincts, I winked. "I know exactly what you're talking about."

Ray nodded. "All right. But this better be serious." He realized this was the best he was going to do and, anticipating something sleazy, was placated enough to continue. "Whitey's the one whose daughter just got jacked. That Brennan guy. Mandy's leaving didn't bother me at the time, because she was being a pain in the ass. Stopped listening. Just did what she wanted. But it broke her mother's heart. Carrie slept in Mandy's bed every night after Mandy disappeared. Years later, I realized Whitey got away with murder." Ray leaned back in his chair, adding, "I loved Carrie as much as I'm capable of loving anyone."

My first thought was that it wasn't a hell of a lot, but I remained silently attentive.

Ray went on, "Hey, I still have friends in Minnesota, so I know what's going on back there."

I had just knocked it out of the park. Ray verified that Al Brennan was Whitey. I took another shot. "Mandy was wearing your leather jacket the night she was murdered, and that jacket was found at a crime scene a couple weeks ago. What was your jacket doing at a crime scene in Minnesota?"

Ray tilted his head in confusion. "What jacket?" he asked. After a minute, it came to him. He smirked. "I got a brown leather jacket as a make-up gift from Carrie, so I was stuck with it. It looked like something some dude in a boy band would wear. Mandy decided if I wasn't going to wear it, she would. I haven't seen that jacket for a decade."

I realized it hadn't been listed among Mandy's missing items because it wasn't her jacket.

Ray was baffled. He finally suggested, "Mandy told everyone that Jon gave it to her, and that was fine with me. Maybe Jon decided to keep it."

I thought out loud. "I don't think Jon took your jacket. It was found on the scene before he arrived. Buttons from that jacket were found in Mandy's bedroom the night she disappeared. Investigators initially hypothesized that the killer had struggled with Mandy in her bedroom the night she disappeared, and in the process, a couple of buttons were torn off." I didn't bother to share that this was before the investigators knew I had picked Mandy up and brought her to Pierz.

Ray breathed wetly through ever-expanding nostrils as a realization came to him. "Hey, that son of a bitch tried to set me up."

"What do you mean?"

"Whitey must have known that jacket was mine. He left buttons off my coat in her room, after he killed her, to make people think it was me. Mandy must have told him no one was home—after all, that's why she had to call him."

"But why wouldn't he leave the whole jacket?"

The answer was clear to Ray, and he laughed at my ignorance. "That's too obvious. Hey, if I was going to set somebody up, I wouldn't leave his winter jacket. Nobody in Minnesota is leaving without his jacket in the middle of winter. You'd realize you didn't have it as soon as you stepped outside. But you might not think about picking up lost buttons."

So, Al Brennan had gone to Mandy's house that night. I was suddenly struck with a terrifying thought. I had honestly never considered that the killer had been in my house, too. It explained why he was comfortable returning to assault me. I asked, "Ray, what does Al look like? I'm not familiar with the Black Crows."

Ray thought for a moment and scowled. "Take a skull and stretch some skin across it like saran wrap, then throw a black mop on top for hair."

Without saying another word, I got up and walked out. My stomach was flipping over like rocks in a tumbler. I had always known who killed Mandy Baker. The weight of that knowledge made the walk to my car seem endless.

I CALLED JON IMMEDIATELY and breathlessly shared what I had. I told him I needed a picture of Al Brennan. He said he'd get one from Tony and send it to my phone. While I was packing at the hotel, the picture arrived. Nightmare after nightmare of lying in bed swirled through my mind, looking up at the face of a man whose skin was pulled tightly over his skull, marionette lines down his chin. It was a caricature of Alban Brennan. My brain had been trying to tell me the answer this whole time. Al must have picked Mandy up that night ten years ago, and stood over me for a moment when I was lying on the couch. In my alcohol-induced haze, I'd seen him. I was a loose end in the Mandy Baker case, a witness who could identify him.

My memory of Al from ten years earlier probably wouldn't be enough to prosecute him for Mandy's murder. Even though we couldn't do a lot with what we had, this was a breakthrough. The focus of the investigation would now be on Alban, and we had just earned Victor his freedom.

Chapter Thirty-Six

Jon Frederick
Saturday, April 19
Little Falls

After leaving Vicki at her grandparents' home, I called Maurice Strock and told him I had new information I wanted to share with the investigators. Maurice told me to be at the makeshift BCA headquarters in an hour.

I laid out the information I had. Al Brennan had worked for Say Hey Ray Benson. Ray said Mandy Baker would have called Al, whom he referred to as "Whitey," if she was stranded. Mandy had told me, when we were dating, that she flirted with the guys who had a weekly card game at her home, and she referred to one of the guys as "Whitey." Al would have been twenty-six years old, while Mandy was sixteen. On the night Mandy disappeared, Serena fell asleep before Mandy left, so she couldn't clearly identify who picked Mandy up. But Al must have hovered over her before leaving with Mandy, because Serena had nightmares of a face resembling Al Brennan since. Serena was assaulted at the same home where Al had picked up Mandy. Serena's attacker told her he liked it rough. Vicki Ament shared that Al sodomized her and stated that he liked it rough during the assault. Al also told Vicki that he had killed before.

The room fell quiet. Then Maurice, sitting back in his mousy gray suit, pointed out that much of what I had was conjecture, and couldn't be used in court. Tony came to my rescue by asserting that convictions are still obtained solely on circumstantial evidence.

I suggested that Maurice send an investigator to interview Ray Benson. Ray would verify that Al had a thing for Mandy. My frustration was becoming obvious, so I calmed myself and said, "Al Brennan returned on the morning Brittany disappeared, covered in black mud. He claimed he was at the south field, but the soil in the south field is sandy. You can brush it off your clothing. But it's heavy clay where we found Brittany's body. And remember, I was shot near the south field when I was checking out Al's story."

Now I had everyone's attention.

I walked over to an aerial view of 210th Street and pointed out how Al could have easily traveled by foot from the farm to the site where Brittany was found, in order to entomb her in the culvert. "My guess is he picked Brittany up on the road and, after he drove by the farm, they argued. Brittany told him she wasn't going along with his abuse anymore. Maybe she even tried getting out of the vehicle. Narcissists, like Al, can't stand being denied. So, he grabbed the awl and stabbed her. Then he tranquilized her while he considered his next step. He probably had the tranquilizer along in case she didn't consent." Hearing the facts out loud sickened me all over again.

Tony picked up the thread. "Then Mary called Al and told him Jason was organizing a search party, so he rushed home and deliberately directed the search away from Brittany's body. Jason's alibi was that he was putting a new stereo in their vehicle. The stereo wasn't replaced in their van, but it was in their truck. Jason had the truck. Mary heard the truck in the yard, and assumed Al had returned. But Al had the van."

Confused, Maurice said, "I thought the van didn't run."

Tony responded, "Not without the awl, or some long tool to start it. The awl wasn't in it when we tested it. But Al knew the trick to starting it."

Sean interjected, "There was a lot of porn on the Brennan computer. Jason admitted viewing some of it, but blamed it primarily on Al. One of their favorite sites was Barely Legal. It's basically eighteen-year-olds who look much younger. Consider the victims—Mandy at sixteen, Vicki at sixteen, Brittany at eleven, and Serena would have been seventeen when he first set his sights on her, and she's still petite."

"We all agree that Al burned Jeff Lemor's trailer, along with their van," I said. "Serena's home was burned after she was assaulted." I clapped my hands together, and asked, "Are we in agreement that Al needs to be brought in?"

Sean nodded approvingly.

Maurice asserted his authority by reminding me, "You're still not working this investigation." He turned to Sean and pointed a gnarled finger at him. "We're here only to listen."

Paula was incredulous. "For God's sake, Maurice, let's finish this."

Maurice leaned forward and told Paula, "Be careful of how you talk to me. I'm your superior."

Paula retorted, "You only need to remind people when it's not obvious."

Tony interrupted the feud before Paula got herself in trouble. "Jason told me they kept an awl in the van. We don't have the awl, but we know Brittany's wound was inflicted with one." Tony stood up and paced. "Jon's version makes sense. Al must have kept Mandy's jacket as a trophy, then realized he could use it to implicate Jon in Brittany's attack. Jon had already been a suspect in Mandy's disappearance after all."

Maurice turned toward Tony. "Didn't I just say we weren't going to share any more information?"

Tony coolly reminded him, "Maurice, you're not my boss. Referencing the Steve Miller song, he added, "Aren't you supposed to be lovey-dovey all the time?"

Maurice hated being disrespected. His face tightened and he blurted, "The polygraph."

Not wishing to humiliate Maurice, I politely interjected, "I think Jeff failed the polygraph because he didn't reveal he had seen Brittany walk down that road before. He was afraid of being sentenced for premeditated murder, not because he actually hurt her. We know Jeff didn't shoot me. Al is the one with a motive. I can prove his alibi was a lie." When no one responded, I turned to Sean. "Sean, what do you think?"

Sean rubbed his chin thoughtfully. "I'm just taking it all in."

Maurice used the pause in conversation to ask me to leave.

Having no choice, I made my exit.

How much more obvious could I make it for them? While I was obsessing over the predicament, my phone rang.

"Jon, it's Vicki. I need your help." She sounded breathless.

I felt bad for the way I had treated Vicki, so, stifling my irritation, I asked, "What can I do for you?"

Vicki frantically said, "I took the quick way back to the shelter with Hannah, because I feel like crap. I had a tire blow out when I was driving by the Brennan farm. It's getting dark, and my grandparents don't drive when it's dark. I don't know who else to call. I'm scared, and I've got Hannah with me."

My pulse quickened. "Keep driving on it. Drive slow, but keep moving as far from the Brennans' as you can. I'll be right there. Lock the doors and stay in your car. Don't let anyone in without calling me first." I had to get her off that road before Al discovered her.

I sped out of Little Falls and soon was driving down 210th Street. Why in the hell would Vicki drive by Al Brennan's farm? The answer was simple. She had a history of making bad choices, and this was just one more. She was also still going through withdrawal, so likely wasn't thinking clearly. It didn't take long before I spotted Vicki cautiously steering her gray Grand Am to avoid the steep ditches on both sides.

She pulled over, and I was relieved to find Vicki, unharmed, huddled next to Hannah in her car, a winter jacket tucked around her daughter's little body. I instructed her to pop the trunk, found the jack and spare tire, and began removing the lug nuts on the rim.

Vicki stepped out of the car and stood over me, thanking me profusely for the help. She periodically blew into her cupped hands to keep them warm. "Boy, am I glad to see you. I was so freaked, I thought I was going to piss my pants. I don't know why this had to happen tonight, of all nights. I was trying to get to the shelter as fast as I could, so I took the shortcut."

I wasn't up for chit-chat. "You can sit in the car with Hannah if you want."

"She's sleeping, and I can see her from here. I feel like the least I can do is keep you company. I kept driving slow, just like you told me."

"You did a great job keeping the car on the road." I worked as fast as I could, feeling the bite of the cold on my bare hands.

Vicki shivered and nodded her head in the direction of the Brennans'. "It happened right in front of their farm. If it wasn't for bad luck, I'd have no luck at all."

Twilight was settling in as I jacked up the car. Vicki looked down the road, lost in thought, her expression pained. She was battling legitimate fear, meth withdrawal, and bitterly cold temps. She was a pretty tough lady. She asked, "When you think about it, what are the odds that I'd know both the killer and the man falsely accused?"

I glanced up at her and kept working while I could still feel my fingers. "Pretty damn good, Vicki—this is rural Minnesota." I didn't add that hardcore partiers know each other well in this part of the state.

"Al isn't like you or Jeff. Al hung around people who used heavily, because that's where he could find victims who wouldn't report the hurt he put on them. He's a predator."

Vicki checked back in on Hannah, then returned to my side. "It's pretty cold in my car, but I think Hannah's okay. The heater's not great."

"Get Hannah and put her in my car. The keys are in it, and it's still warm," I said. She gratefully did as I suggested.

When Vicki returned, I told her, "Once I get this tire changed, you drive my car, and I'll follow you to the shelter in yours, so you can keep Hannah warm. We can switch when we get there. If you want, I can have my dad look at your heater. He can fix anything, and he enjoys helping people."

Vicki nodded gratefully. "Thank you."

I removed the tire and carefully examined it. I had a feeling this wasn't simply bad luck. I saw what appeared to be a bullet hole in the side of the tire but said nothing to Vicki, not wanting to alarm her further.

Vicki questioned, "How many girls do you think Al Brennan has raped?"

"I need you to not talk for a minute, so I can think." I glanced down the road. I didn't see anyone, so I went back to work, fumbling slightly as my fingertips began to numb.

Vicki didn't notice the tire. Instead, she was openly contemplating not talking. "Do you mean not talking right now, or when you're done? Because I'm cold and I'm freaking out, being on this road, and it helps me to talk about—"

I interrupted her. "Vicki, I want you to go. Drive to the shelter. I'll meet you there."

Vicki abruptly froze. In cold fear, she slowly put her hand on my shoulder and whispered, "Jon. He's coming . . ."

I turned slowly to see a figure in a camouflage jacket with a crazy head of hair step out of the ditch, carrying a rifle. A silhouette of that hair was all I needed to know it was Al. If Vicki and I ran together to my vehicle, he would have plenty of time to kill both of us. I decided to make him choose. This time, Vicki wasn't going to get a raw deal.

I turned to Vicki. "Take my car to Little Falls. Be careful not to go in the ditch turning it around—it's a tight U-turn. Hannah's life may depend on it. My cell phone's sitting on the seat. When you're on the road, call 911, and tell them where I'm at. Go!"

"But what about you—"

"Just go!" I gave her a harder shove than I'd intended, but she grasped my sense of urgency. She ran to my car, ripped open the door and jumped in. She began turning the vehicle around.

Al started to lift his rifle, but then looked back at me.

Vicki almost caught the edge of the ditch with a front tire.

Al studied me as he hesitated, still weighing his options.

Vicki made the turn and straightened the wheels out. Icy gravel shot out from the under the tires as she sped away.

With Al focused on me, I couldn't chance going for my gun. The distance between us was too great for my handgun to deliver a lethal shot, but his rifle certainly would. I couldn't afford to escalate the situation. Since Vicki's car was now my only mode of transportation, I decided to finish changing the tire. I slid the spare on the bolts, hyper-aware of Al's movements.

As Al approached, he asked, "Can I help you?"

I stopped working on the tire and turned cautiously to face him. "Do you always bring a rifle when you're being a good Samaritan?"

Al's eyes were dilated black, and he smirked in giddy gratification. He continued to hold the rifle at his side with his finger hovering over the trigger. He remained at a distance where he could easily raise it and fire before I got to him. Al responded, "I think it's in my best interest to stay armed."

I tightened the lug nuts, willing my fingers to continue working.

Al commented, "A real spare tire. Not one of those doughnuts."

"I have a feeling she can thank her grandfather for that."

"Why did she take off like a screaming banshee?"

"Her daughter's sick and she needed to get to Little Falls. I told her to just get going. I'll switch vehicles with her later."

After lowering the jack and tossing it in the trunk, I turned back to Al.

He gave me a menacing smile, deepening the lines around his mouth. "I saw you studying the tire. Guessing you found a bullet hole." With his finger now securely snugged around the rifle's trigger, he aimed the weapon at me and instructed me to slowly remove the gun from my shoulder holster and toss it in the ditch. I reluctantly complied. Then he tilted his head at me. "Why didn't you leave with Vicki?"

"I didn't think we'd both get to the car without getting shot. But if I stayed, you'd let her go and focus on me, since I have a gun."

"The smart thing would have been to leave the whore for me. We would have both been happier." In his grating tone, he said, "I had a feeling you boys were coming for me. So, I grabbed my rifle and walked out to the road to see if there were any squad cars sitting out here. I was thinking I could really use a head start. I needed a car that wouldn't be immediately traced back to me, and here comes Vicki. It was like being handed a gift. I knelt down, and hit that tire with a perfect shot." Al looked at me for adulation. When I didn't respond, he continued. "Then the stupid bitch tries to drive away on the flat tire! She wasn't going to get too far, so I figured I'd take my time and let her change the tire. Save me some work. But she just kept rolling along until you showed up."

Al was comfortable spewing information to me because he intended to kill me. He asked, "Where's your phone?"

"In my car," I said, pointing down the now-empty road where Vicki had driven away.

He gestured the rifle at me, and I felt my insides clench. "Empty your pockets."

I pulled my pockets inside out, showing him my billfold, some change, and a pen. Al was satisfied that I didn't have a phone. This meant he could take me anywhere and the police wouldn't be able to trace my location. He maintained his distance, so I had no chance to make a move.

Trying to buy some time, I said, "I'd bet you could survive for a long time off the grid, with all the hunting and trapping you do."

"I've walked through woods no other human has ever seen."

Al's finger flexed on the trigger, so I talked faster. "Don't you think it would be too much of a coincidence to have my body, or blood, discovered so close to your farm?" His trigger finger had almost passed the point of no return.

Al smiled and relaxed his finger off the trigger a fraction.

I continued. "You may be the luckiest criminal ever. You left Mandy Baker just lying there, but my crazy brother came along and buried her for you."

Al snorted, "Your brother saved your ass. They came looking for you even without the body. If that body was found on your farm back then, you'd be in prison."

I pointed out, "Brittany isn't saying anything."

"If I had to do it again, I'd put her in a place they'd never find her. Water by a road is too risky." Al considered it all. "But there's the whole issue of the bullet in the tire. How am I going to explain that?" He repositioned the rifle, pointing it at my heart.

"I can help you walk away clean. We'll burn the tire."

"You have no spine, do you?" Al laughed. "I've stripped and ridden your woman, and here you are kissing my ass." He stepped back, and with an arrogant smile, said, "You can destroy some evidence for me, if you can do it quick."

A man who reacts with impulsive anger is easy to manipulate. I wasn't going to be that man for Al. I carefully bent down and picked up the tire. I was hoping to hear sirens, but it wasn't happening. As if reading my thoughts, he backed far enough away from me so throwing the tire at him ceased to be an option.

I showed him the damage to the tire. "There's no bullet in the car. It must have fallen out somewhere on the road. You live on this road and hunt on the land surrounding it. It would be easy enough to explain why a bullet from your rifle might be found around here. Once the tire's destroyed, so is the bullet hole." I hit the trunk. "There's an emergency kit in the trunk, probably put there by her grandpa. It has cloth and matches in it. I'll dip the cloth in the gas tank so it soaks up some gas, then lay the cloth over the bullet hole. It won't be long before the tire's burning and the evidence is gone."

Al nodded and, with a sardonic grin, spat, "All right, do it."

I took as much time as I could, without angering him to the point of shooting me, while I soaked up some gas and set the tire on fire. The black smoke stunk up the cool air as it billowed into the breeze.

Al said, "I still have a problem, because you're the one investigator who can find the error in my alibi. They had to bring in a damn farmer."

Acting as if I still hadn't figured it out, I said, "You don't have a nine-millimeter registered to you."

Al laughed gleefully. "Won it in a card game! They'll never find it."

"I assumed that. Probably with Say Hey Ray and the boys?" I sank my fingers into my empty pockets, searching for warmth.

The black tire smoke swirling around his raggedy hair created a picture of pure evil. "Mandy used to enjoy it. Then all of a sudden she was too good for me? She fought it, and it cost her. I was at her beck and call. She owed me."

Al realized I was stalling and an angry storm began to develop across his face. He hastily ordered, "Get in the car," gesturing toward Vicki's Grand Am. "You're going to drive me to my hunting shack, and if you can follow directions, I'll let you walk away. You're going to have to walk back to town, though. I want a head start."

Al was an accomplished liar. Regardless of what he said, he was going to kill me. After everything he had disclosed, he had to. I got in the driver's seat, while Al slid into the back passenger seat, keeping his rifle fixed on me. He instructed me, "Start driving, nice and slow, toward the south field."

I put the car in drive and slowly started down the desolate road. If Al had sat in the front passenger seat, I could have grabbed the barrel of the rifle. If he had sat directly behind me, Al would have struggled to turn to get a good shot at me if I jumped out the driver's side door. His decision to sit behind the passenger seat made it more difficult for me to get out of this alive, but I had an idea that would involve some physics. The doors automatically locked when the car went into gear, so I unlocked my door and locked the windows as I spoke. I then reached over and closed all the vents;

Al's rifle came up at my unexpected movement. I explained, "Don't freak out, here. I was adjusting the heat, and now I'm going to bend down and adjust the seat. Vicki's legs are shorter than mine." Pretending I was having some difficulty with the seat, I bent down toward the door, slightly opening it. In a sequence of quick moves, I cranked the steering wheel toward the ditch, stepped on the gas, and dove out, slamming the door behind me. I just needed Al to miss me with his first shot, so as I hit the gravel, I rolled quickly at an angle. My body was pummeled by rocks as I hit the road, but my will to survive kept me in motion.

A rifle blast struck up a puff of dirt from the ground next to me. After watching the car slowly roll onto its side in the ditch, I considered running, but didn't. I was a little dazed, but I needed this to be over. I ran to the car, which was now resting on its side, and waited for Al to try to climb out. Had my plan worked? When a rifle's fired, an explosion puts the bullet in flight. If that explosion occurs in a small, confined space, such as inside a car with the windows rolled up and the vents closed, it should rupture the eardrums of the passenger. I glanced through the window to see Al crumpled against the door, holding his ears.

In one fluid motion, I jumped up on the side of the car, pulled open the door and reached in, quickly grabbing the rifle. Al lay helplessly inside, still cupping his ears, his face contorted in agony. I stood over him ready to fire. I wanted to kill him for hurting Serena. I wanted to kill him for taking Mandy's life. I wanted to kill him for raping Vicki. I wanted to kill him for trying to kill me. But what I wanted wasn't the same as what was right, and when the two conflict, I try to do what's right. Al wasn't a threat to me at the moment, but he damned sure was evil. I told myself, *Don't play God. Just do your job.*

While I contemplated this, the crunching sound of tires rumbling heavily on gravel interrupted my silent inner battle. I was never so happy to see Tony's ugly Chevy Celebrity. He led an ominous caravan. Tony's unmarked squad car was the only one in this parade with its lights on. Behind him, half a dozen squad cars rolled at a safe distance through the dusk.

As the Chevy came to a stop, Tony and Sean stepped out simultaneously. Police officers fanned out in a half-circle around us. It must have been a sight, me standing precariously on the rocker panel of a car resting broadside, aiming a rifle inside it. Tony ran to the car and scrambled up to join me.

Without taking my eyes off Al, I commented dryly, "Could have used you ten minutes ago."

Tony gave me a curious look, something like a combination of respect and disappointment, and said out of the side of his mouth, "When I saw you holding that rifle, I was thinking we arrived ten minutes too early."

Together, Tony and I dragged Alban out of the car, depositing him roughly onto the gravel road. Sean calmly addressed the man on his knees. "Alban Brennan, you are under arrest for the attempted murder of Brittany Brennan." At least a dozen officers now had their guns drawn on Al.

Sean turned to Tony and said, "Read him his rights. Hold the card in front of his eyes. With that blood dripping out of his ears, he probably can't hear us."

Tony read Al his rights as the officers quickly cuffed him.

Sean told me, "The sandy soil was the piece that finally convinced me. It gave us a motive for the attempt on your life. But I was starting to come around. I could never reconcile the fact that once Brittany regained consciousness, she still wouldn't help us make a composite sketch of her abductor, even when we set it up so all she had to do was nod. That told me she knew her abductor personally. I showed her pictures of a variety of offenders and she had no reaction to any of them. Not even Jeff Lemor. This convinced me he wasn't our guy."

I felt a euphoric sense of relief for having survived. Two thoughts occurred to me. The first was that Sean held his cards close to the vest. He only let out what he was holding when he felt he needed a little more information from others. My second thought was, is it over? Maybe Tony was right, and when it started to fall, it fell like a house of cards. With everything I'd been through, I still wasn't ready to believe it. Regardless, I was damn glad to be alive. I needed to go to the law enforcement center and make a report of everything that had just happened, and then I was going to find Serena. I liked it better in the movies, where detectives and their lovers walked off into the night together after the big event, and no one had to do paperwork.

Chapter Thirty-Seven

JON FREDERICK
THURSDAY, JUNE 5
BUREAU OF CRIMINAL APPREHENSION, ST. PAUL

SERENA AND I HAD DEVELOPED a nighttime routine. At the end of the day, we'd lie together on our new couch, watching *Homeland* on Netflix. Serena tells me it's good. The comfort of her body, after an active day, always put me to sleep in minutes. When the show was over, she'd wake me and we'd go to bed. I'd wake when she had a bad dream, gently calm her and then give her a few minutes to compose herself before we snuggled. After her anxiety dissipated, we moved to positions of slight contact, and both fall back to sleep. Over the last month, her bad dreams had become fewer, so we're both sleeping longer. I've concluded that you can't make anybody love you exactly how you want to be loved, and it's probably for the best. Serena's love for me is beyond what I could have imagined, or created, and I accept it with gracious humility.

I was back at work for the BCA. Maurice still didn't like that I was so close to everything that happened with Mandy, but accepted that I hadn't done anything wrong. I was just happy to be back.

Tony met me at the BCA office in St. Paul to discuss Al Brennan's prosecution.

Al was pursuing a not guilty by reason of insanity plea. Apparently, his attorney had found a psychologist who supported this. I never liked this plea. It should be *guilty* by reason of insanity.

If a person was murdered, they were no less dead because the killer was mentally ill. The truth was, people who took the insanity plea generally served more time in a locked facility than people who went the prison route. Still, I wanted to see this case called as it was. Al wasn't insane. He was vile.

Tony paced back and forth, grumbling, "It pisses me off to see psychologists sell out to defense attorneys. Where are their ethics?" He tossed Al's psychological assessment on the desk in front of me. "This guy claims Al's a schizophrenic who has command hallucinations that tell him to harm others. Al Brennan is no more schizophrenic than you or me." Tony sarcastically added, "You, anyway. It's all bullshit. Now we need to find a therapist who can see through this crap."

"I know someone who can. Dr. Nicole Lenz."

Tony stopped pacing to ask, "How do you know her?"

"She worked with my brother. Dr. Lenz is a psychologist who was able to identify the exact areas of concern for Victor. Not only was she able to see the issue clearly, she was able to explain it to our family in a manner everyone understood. It'll take someone who can identify a schizophrenic in exact terms to call someone out who's malingering."

Tony pondered this. "It's damn hard to get a psychologist to say someone's faking it. Making that assertion is just setting yourself up for a lawsuit."

"I'll call her." Fortunately for us, juries were skeptical. If one psychologist out of six said a defendant was faking it, that was usually enough to sway a jury. People liked to see consequences for violent crimes.

Monday, June 30

Tony and I sat in an observation room behind mirrored glass at the Morrison County jail, watching Dr. Nicole Lenz conduct her second interview with Al Brennan. Dr. Lenz told us she couldn't give us any hint of her opinion until both interviews were completed. Al and Dr. Lenz were seated across from each other in an interview room with gray cement walls. The psychologist was a thin, fair-skinned woman in her late forties, with light freckles and shoulder-length brunette hair streaked with silver. She sat back in a plastic chair with her legs crossed, looking perfectly at ease. Sitting next to her, Al looked troll-like in his jail orange and his unsightly hair.

Dr. Lenz presented as paradoxical, appearing physically relaxed, while intensely scrutinizing Al's behaviors. She asked, "Have the visions persisted?"

Al carefully thought out his answer and then replied with a simple, "Yes."

"What is your emotional reaction to the hallucinations?"

"Scared. It makes me question my sanity, you know."

I turned to Tony. "He's faking well. Most people who fake it make the mistake of over-attempting to act crazy. He's acknowledging an emotional reaction to his hallucinations, which is typical for someone who's psychotic."

My comments bothered Tony. He countered, "How is it that you know so much about the insanity plea?"

"I volunteered for a lot of tasks at the BCA before I was promoted," I said. "One was to help prepare one of the investigators for a case where they felt a perpetrator was malingering. Plus, I also have an insane person in my family."

Tony chuckled. "That just makes you like everyone else."

On the other side of the mirrored glass, Al nervously sputtered, "Last time you said that schizophrenics typically hear more than one voice. I didn't want to admit this, but I do, too. Sometimes it's my dad. Sometimes it's scary political figures like Idi Amin."

Tony spat in annoyance, "Man, is that a line of crap! Do you think Al knew who Idi Amin was before he went to jail and found old magazines and books to read through?"

I put a hand up and whispered, "I think that was a point for us. She's setting him up."

Dr. Lenz asked, "Are the voices constant, or are there situations that make them worse?"

Al swallowed hard. "The voices are constant."

"Is there anything you can do that helps you cope with them?"

Al thought long and hard on this question. The tension was palpable. I could sense the wheels spinning in his head. If he answered that he could cope with them, this might suggest that he should have coped with them, instead of attempting to kill Brittany. Al finally said, "There's nothing that helps."

Dr. Lenz got up and glanced back at her empty chair as she spoke to Al. "You said the voices are constant. I want you to speak directly to them."

Looking slightly uncertain, Al stood up and yelled at the empty chair, "Leave me alone! I'm not hurting anyone anymore!" He looked back at Dr. Lenz for approval.

For the first time, Dr. Lenz exhibited the glimpse of a smile. She told him, "I don't have any other questions," and dismissed him.

Dr. Lenz joined us in the observation room a few minutes later bearing a smile of satisfaction. "Well, do you want to know what I think?"

I nodded. "Of course."

She stood over us like an elementary teacher. "He's malingering. Let's see how good you guys are. How do I know he's malingering?"

I suggested, "The visual hallucinations. Schizophrenics primarily have auditory hallucinations."

She nodded. "That's good, but keep going."

Tony joined in. "His confronting the voice in the chair. I don't know a lot about malingering, but I do know that real crazy people hear the voices in their heads. They wouldn't approach a chair to talk to their voices."

Dr. Lenz smiled with approval. "Very good. I particularly liked the way he followed my suggestion. The first time I met with him he heard one voice. After I suggested that an insane person might hear more than one voice, he made sure to have another voice this time."

I added, "He claimed the voices are constant. Schizophrenics typically have voices that come and go."

"Also good," she said. "Further, he doesn't have a strategy for dealing with them. Someone who actually hears voices has a strategy. For people with schizophrenia, the voices are always worse in some situations." She turned to me. "When are the voices worse for your brother?"

"When the radio's on or when he's in any building with an intercom system. It seems to trigger them."

She smiled. "People who truly experience mental illness know this. He also reported two kinds of psychoses which typically don't co-occur, command hallucinations and visual hallucinations. Plus, he has no prior history of mental illness. As with most malingerers, he isn't faking the most common characteristic of schizophrenia: a flat affect. When people fake, they focus on what they should do, rather than recognizing the lack of emotionality and avolition of schizophrenics. However, the *coup de gras* is the crime itself. An insane person would attempt to kill someone for an illogical reason, but then stay at the scene. To an insane person, the murder was justified. There would be no reason to run. A sane person cleans up the scene and takes elaborate steps to avoid being caught, because he knows the consequences. He had a sane motive. Alban attempted to kill his daughter to cover up his crimes."

Tony smiled. "We look forward to your report."

Alban Brennan's effort at an insanity plea had just been destroyed.

Chapter
Thirty-Eight

Jon Frederick
Wednesday, July 2
Morrison County Jail, Little Falls

Jason Brennan agreed to testify against his father, solidifying the case against Al. Brittany's therapist reported that she was still too traumatized to testify. Knowing we could get a conviction without her testimony, we decided to leave her out of it and let her heal.

I could have gone to Little Falls any day this week, but chose this particular day because it was Jeff Lemor's release day. Jeff had been sentenced to ninety days for violating his probation by using alcohol but was released early due to good behavior.

When I pulled into the jail parking lot, Vicki was anxiously adding to her already ample makeup in the rearview mirror as she sat in Jeff's blue "FO D" pick-up, waiting for his departure from jail. I quietly approached her and pounded on the window.

Vicki let out a sharp, shrill scream, then jumped out of the truck, laughing. "Jerk! I've probably got lipstick all over my cheek." Vicki was conservatively dressed in a mid-length denim skirt and western-style blouse, with battered brown cowboy boots that had been through some tough days, looking like she was headed to a rodeo. She looked clear-eyed and healthy. I was relieved to see she had put on some weight. After shaking her fist at me, she gave me a big hug.

Vicki softly added, "I never did thank you for coming to my rescue that night."

"I know. I came back here just for that," I teased.

Vicki furrowed her eyebrows and asked, "You didn't really, did you?"

I couldn't help it, I ruffled her hair. "No, I've got some papers to deliver to the county attorney."

"Ugh. You're so mean!" She set about fixing her hair in her reflection in the truck's window.

"You're looking good, Vicki. Big day today."

"Yeah. I'm so excited I could piss my pants. You should read the letters I've gotten from Jeff. So nice . . ." There was a glimmer of hope in her eyes.

"Vicki, promise me you'll take care of yourself and your daughter, all right?"

"Oh, you can bet on it. It's going to be so fun having Hannah outside this summer," she beamed. Vicki caught herself. "I'm sure you didn't come here to talk about Hannah. Thanks for caring, and thank your dad again from me, for fixing my car."

I pulled a manila envelope out of the stack of papers I held and handed it to Vicki. "Would you mind giving these to Jeff?"

Vicki peered into the envelope. "They're his pictures of his mom. I thought they burned up."

"Before Sean left the trailer that day, he took the pictures to the lab and asked the CSI crew to go through them for any possible prints of Brittany. Of course there weren't any, so the pictures ended up being filed away with the rest of the evidence used in the investigation. I wanted to make sure Jeff got them back."

"Thank you." Vicki gave me another quick hug, and I headed into the jail.

I STOPPED TO SPEAK BRIEFLY to Jeff before he was released. I wanted to give him some information that would help him let go of resentments. If you want to move forward, you need to let go of the past. I explained to Jeff that he had been headed to prison on a probation violation for possession of a weapon, until his trailer burned down. I also wanted him to know that Vicki was the one person who stood by him when everyone else wanted him lynched. He was lucky to have someone who loved him so much. If he honestly wanted to make amends for his past sins, he could do so by treating Vicki and Hannah honorably.

A Christian ministry group that assisted inmates adjust to life in the community had helped Jeff find a home and employment while he was in jail. Now it was up to Jeff.

When I returned home, Serena was in bed, napping. Today was a day of resolution for me, so I couldn't let her sleep. I gave her a nice, long backrub, and then kissed the back of her neck and whispered, "I need to ask you something."

Serena acknowledged that she'd been extremely tired lately, and apologized for it. She sat up and stretched as she told me, "I think I know what this is about."

I interrupted her. "You've been through so much, it's no wonder you're tired," I said. "Besides, it has to annoy you that I fall asleep every time we lay on the couch together to watch a show. I've always had difficulty falling asleep, but when I'm next to you, this soothing, cathartic tranquility overtakes me, and I just give into it. It's like lying on the porch of heaven."

Serena laughed in confusion. "It doesn't annoy me. I think it's sweet, because I know you've always had a troubled soul. It comforts me."

"Please bear with me a little longer," I said. "I think I've loved you for as long as I've been capable of love, and I love you more than ever right now. I need you." I sighed, "I've always taken pride in being independent, but I can't get around it. I need you. You make me feel like I'm giving you the world when I really haven't given you much of anything."

I dropped to my knee. "Serena Bell, will you marry me?" I slowly opened my hand, revealing a small, black velvet ring box.

Serena's emerald eyes glistened as she responded, "Yes . . ." She took the ring box from my hand and opened it. She studied it and, with genuine pleasure, told me, "It's beautiful. I love it. I love you."

"I thought about proposing to you by the curve of the river at my parents' farm, where we used to sit by the fire on summer nights. It's where I first realized I'd be the luckiest guy in the world if you would marry me. But I couldn't wait. I didn't want to go another minute without knowing." After giving it significant thought, I didn't want the proposal process to overshadow the proposal. Big, dramatic marriage proposals make it hard for those on the receiving end to say no, even if they want to. It needed to be discreet enough to allow her to decline without pressure. I wanted Serena to be focused on the merits of sharing her life with me, with no pressure to accept. It had to be what she wanted.

Serena smiled. "When people ask how I reacted to the proposal, I can say, 'I damn near fell out of bed!'" She laughed, and I joined her.

Serena pulled her shirt up slightly above her waist, baring her midriff. She placed my hand on her stomach and looked at me expectantly. "We're having a baby." She beamed. "I absolutely couldn't tell you until you proposed. I didn't want you to propose to me just because I was pregnant."

This time, the adrenaline rush that spiked through me was saturated in the purest form of joy.

Chapter Thirty-Nine

Jon Frederick
Wednesday, August 4

Al Brennan was convicted of attempted first degree murder, and sentenced to life in prison without the possibility of parole.

My contentment was short-lived, as Paula contacted me and told me that Jason Brennan had been arrested and was asking to speak to me. The night before Al's sentencing, Jason sexually abused Brittany. I agonized over this news, and then offered to help. Tony asked if I would travel to Arrowhead Juvenile Center in Duluth to interview Jason—he was unable to, as he would be attending an appeal hearing filed by Al's attorney. Upon hearing the news about Jason, Al's attorney had immediately asked for a new trial, suggesting Jason had perjured himself in court when he claimed he didn't have sex with Brittany. Jason's testimony that Al had left at ten thirty in the van the morning Brittany was abducted was our strongest testimony. We hadn't brought the case against Mandy Baker forward yet, or the other assaults, as they would be easier to prosecute with this conviction. Still, Tony wasn't concerned over our ability to keep Al in custody. He described the court hearing as a formality to appease Al's attorney.

People wanted to believe everything was wonderful for an unhealthy family after the perpetrator was removed, but that was rarely the case. No family member comes out of a bad situation unscathed and, without proper help and enforced boundaries, bad things happened. I was initially frustrated that Mary had left Jason and Brittany alone at night. Then I discovered Mary was unable to find daytime employment, so she ended up leaving the kids alone while she worked the night shift at a nursing home. Mary was trying to avoid being a welfare mother.

Brittany had unbearable nightmares. The tortured little girl would go into her brother's room at night and sleep on the covers of his bed for companionship. Then one night, she crawled under the covers with Jason, and Jason engaged in sexual intercourse with her while she lay there and said nothing. Jason claimed she initiated the contact. *Come on, Jason, she's twelve years old, and she's your sister*, I thought in disgust when I heard this. Mary had brought Jason to therapy a month ago, and even told the therapist she had concerns that Jason struggled with some sexual issues related to his past viewing of pornography. What she didn't know was that a number of providers, such as Medicare, won't cover services if concerns were expressed about sexual issues. So, instead of getting badly needed help, Jason was left home alone at night, with his untreated sexual issues, to take care of a twelve-year-old girl who had experienced severe victimization.

Jason still claimed he hadn't had intercourse with Brittany prior to testifying, so he hadn't perjured himself. After interviewing Jason and Brittany again, I believed him. But would this new offense be enough to create reasonable doubt in the judge ruling on the matter?

Additional charges could be added against Al Brennan, but as I examined them one by one, I realized they all were problematic. First, the DNA from the assault on Serena had been misfiled, and the BCA lab techs were trying to locate it. It had been delivered to the lab, so it was a matter of tracking it down. This occasionally happened with DNA that wasn't high priority, and a physical assault without a confirmed rape was not considered a high priority. Second, Al never admitted to the arson of Jeff Lemor's trailer, and he likely wouldn't be held in lock-up for being suspected of burning an unoccupied trailer, as he had no prior charges. Third, the prosecutor had been reluctant to add Al's attempt on my life, as well as the murder of Mandy Baker, to the case of Brittany's attempted murder, because Mandy's body was discovered on our farm. The prosecutor had concerns that officers who came to the scene witnessed me holding the rifle on Al, and the defense attorney would use this scenario to create reasonable doubt of Al's guilt. At the time, I wasn't even working as an investigator, as I had been suspended. Finally, Vicki had lied to investigators by attempting to provide an alibi for Jeff, making it difficult to prosecute the rapes she suffered through based solely on her word.

It was all disconcerting, and I began to fear that Al could eventually be freed, at least until charges came forth in Mandy's murder.

Chapter Forty

Serena Bell
5:30 p.m.
Wednesday, August 4
Birmingham Apartments, Minneapolis

I had gone into work early this morning so I wouldn't have to take time off for my check-up with my obstetrician. Everything was good with the baby. Now that I was finally home, I was tired and was going to take a nap before I did anything else. I decided to leave the bedroom door open to make certain I would wake when Jon returned from Duluth.

Chapter
Forty-One

Jon Frederick
6:25 p.m.
Wednesday, August 4
Interstate 35 south of Duluth,
headed toward Minneapolis

I tried calling Tony a couple times to see how court went, but the calls went immediately into his voicemail. Serena had texted and said she was home and was going to lie down for a nap, so I thought I'd give her another half hour before I called. Her pregnancy had significantly increased her need for sleep.

My cell phone buzzed, so I retrieved it from the console. "This is Jon Frederick."

"Jon, it's Paula." She was distraught, her voice vibrating with unchecked emotion. "Tony was shot and left for dead." She managed to choke out, "He isn't going to make it."

My brain immediately went into crisis mode. "I'm on my way back from Duluth, about an hour away from the Twin Cities. I promise to get there as fast as I can. Where is he, and what happened?"

It was silent for a moment as Paula gathered her composure. "He was airlifted to Fairview. Tony was shot in his vehicle—a couple shots through the window and four more through the door. It all went down about two hours ago. Al Brennan's on the run in his pick-up truck, so we've issued an APB on it. From what I've read in the report, you'd think they'd be able to hear it a mile away," she sniffed.

Shocked, I asked, "Wait, what? How did Al get out of prison?"

"He was released at the hearing. After reviewing the evidence, the judge determined Jason likely committed perjury. He didn't feel it was fair," she said in a mock whine, "to make Al wait in prison for a retrial. After all, with the verdict thrown out, Al isn't guilty of anything."

"I thought this was a preliminary hearing!" I was incredulous. My foot automatically pressed down on the accelerator.

Resigned, Paula sighed raggedly. "No one thought he'd get released. You know how Tony can get. He and Al got into it in the parking lot after court," she sobbed slightly. "And Al came back and found him. I'd love to go after Al, but Tony's more important right now. I want to spend the last few moments I can with him. I probably won't call again." She was choking up.

"I'll get there as fast as I can."

First, I was going to call Serena to make sure she was behind the secure doors in my apartment, then I'd pick her up and we would go to the hospital together. My hands strangled the steering wheel in desperation as I sped toward my home.

Chapter Forty-Two

Serena Bell
6:28 p.m.
Wednesday, August 4
Birmingham Apartments, Minneapolis

Something woke me from a sound sleep. I think my phone was buzzing. When I reached for it, I knocked it off the night stand and onto the floor. The apartment door was closing, and the anticipation of Jon's return brought warmth that flooded through me like a pleasant tea. I slipped out of bed. Not bothering to dress, I stepped toward the bedroom doorway in just a t-shirt and underwear. It sounded like Jon's apartment manager was talking to him just before he entered.

Jon usually called my name when he came in, to alert me that it was him. Tonight, he must have forgotten. A prickle of unease began to crawl up my spine. Something wasn't right. I slid back behind the bedroom door, heart hammering, and peered around it.

I stifled a gasp, stunned by what I saw. Even from behind, there was no mistaking that mass of crazy hair—Al Brennan was inside the apartment, hands on his hips, looking into the empty living room. Ice-cold terror shot through my limbs and froze me in place. Al wore the standard gray prison-release button-down work shirt and jeans. Once the lock on the apartment door clicked into place, he removed a gun from his waistband. Acid crawled from my stomach to my throat, choking me. This couldn't be! He still hadn't seen me, so I quietly backed into the bedroom. I only had a second to make a decision. I was in trouble. If I locked the bedroom door he would hear me, and he could get to the bathroom door before I could lock that, too. There was no doubt in my mind that this was the man who had assaulted me, and this time he had a gun. And this time, I was pregnant. I needed to hide.

I glanced over at the large armoire against the wall, at the foot of the bed. It had a large door on the left side, and drawers on the right. I gently opened the door, and there was only one t-shirt inside. Only a guy would have a large empty space in his armoire. I slid inside, noiselessly closing the door behind me. It was a tight fit, with my knees pushed against my chest and forehead, with little room for movement. I fumbled with the t-shirt and began to wind it tightly around the latch from the door and the inside catch, willing my trembling hands to cooperate and hoping to make the door impossible to open. *Kyrie eleison*, I prayed. *Lord, have mercy.*

It wasn't long before I heard Al moving into the bedroom. I held my breath and kept my contorted body still. I couldn't see what he was doing, but I imagined, with revulsion, Al standing at the bed, feeling the mattress to see if it was warm. It was then I realized I didn't have my phone. It had to be by the bed. Did he now have it? Then I remembered I had knocked it on the floor. Maybe he didn't see it.

I heard him opening and closing the closet doors, and imagined him looking under the bed. I finally breathed a sigh of relief when I heard him leave the bedroom. Contorting my body into that tight space had worked!

Suddenly my phone rang, the sound jangling through me like a shockwave. It was my mom's ringtone, which had never clamored so obnoxiously. I closed my eyes tightly, praying he hadn't heard it from the other room.

No such luck. Footsteps clomped into the bedroom, stopping around the vicinity of the nightstand. Al had picked up the phone, but said nothing. I imagined my mom asking, "Serena?" when there was no response. I heard a small thud and figured he tossed it back on the floor.

Al was moving items about. His footsteps approached the armoire, until he was inches away from me. I knew the slightest twitch would give me away, and my legs were starting to cramp. After thirty torturous seconds, I heard his footsteps retreat into the bathroom. I considered making a run for it, but I knew by the time I could get out, he would be right in front of me.

I heard the shower curtain slide aside. I continued twisting the t-shirt as tightly as I could around the inside latch. Al returned to the bedroom once again. While walking by the armoire, he pulled on the doorknob. It didn't move. My breathing was becoming jagged, and I struggled to keep it silent. I ground my forehead into my knees, trying to think of any possible way out of this. He immediately stopped, and I could hear him walking over to the bed. Did he see my clothes on the floor? He returned, and again, pulled the knob on the armoire door. Thank God, it didn't budge.

I could feel my heart pounding against my thighs, somewhat surprised Al couldn't hear it thundering. I caught my breath, and beads of sweat formed on my upper lip. He began opening and closing the drawers next to me, then walked away. I felt a split second of relief before he was suddenly back in the room, and couldn't stop myself from gasping softly as I felt the armoire being dragged away from the wall.

Chapter Forty-Three

Panthera (Alban Brennan)
6:45 p.m.
Wednesday, August 4
Birmingham Apartments, Minneapolis

Tony Shileto had to die. He wasn't going to leave me alone. Jon Frederick has to go too, and then I could disappear. I'm not that important to the rest of the investigators, so they'll eventually get bored and move on—just like they moved on after I killed Mandy. My plan is to sit in the apartment and wait for Jon, shoot him when he walked in the door and then disappear. It didn't take much of a lie to get his landlord to let me in. I brought the tranquilizer needle just in case Serena showed up instead. I wouldn't mind one more shot at her.

As I walk through the apartment, I can feel Serena's presence. It might be just a slight scent, but the hunter in me can smell fear. I swear Serena's a damn ghost. I left her zip-tied, and when I returned I couldn't find her again. And today, I feel her warmth on the bed, see her clothing on the floor. Her cell phone's here. She's here. Okay, focus. What structures are large enough to contain a person?

I return to the bedroom once again. The door on the armoire doesn't budge. It's a big waste of space if it's just for design. I lift as I open the drawers of the armoire and realize it's unusually heavy. The little bitch is inside this thing! I glance over at the bed and briefly fantasize of finishing what I started with Serena. The problem is I can't enjoy her right here, knowing Jon could walk in at any time. Still, the fantasy of Serena begging for her life, offering to pleasure me, is so gratifying, I abandon thoughts of Jon. So, how am I going to get her out of here?

I go back into the kitchen closet and see what tools are available. I find some Gorilla tape. This is a lucky find—it's stronger than duct tape. I'll just package her up in her crate, like a dog, and take her with me. And here's a hammer. I'll need this, too.

I return to the bedroom and hear her gasp as I bounce the armoire away from the wall. Her weak utterance of fear increases my arousal.

I press my cheek against the armoire and speak to her. "I could have had you ten years ago, but Mandy told me, 'If you touch that bitch, you're going to jail.' I wasn't sure if you looked up at me when I was talking to Mandy. At the time, it didn't matter, as I didn't have any idea how that night was going to end. If Mandy would have just cooperated, she'd still be alive. Now you get to make that call, too."

I take a rough guess where her ass is sitting, pull the hammer back, and pound a hole through the flimsy back of the armoire. She starts screaming, but I quickly take out the needle and inject her with the sedative. There's no way for her to dodge the shot in that tight space. Her compartment helps drown out the screaming, and it isn't long before it stops. I wait a minute, then pinch her through the hole, but her only response is a sleepy groan. I take the Gorilla tape and wrap it around the dresser again and again, to make sure the door won't open. I have to grin at my success. This is my first victim in a "to go" container.

Serena's an opportunity too good to waste. I'll have another shot at Jon. He'll come racing to me, angry and out of control, and I'll be ready. Okay, I need a two-wheel cart to haul this out. I bet I can get one from that dipshit of a landlord. I'll just Gorilla tape this whole dresser to the cart and push it all into the back of my truck.

Chapter
Forty-Four

JON FREDERICK
7:04 P.M.
WEDNESDAY, AUGUST 4
INTERSTATE 35

I TRIED CALLING SERENA AGAIN, but she wasn't answering. We had both installed the "find the phone" app, and I could see her phone was turned off. I called the Minneapolis police and explained the situation. They agreed to go to my apartment. I then called my chronically agitated landlord, Loren Ronbauer, and asked him to let the police in so they didn't have to kick in the door.

I was surprised when Loren spat, "I've been letting people in for you all day. I have things I need to get done!"

I kept my voice steady and asked, "Loren, who did you let into my apartment?"

"The gas guy. You called and told me you damaged a pipe, but you had already called a gas guy and I should just let him in, so I did. It sounded like I didn't really have much of a choice."

"I never called you."

"I called right back to make sure it was you."

"You called the number you have for me on record, or the number that had just called you?" Dread settled into my stomach.

It was silent on Loren's end for a moment before he stated, "He answered with your name."

"Brilliant," I said sarcastically. "Loren, what did this gas guy look like? What was he wearing?"

"Am I a fashion critic?" He was still irritated, but had lost some steam.

"No, but you might be an accomplice to a crime. What did he look like?"

"I don't know, average height, maybe five-ten. Gray shirt, jeans. Thick, shaggy hair. His face was weirdly white."

"I'd imagine. He's been in prison all summer. You need to get to my apartment to let the police in. Call me as soon as you get there, and tell me what you see." He started to protest, but I cut him off. "Look, my pregnant fiancée is at my apartment. You let a stranger in. I need to make sure she's okay."

Loren stuttered, "I, I let him in a second time. He needed to borrow a two-wheeled cart to haul out a piece of furniture. And he never returned the cart!"

"Son of a bitch!"

"All he took was an old dresser. He said there was gas on it. It didn't look like it was worth anything. Why would he steal it?"

Was this guy a complete idiot? Natural gas is a gas. It wouldn't spill on a dresser. It was all I could do to not start beating my phone on the dash of my car. If my grip got any tighter, my phone would disintegrate in my hand.

Loren whined, "I thought I was doing you a favor."

"Okay," I said. Trying to keep steady, I asked, "What did he load it into?"

"A black truck."

"Did you get the plate number?"

"No."

It was probably Al Brennan's black truck. "How long ago was this?"

"Fifteen, twenty minutes ago."

"Okay, get to my apartment and call me." Al had Serena. I stood on the gas pedal, threatening to put it through the floor. I silently apologized to Tony. He would have to wait. I prayed he could.

I called Maurice at the BCA headquarters and told him what had transpired. He said he'd make sure law enforcement was looking for the Brennans' pick-up on the freeways surrounding Minneapolis. My sense was that Al was headed to Morrison County. It was his territory—he had never lived outside of Morrison County. I called the county sheriff, who agreed to have officers look for the truck, particularly on Highways 10 and 25, as they would be the most common routes to take from Minneapolis to Little Falls.

I called Vicki and told her Al had been released. After I calmed her some, she agreed to have Jeff take her and Hannah to stay with a sober relative in northern Minnesota until Al was back in custody.

Loren called me back and reported that Serena wasn't in my apartment. There was no sign of a struggle and no blood, but Serena's shoes were sitting by the apartment door. Her jeans, stockings, bra, and cell phone were all on the floor of my bedroom.

I had to make a decision. Should I go to my apartment to see if I could glean any evidence from what was there, or should I try to guess Al's destination? I turned off Interstate 35W and headed west to Morrison County. If Al brought Serena somewhere else, I'd lose her, because I couldn't think of another possibility. I had to inform as many people as I could, take my best guess, and pray. Al had a head start on me, but I had a siren in my unmarked car and could make up the time. I just needed to figure out where he was headed.

Chapter Forty-Five

Serena Bell
9:15 p.m.
Wednesday, August 4
Morrison County

I came back to consciousness still wedged tightly in the armoire, engulfed in complete darkness. My body was stiffening from the cramped quarters, which was rattling like a paint-shaker. My weight was on my left side, so the armoire was lying flat on its back. From the engine and wind noises, I had to be in the back of a pick-up truck, rumbling down a gravel road. As a teenager, I'd ridden in the back of a four-wheel-drive truck on unpaved roads with my cousins. Back then, it felt like my teeth were going to rattle out of my skull, and that was just how I felt now. The humid, stale air in my cramped space heightened my claustrophobia. I tried a couple of deep breaths to stem my panic, but it wasn't working. I felt like I was going to be sick, but I had to find a way to survive this—not just for me, but for our baby. I was wedged in so tightly, I couldn't get any leverage to push myself in any direction.

The easiest way to break out of this armoire was through the backing, a sheet of wood less than a quarter inch thick. However, I was lying on that side, and besides, I could feel through the hammer-hole that it had been heavily wrapped with tape.

I carefully unwound the t-shirt from the lock and tested the door. As I suspected, the tape was wrapped all the way around the armoire.

My best bet was to try to push the top of the armoire up, since it wasn't made to take force from that direction, and I doubted Al had wrapped tape over the top. I pushed up hard with my head, but it didn't budge. If I could turn my body upside down, I could push with my legs, but my skin burned against the wooden sides when I tried to change my position. I was just wedged too tightly in one damn spot. Hitting my head against the top would only knock me out. *Come on, think.*

I tried the door again, managing to push it open a quarter of an inch so I could gulp some badly needed fresh air. It was getting dark. I stuffed the t-shirt partially into the slight opening, to make certain the door remained at least that much ajar. This helped my stomach some, and the fresh air and deep breathing also reduced my panic.

I wished I had something to cut the imprisoning tape. I worked a finger through the crack and started scraping on it with my fingernail. There was a lot of tape, so this would take time, but it could work. Something had to work.

The truck stopped. Al got out and smacked the dresser door hard, scaring the hell out of me. It was all I could do not to react.

I anxiously thought about the sexual predator on the other side of this door. Jon had told me that Al had brutally sodomized Vicki without having any reason to be angry with her. My fiancé had sent him to prison, and I could testify that he picked Mandy up on the night she disappeared. What form of hell awaited me? I was sweating with fear, and my hands were clammy. I decided it would be best to let him think I was still unconscious.

My wooden tomb was pushed out the back of the truck bed and fell hard to the ground. It knocked the wind out of me, but I willed myself to stay quiet, gasping silently. I was now able to see more light through the hole in the back of the dresser. I saw gravel for an instant, then heard scraping as the armoire slid along. I was then tipped upside down, my body shifting and sticking with each jostle. I tried to brace myself, palms flat against the side. All of a sudden, I was flipped quickly back, right side up, but the landing felt unstable. Whatever I landed on gave under the weight of the armoire, and bounced fluidly a few more times. The scent of rotting fish and something mossy seeped into the openings, reminding me of days playing in the pond behind our house. I could only guess the armoire had been tipped into some kind of a boat. The buoyancy started to give me motion sickness, and I again fought the urge to throw up, swallowing it out of fear he would hear me. Then I couldn't hear him moving anymore. Had he left me? What was he going to do? I clawed desperately at the tape again. It was too thick.

I heard movement, so I quickly pulled my finger back in, hoping he hadn't seen it in the dark.

Al grandiosely said, "It's time for you to beg for your life, Serena. After that kick to my groin, you've got to deliver on something so erotic, I'll never stop fantasizing about it. Tell me what you can do for me."

I despised everything about Al, and found myself deliberating over what would frustrate a sadist the most. I took pleasure in not responding.

After a couple minutes, the drawers were pulled open and something clunked heavily as it dropped inside them. Oh, God, he was filling the drawers with, what, rocks? Concrete blocks? Something heavy. When this stopped, I could hear the ripping of tape again. He was taping the drawers shut. Suddenly, it dawned on me that I was going to be dropped into a lake in this weighted cage. I was completely unravelling. A new wave of hysteria threatened to escape from me in a primal scream.

Al's voice slid through the armoire like a lazy snake. "Now, I imagine you're wearing very little in there, and I planned on having you under me on the ground, ass up, by now. But, I'm having a little trouble getting it up from your kick to my balls last time. So, it's time for you to do your best sweet-talking. First, you can tell me everything you'd beg to do for me, and then you can show me."

When I didn't respond, the boat was pushed from the shore. This was my worst nightmare. I was cramped into a small, dark container and about to be deposited into a smelly body of water. The combination of my claustrophobia and inability to swim shot a paralyzing fear through me. I wished I would have done so many things differently. I wasn't ready to die. *God, please help me,* I prayed. *Kyrie eleison.*

Al started talking to me again. "If you can hear me, this would be a good time to talk. I don't like dumping a nice piece of ass without using it first. Beg!"

I should beg, I thought, but I just couldn't give him the satisfaction of giving in. Instead, I closed my eyes and prayed. My trembling body was cramped and sore, but I tried sliding myself upside down one more time. I still couldn't turn. It was useless. I thought about pleading to Al, just to get out of this damn dresser, but I was both angry and terrified to face him. I imagined what he'd do to me, and feared it would be even worse. I had held out hope to the very last second that someone would save me. I didn't want to die. I didn't want my baby to die. But if I left this crate now, I knew I'd soon be begging to die.

Al kept talking. "You should have recovered from that tranquilizer by now. It wasn't any more than I gave Brittany. You gave a good fight, but now you either give it up, or I'm just going to watch you die. At your parents', you damn near knocked me out. My balls were swollen for a week! Today, I can't even get you to try to plead your way out of a dresser that's destined for the bottom of Green Lake. Adios, bitch!" He started to tip the armoire into the water.

I called out. "What do you want?"

Chapter Forty-Six

JON FREDERICK
9:20 P.M.
WEDNESDAY, AUGUST 4
MORRISON COUNTY

WHERE WAS AL TAKING SERENA?

During our last conversation, Al said he made a mistake leaving Brittany's body in water beneath a road. I had the impression he still would opt for some kind of submersion. He put Brittany underwater alive. Would he do that again? The Mississippi River runs through the heart of the city of Little Falls. If he was going to dump her in the Mississippi, he would have to do it either north or south of the city, which wouldn't be convenient for him. I called Dad, and he agreed to get friends to the roads that access the Mississippi. Dad said he would go to Fish Lake, between Little Falls and Pierz.

I would give my life for hers in a heartbeat. I envisioned myself with Serena. She was holding an infant she recently gave birth to. At first, I dismissed it as wishful thinking, then the number 195 flashed in my brain. One-ninety-five could mean straight man with a woman, holding a baby she'd recently given birth to, or it could simply be a road.

With my siren wailing, I cruised through Morrison County. Tony had mentioned off-hand that Al fished Green Lake. It would be an easy spot to dump a body unnoticed, especially at night.

There are no houses on Green Lake. It's a small body of water completely surrounded by farmland, and fewer than two miles from Al Brennan's home, off of 195th Avenue. That had to be it.

I called the Morrison County sheriff, and he sent the closest deputy to meet me by the dirt road that ran to Green Lake, just off of Highway 27. I asked that the deputy leave his sirens and lights off to give us the element of surprise. I prayed to God I wasn't wrong about this, and that I wasn't already too late.

Chapter Forty-Seven

Serena Bell
Wednesday, August 4
Green Lake

Al silently considered my pleas, then finally told me, "Okay, I'll knock a hole big enough so you can stick your hands out, and then I'll zip tie your wrists together. Then I'm gonna pull you out and bend you over one of the bench seats in this boat, and if you're really good, I'll take you with me instead of dumping you in this lake."

Al's response gave me an odd sense of relief as I resigned myself to my fate. He was going to rape me, and deposit me in the lake when he was through. That's why he wasn't taking me back to shore. I had no chance of surviving if I went into the lake with my hands bound. *How do I want to die?* I was fed up with Al and every other misogynistic jerk who abused women, so I considered what response would create the greatest narcissistic injury. I calmly responded, "Beg me."

I could hear the anger in his breathing, which had gotten heavier and was whistling through his nose. He ground out, "What did you say?"

I responded, "Get on your knees and beg me, asshole." I had decided to take my chances in the dark lake.

Al's voice was dripping with cold rage. "It's time to put you down, bitch."

I felt the armoire being lifted and heard the loud splash as I hit the water. Dank, fishy water began seeping through the cracks in my tomb, and I realized I would soon be submerged. I took a deep gulp of air, wondering how many more of those I would get. Adrenaline fired through my body as I realized this was it. My only way out had to be through the top of the dresser, so I banged my head against it. I couldn't get enough leverage to push and force the top off. No matter how frantically I struggled, I still couldn't turn my body.

An explosion of gunfire shocked me into stillness, ripping a hole through the door right in front of my face. Al was going to make sure I was dead, and I couldn't do a thing to prevent it.

Jon Frederick

Officer Tom Cannon and I spotted Al's black truck in the dark, on a gravel boat landing at Green Lake. As we ran toward the lake, we could hear a boat. Tom used his flashlight to scan the lake surface. A beam of light caught Al pushing the dresser into the lake from the boat. If that boat moved before we found Serena, there was no chance of finding her alive in that murky cesspool. You couldn't see a foot in front of you in that water in broad daylight, let alone at night. I raised my gun.

I'm not certain what happened first. Al leaned forward to fire at the dresser, and I began to mercilessly fire at him until his body toppled into the lake. Then, I dove into the murky water and swam as fast as I could toward the splash, praying God would help guide me to Serena. Still fifty feet away, with Officer Cannon's flashlight trained on the boat and dresser, I helplessly watched the dresser sink beneath the algae-covered water.

Serena Bell

As the armoire sank into the dark water, I tried flipping myself one last time. My lungs burned and I was running out of air. This time, the slimy water provided enough lubrication to allow my body to turn, and I was soon upside down stomping at the top of the armoire as hard as I could. It loosened! With one last push I kicked it free, and now, upside down, I used my arms to push myself out. I was momentarily disoriented, not knowing which end was up. Buoyancy righted me, though, and I kicked to the surface as the armoire descended below me. When my drenched head broke the surface I greedily swallowed mouthfuls of air. I still had a major problem, though—I couldn't swim. I could dogpaddle a little, which got me to the surface, but I couldn't maintain it long enough to make it to shore. I grabbed hold of something floating by, only to realize it was Al Brennan's body. He didn't move, but I swear his now-vacant eyes looked right at me. I immediately let go with a scream and started panicking in earnest.

Someone was swimming toward me in the dark, calling my name. I just had to tread water. I thought I could do this, but found my mouth filling with the sour lakewater as I struggled and yelled for help. If I went under, they'd never find me. I flailed my arms, but my head slowly slipped back below the surface. This couldn't be happening. Not now.

Jon Frederick

My first dive down toward the armoire was unsuccessful. In desperation, I resurfaced for air. Terror struck when my fears were confirmed—I couldn't see a damn thing in the water. I had to find her, *deo valente*—God willing. As I was about to dive again, Serena's dark head popped above the water just twelve feet from me. It was an incredible relief to see her surface, but before I could get to her I watched her sink under again. I dove after her, and with God's grace, caught her t-shirt and pulled her above water.

Serena was panicking and I had a hard time keeping her afloat. I tilted her head back and yelled "Breathe!" before she pushed me back below the surface as she desperately clawed her way upward. I fought my way back above water. She still struggled, but her fight had slowed to the point where I could hold onto her with one arm. I slowly began to make my way to the boat, which had mercifully not drifted too far away. Officer Cannon's light remained steady and trained on the boat for guidance. If he hadn't been there with the flashlight, this could have ended tragically. Once I got close enough, I grasped the edge of boat and simply hung on until Serena finally calmed down enough to work together to get into the boat.

When Serena and I finally made it to shore, Officer Cannon and I dried her off with one blanket and then covered her with another. The officer retrieved his car and kept the headlights on so we could see what we were doing. While we worked, Officer Cannon tried to offer me an out, saying, "I saw him shoot at the dresser before you started firing," but I wasn't interested. He also saw me raise my gun and repeatedly fire until Al was in the lake.

I told him, "Just report what you saw. I don't regret what I did, and I'll stand by it. We need to get to the hospital."

Officer Cannon pressed, "Byron Smith was convicted of murder in this county for shooting two people who broke into his home. You're going to need my support."

He was probably right, but at the moment I didn't care. My only concern was getting this toxic muck washed off Serena.

I rushed Serena to the hospital in Little Falls. At my speed, it was only ten minutes away. Once at the hospital, Serena immediately showered to make certain all the toxins were washed off. She requested solution to rinse out her sinuses.

I never had a desire to kill anyone. The commandment "Thou shalt not kill" doesn't have any footnotes identifying exceptions. But I didn't regret killing Al. It was what I had to do to save Serena. If I was put in that same situation a hundred times, I would shoot him every single time. This was something I'd have to work out with God.

The Morrison County sherriff interviewed me at the hospital. They had recovered Al's body. It would take time for the official autopsy to be completed, but it appeared I had hit him twice. The first bullet had gone through his torso, but wasn't fatal. The second appeared to have severed his spinal cord at the neck, resulting in his immediate paralysis and his drowning in the filthy soup of Green Lake. Officer Tom Cannon estimated I fired six to eight shots. I wasn't keeping track. I just fired until he wasn't standing, hoping to keep him from interfering with Serena's rescue.

It was finally over.

When my interview was over, I met my parents outside of Serena's room.

Mom pointed out, "Serena is being examined by Dr. Philippi. She's an obstetrician. Why did she ask to see an obstetrician?"

I matter-of-factly told Mom, "Serena's pregnant."

Mom slapped me and scolded me. "This is your fault. You've been trying to get with her since she was sixteen years old."

I couldn't argue with that.

Exasperated, Dad smiled and told Mom, "He just saved Serena's life. He saved your grandchild."

Mom fussed, "Thank God she's okay." She put her open hands on each of my cheeks like she was addressing a small child who needed to hear her message. "Slow down. You've been going a hundred miles an hour since you left home. Please—for Serena's sake, and for your family." An unexpected lump formed in my throat, so I averted my eyes and nodded.

Dad shook my hand and clapped my shoulder. "Congratulations."

Serena called for us to join her. She was wearing light blue scrubs and hospital slippers and sitting on the edge of her hospital bed. I bent down and gave her a hug. She pulled away and said, "Everything's okay. I can go now."

Mom went directly to Serena, nudged me aside and hugged her. "Thank God you're okay. You are one tough girl." Mom had expressed her immediate frustration with me, but had quickly moved on and was looking forward to the opportunity to both teach and pamper a grandchild. With Serena's hands clasped in hers, she said, "Bill and I will get to work on making a room baby ready." Adding, "for when you regularly come with the baby to visit."

Serena met my eyes, and I gave her a reassuring wink.

Chapter Forty-Eight

Jon Frederick
3:30 a.m.
Thursday, August 5
Minneapolis

When we were finally able to leave Little Falls, Serena and I drove directly to Fairview Hospital to pay our respects to Tony. I needed to see him, and Serena had been through enough that she didn't care if she visited still wearing the scrubs the nurses had pulled together for her at the hospital. I was frustrated over not being informed of Al's release from prison, until I was told Tony had agreed to notify me but never had the opportunity.

Tony's status hadn't improved any. Paula shared that he had threatened Al, saying he would have him back in lock-up before the day ended. It didn't take Al long to recover his gun, along with the tranquilizer he used on Serena, from somewhere near his farm. Al returned to Little Falls, and when he found Tony getting into his car, Al opened fire. Tony had taken a bullet to the head, and two more to the body. He had not yet regained consciousness. Al then drove to Minneapolis looking for me, but instead he found Serena.

Tony always did what he felt was needed to resolve a situation. In movies, the rogue cop is the hero. In real life, a cop who threatens people gets shot. But, who am I to say? I got shot sitting in a field by myself. I had hoped Tony would one day find peace. Maybe he would, now. We agreed to keep Tony in our prayers, and Paula promised to keep us updated.

11:35 A.M.
Birmingham Apartments, Minneapolis

Serena was still asleep, tousled hair and peaceful face resting on a pillow. I kissed her forehead and slipped out of bed. I picked my clothing off the floor and, in my usual obsessive manner, put them away. I stopped and appreciated Serena in my bed. I glanced at her clothing disarrayed about the floor on her side of the bed, and smiled. Yesterday, I almost lost her. Being with Serena made me the luckiest man on earth.

Psychologists point out that we are driven by thirst, hunger, and sex. But it's not that simple. I had all of those desires met before I sought out Serena. Sociologists would add a desire for power to the formula, but they're wrong. It only feels like power from the outside. Our most powerful drive is a desire for affirmation—to be heard, understood, comforted, and soothed. Serena and I shared an affirming, passionate synchrony I couldn't experience with anyone else.

Both Tony and Clay accused Serena of manipulating me, and accused me of mindlessly following her lead. I feel like I can be the man I was meant to be in her presence. Is my driving force an engrained sense of morality, or simply a codependent desire for affection from a compassionate partner? Driver or driven? I didn't care. As a result of her influence, I was happy, sleeping soundly, free from my past . . . and unconcerned how it appeared to others.

The End

About the Author

Frank Weber is a forensic psychologist who has completed assessments for homicide, sexual assault, and physical assault cases. He has received the President's award from the Minnesota Correctional Association for his forensic work. Frank has presented at state and national psychological conventions and teaches college courses in psychology and social problems. Raised in the small rural community of Pierz, Minnesota, Frank is one of ten children (yes, Catholic), named in alphabetical order. Despite the hand-me-downs, hard work, and excessive consumption of potatoes (because they were cheap), there was always music and humor. Frank has been blessed to share his life with his wife, Brenda, since they were teenagers.

CPSIA information can be obtained
at www.ICGtesting.com
Printed in the USA
LVOW03s0549010917
547181LV00006B/6/P